I0780840

WORLDS APART, WORLDS TOGETHER

LORNA HOPKINS KEITH

copyright © 2025 by Lorna Hopkins Keith

All rights reserved.

No part of this book may be reproduced or transmitted in any form or by any means, electronic or mechanical, except for the purpose of review and/or reference, without explicit permission in writing from the publisher.

Cover artwork design copyright © 2025 by Niki Lenhart
nikilen-designs.com

Published by Water Dragon Publishing
waterdragonpublishing.com

ISBN 978-1-964952-05-5 (Trade Paperback)

FIRST EDITION

10 9 8 7 6 5 4 3 2 1

Again, special thanks to all those in my critique group, Wordsmiths, who helped shape this story and my writing, especially my husband, Greg.

LIST OF CHARACTERS

THE PHREN (FURRED HUMANOIDS)
Ping, researcher in Exo
Eler, Ping's chief
Adar, Elar's chief
Mola, chief of Science
Mater, Ping's mother (Kati)
Aunt Lee, Mater's sister, education
Aunt Dela, Mater's sister, medic
Bede, Ping's sister, 3D printers
Zee, Dela's daughter
Juni, Ping's sister, child care
Cori, Bede's daughter
Gran, Mater's mother
Nela, clerk in physiology
Miki, chief of Computer Central
Rody, chief of Exterior Maintenance
Bolo, chief of Interior Maintenance
Essi, Ping's coworker in Nutritional
Kile, medic
Cura, Ping's helper in Nutritional
Peni, Juni's baby
Caleb, physics
Mang, education
Otre, Nutritional
Akoi, chief of Medical
Assorted Phren citizens

HAVEN (HUMAN)
Sam (Samanda), retired leader
Brad, her twin brother
Hal, leader, her significant other
Tim, the boy's father
Dian, the boy's father
Lian, the boy
Maxee, a furred Klocti (humanoid)
Glenda, construction

Ben, her son, head of construction
Todd, Sam's 'other' brother
Zack, head of Security
Abby, construction, new head of police
Aunt Linda, Todd's mother
Braxi, Maxee's oldest kub
Felicia, Brad's older daughter

THE HUMAN CLAN
Kaylyn, captured by Phren
Jan (Janni), Kaylyn's mother
Glori, Jan's best friend
Susan, head medic, Glori's mother
Betsy, Kaylyn's daughter
Barry, Kaylyn's son
Marisa, Jan's mother
Old Allen, Marisa's mate
Adam, Kaylyn's mate
Gramma Perri, Marisa's mother
Grampa Charley, Marisa's father
Uncle Peter, Perri's twin
Granlyn, original matriarch and Perri's mother (deceased)
Rorey, from another world, helped Marisa find Peace
Ricky, Marisa's brother
Loren, Kaylyn's brother
Grampa Bay, first generation from Earth (deceased)
Grampa Larry, Granlyn's mate (deceased)

WORLDS APART,
WORLDS TOGETHER

1

O N THE PLANET OF PEACE, a green world with grassy plains, deep forest, high mountains, and a large sea, there lived four communities of intelligent beings. Two were humans from Old Earth, and another was Newamb, home of the humanoid Ambaak. Under the sea, lived the Phren, stocky, furred humanoids, in a three-module habitat.

The world became unpeaceful.

Inside the habitat, a Phren called Ping sat in her tiny blue cubicle and pulled down a blue-green helmet over her head which connected her to the bioputer. One of the many cogs in the place that kept the habitat functioning, her main task was research for any chief who asked a question or ordered a report.

Once again, she pushed away the ache of childlessness. She had not been chosen to reproduce; she had not been told why.

The Phren, as young children, were instructed to follow the rules of the society and always do their duty without question. When everyone did so, the community would prosper. Ping always did her duty without thinking about it. It was what was done. It was her life.

Until one day, an error caught her eye. She knew she'd entered a numeral four, but the screen showed a nine in its place in the long string of numbers. Making note of it, she returned to the field and corrected it. The event was not important enough to report to her chief.

But bioputer never made mistakes.

Other than the subdued hum of the air mover, silence surrounded her. Ping's pale violet fur, covering all but her face, palms, and soles of her feet, kept her comfortable. She didn't need to taste the air to know it was flat and metallic.

Ping noted another small error, corrected it, and moved on. *This cannot be*, she said to herself. Ping knew she should report this to her chief, but found she wanted to keep it to herself for a while longer, to see if it happened again. A rebellion against duty was unheard of, the rules were so strictly enforced from early childhood.

Why I feel this way?

Ping was different from most of the other citizens, in that she could recall every event in her life back to infancy. But still, she was just a cog in the machinery of Phrena, doing her daily duty. She continued her tasks. She was required to, she must.

•　　　•　　　•

The next day, as she settled into her sitnest and pulled down the bioputer, she remembered the errors and kept a watch out for more. She felt no concern, having been taught to keep emotions hidden and uncalled upon since childhood, but something stirred inside. However, she found no errors that day.

Two days later, checking the date of birth of an ancient chief from the original source against the report information, Ping came up with two different dates. "That not possible," she said aloud.

Ping removed the blue-green bioputer helmet from her head and took a deep breath. The ovoid device rose to the ceiling of her tiny blue cubicle on its stem-like cord. As one of the top researcher in the Phren community, she dealt with everything from solutions to everyday problems to ancient history. According to her researches, the habitat was not as perfect as the high chiefs believed.

Impossible as this was, the error must be reported to her chief. Duty demanded it.

She rubbed her chest fur and *mind reached* for her chief in the next cubicle.

"Eh?" Chief Eler stepped to her doorway.

"Here is incorrect date of birth of Head Chief Soto, along with correct date," Ping said. "How we delete wrong one?"

"Cannot be wrong. Bioputer always correct."

"No. Come see."

Chief Eler, a pale tan furred humanoid with round dark eyes and a tiny button nose, peered in and scanned the entries. "Cannot be."

"Is. Can us correct?" The tickle inside her grew stronger.

Chief Eler punched an entry into his personal pad. "Yes, is problem. I send to Chief Adar. He deal with it." Chief Adar was his chief. "You so good at finding things."

Ping warmed and touched her identity necklet of lavender and pale blue swirls. *At least this I can do well.* Her research work soothed her. Her world, Phrena, needed her services. In this bio world under the sea, little changed, but there were always questions.

"Continue with next assignment." Chief Eler returned to his cubby.

Ping pulled up a new report form. As she set it up, something twitched in her exo hind brain. Since she didn't know what to make of it, she ignored it and continued working on the new report. This one had no errors.

Sometime later, the wall screen chimed. "Alert. Alien arriving at Xenocomplex."

"Eh?" Chief Eler trotted out to prepare a table in the large, central exam room. The outer hatch slid open. A grav sled carrying a being oozed over to the table, slid off its burden, and oozed back out to hunker just outside the doorway demanded.

"What this?" Chief Eler.

Ping went to look. Her jaw dropped. A child without fur. She stared at it. She'd never seen a live land person before, although she'd seen many images in her researches. What in Phrena was going on? Her exobrain twitched again.

Chief Eler, beside her, peered at the being encased in a clear cocoon with a breathing bubble over his face. "Why he here?" He looked around as if to seek a thought. "I call Chief Adar. Chiefs need to know. This not supposed to happen. Go back to assignments."

Ping obeyed, but could not get that smooth little face out of her mind. Unable to focus on her task, she made mistakes herself. And corrected them.

Chief Eler returned after a little while. "Come."

Ping followed him to the exam room.

Chief Eler examined the boy, who opened his eyes wide. "Greetings."

The boy cried out and shut his eyes.

Chief Eler checked the boy's mind. "No mind link." He pulled down an instrument from the ceiling and ran it over the boy's body. "Similar arrangement of organs as we. Longer limbs for child."

"How no mind link?" Ping asked. "How can that be?" It had taken her a few minums to process that.

The boy opened his eyes, glanced here and there, and yelled, "Mommy!" He fought to rise, but the cocoon held him. He stopped struggling.

Ping had never seen a live sentient being other than Phren. Always before, she had only been allowed to access dead samples, mostly lower level. His cry sounded like a small child calling for his mater. She yearned to hold him, but she was not allowed to have anything to do with children.

"Watch him, tell me when he wakes," Chief Eler said. "I have tasks."

"Yes," Ping said. Something fluttered in her chest. She had never come across a mention of a land person being brought to the habitat. *Why did drone bring boy? Had someone reprogrammed it, or had it become aware?* She shivered. Things were changing faster than she could process them, and she wasn't sure if this boded well for the future of her community.

Ping looked around as if she could find answers on the walls. This room, like all the others in Phrena, was flattened spheres or ovals with pale walls of different hues. She found the pale blue of this exam room soothing.

Ping examined the boy. Bipedal, like herself, the major difference was his lack of fur. His pale body held only a mop of brown fur on his head and a light dusting of hairs on his limbs. She ran her four fingered hand down the soft, silvery fur of her arm. The land people wore body coverings instead, but he wore none. *Why?*

The exam rooms and work cubicles surrounded the round central room where the safe boxes sat around the cold room in the center. Ping trotted to her cubicle, downloaded a block of data into her exobrain and returned to the exam room. She processed the data and watched the boy at the same time.

Evening mealtime came, and the boy still slept. Chief Eler emerged. "You go eat. I stay here and eat after."

Ping shut off her data stream and rose. "I not be long."

Twice a day, the Phren ate concentrated food nuggets and drank a fortified beverage. Food was only important as a means of energy and body repair.

She retired to her sleep pod and tapped the dispenser in the niche in the wall over her sleepnest. A brown and green ball dropped into the palm of her hand, and she ate it in four bites, followed by a cup of nutridrink.

When she returned to her workstation, Chief Eler was probing the boy. "He not wake."

"Did us harm him?" Ping hoped not. "Perhaps cocoon?"

"Cocoon to keep his microbes from we."

Ping gasped. "Look, he not breathing." The breathing bubble lay flat on his face.

Chief Eler peered at the boy and stepped on a flat plate in the floor. A small box rose out of an opening that appeared in the floor next to the exam table and opened out like flower petals into a much larger box. The clear structure with rounded corners opened and the two slid the cocooned boy into it. Chief Eler used a sharp metal digit to slice open the covering and put a breather over the boy's face, then closed the container.

The breather pumped air into the boy's lungs as he gasped and struggled for air. When he began to breathe normally, the breather detached and slid away. The boy fell into a deep sleep.

Chief Eler brought a round, green object from a cupboard and set it in a sitting nest near the box. The green thing waved eyes on stalks at the box and settled its four thin limbs in the round, padded seat.

"Opti watch box and send alert if movement. You may go now," Eler said. "Sleep well."

"Yes." Ping trotted to her cubicle, shut down her equipment, and trotted to her sleep pod. Besides her sleep nest, it held a small cleaning room and an even smaller storage area. She did a quick cleaning with the forced air brush and sat on the side of her nest.

Ping stared at the green forest on her screen and pondered the day's events. Always, the days were the same. She reported to her workstation, she did her tasks, she returned to her sleep pod. On off days, she went to Park to enjoy nature, and every other eight-day she visited with her family. This was her life.

Now, things had changed. Ping wasn't sure how she felt about it. The same things every day were comforting, but changes were interesting. Would there be more changes, or would they go back to what she suddenly found dull. She had seen a few minor glitches before and hadn't bothered her chief with them. This time, involving a chief, she'd thought she better tell him. *Maybe they fix it, delete wrong date.*

The boy was a major intrusion, an event that did not belong. She had never thought about the land people, just knew they were there. Now a desire to learn more about them surfaced in her. She had always enjoyed learning, and she'd learned a lot while researching. This was different. This was something from outside the habitat. For the first time, she felt there was more to the world than just the habitat.

Ping sent her gratitude to the Great One and curled in her nest. She closed her mind and slept.

2

WHEN PING AWOKE, the events of the previous day came back to her. A land boy—no, it must have been a dream. *That not happen in habitat.* She pushed the thoughts away and prepared for the day.

At her workplace, Ping glanced into the exam room and saw the boy. *No,* she thought as she continued to her cubby. *How he still here?* When Chief Eler brought her assignments for the day, she asked, "Boy yet sleeps?"

"Deeply. Unable to access his mind. Took images of boy with minicim," he replied.

"His people," Ping began.

"Your assignment's here." He cut her off.

"Yes, Chief." She pulled the bioputer helmet down over her head and set her screen to forest. The mass of green soothed her. She accessed her assignment, but a concern for the boy remained in the back of her mind, along with a sense that this could not possibly be real.

In all the hundreds of years of the habitat, never had the land people come, or had been brought to the habitat. It was not done. The Phren sent drones out to watch and study land people for threats to the habitat's safety. But never had one been brought inside. Small animals, yes, but usually dead.

At midday break, Ping removed the bioputer and blinked. The boy still slept. She walked around the Exo complex and as she returned, heard someone at the main entrance. A grav cart entered, and the AI announced, "This Kay from land people. Caught it swimming from land." The cart decanted the being onto the nearest table and left.

"What?" Chief Eler trotted out of his cubby.

Ping followed and stared at the long, narrow individual enclosed in a clear cocoon. A pair of lumps on the front of the body told her the person was female. She herself did not have the fem lumps; on her species they only grew when one was ready to reproduce. The land fem was also furless, a wide piece of cloth around her body. Black curly fur on her head, a little on her thin limbs, so easily breakable. She felt the fem's distress.

The Kay glanced around and strained to see the boy. She squawked so loudly Ping clamped her hands over her ears and used the probability code in her mind to decode the noise. She moved the table around so the Kay could see the boy and sensed the Kay scanning and entering the boy's mind. *She can do that?*

The Kay turned to Chief Eler and Ping and spoke. She made a motion to move the box toward the exit.

"She want to take him home," Ping said. She found it easy to connect with this fem. The fem-to-fem mind connection was the strongest of her species. The Kay touched her mind, and Ping knew they would meet again. She couldn't tell whether this was for the good of the community or not.

Chief Eler called the anti-grav cart back, and he and Ping moved the two onto the cart. He instructed the AI to take them to the exit and have someone take them back to the land.

Ping returned to her cubicle and stared at her screen. Not one, but two people from the land here. So much in so short a time. Ping shivered. These events were too much for her to process now. She pushed the thoughts of them away and pulled up her first assignment. The words did not make sense.

Focus, Ping told herself. She set up the report, but the two faces popped up in front of her. She pushed them away, but every so often they popped up again. What did it mean? *Why these other things come into my mind?*

This was not how her life should be. Every day, she rose, ate her nugget and prepared for the day. She went to her workplace and did her assigned tasks, with a break at midday. On her day off, she went to Park, a place of trees and other plants. In the evening she returned to her sleep pod and watched or experienced virtual reality entertainment on the screen. Every second eight-day, in the evening, she would meet with Mater, her sisters, aunts, and grandmothers. This was her life. This was the way it was supposed to be.

Now things were changing. Events that didn't belong occurring. *Why to me?*

Ping pushed all thoughts back into her exobrain and focused on her task. This time she made no mistakes. The future would be what it would be.

3

O NE MORNING, on the land above the habitat, on the world the humans called Peace, Kaylyn had gotten up to take a break from mending tunics when she received a mental call from her mama.

'Come to the plaza. Sam and others are coming down. We must go down to the beach as soon as possible.'

'Why?' Kaylyn tugged a curl.

'A boy from Haven has been abducted by a flying beast and taken down to the sea.'

'There are no such things as flying beasts. I'm coming.'

'The father says there is.'

Kaylyn trotted out to the plaza, where she met her mama, Jan, and aunt Glori.

"That's what Sam's quine told me they said." Jan looked toward the north. "Here they come."

Kaylyn heard the thundering of the quines, the four-legged people who allowed the humans to ride them, approaching through the village. Sam, on Qiota, in the lead, pulled into the plaza and barreled to a stop. Brad, her twin, was right behind her followed by a couple of people on a single quine, the boy's parents.

The woman had her face buried in her husband's back, arms tight around him, and his face and fists shone white. Several people who came out to see the arrivals helped them off the quine's back after she knelt to make it easier for them to dismount, and led them to a bench.

"Welcome," Jan said. "I am so sorry about your boy. I'm Jan, this is my daughter, Kaylyn, and this is Glori. We will help you any way we can."

The man nodded. "I'm Tim, and this is Dian. We appreciate anything you can do."

Dian hid her face in Tim's shoulder.

Jan and the other women sat on a nearby bench. "What happened?"

Tim gulped and took a deep breath. "Little Lian, he's only six, likes to go out in the dawn. If I'm awake, I follow to see he doesn't get into trouble. He was half under a bush when this thing swooped down, grabbed his legs, pulled him out and swallowed him."

Jan and Glori looked at each other with raised eyebrows. Jan frowned and Glori wrinkled her nose.

Involuntarily, Kaylyn's mind touched the image from Tim's. After a quick look, she sensed it was a machine. *But from where?* A hint of guilt intruded her senses.

"Was it a creature or a machine?" Glori asked.

"I couldn't tell. It was dark and the thing moved so fast." Tim twisted his hands.

"May I look at the picture you have of it in your mind?" Jan asked Tim. "It may help us identify it."

Tim glanced down at Dian, then back at Jan. "Very well. Just that."

"Of course. Think about it, put it foremost in your thoughts." Jan closed her eyes, sent a tiny, gentle probe from her mind to his, found the image, and brought it back to her own mind. After studying and returning it, she said, "I think the thing's mechanical. Probably just taking him somewhere. We need to go down to the beach. Up for another ride?"

Tim sighed. "That gives us hope. Did you hear that, Mother?"

"Yes," Dian whispered, sitting up. She drew in a deep breath. "Can we go on now?"

"Are you sure you wouldn't like to rest a little before we go?" Glori asked. "We need to collect a few things."

"We need to find him." Dian sagged against Tim.

"You need to rest and eat something," Tim squeezed his wife. "How far down is it to the sea?"

"Quarter day ride," Jan said.

"I think we can spare a little time," Tim said. "Where ..."

"Over here." Jan and Kaylyn led them to the medical clinic where Jan explained the situation to Head Medic Susan, who led them to a pair of beds. "Rest," Jan said. "I'll be back in a little while."

Kaylyn and the other two assigned their tasks to assistants, gathered food and water, and called the quines. Sam's quines had joined the local group under the grove of trees where they lived.

A short time later, Jan collected Tim and Dian from the clinic.

"I feel much better," Tim said. Dian nodded.

The quines trotted into the plaza, swishing their long blond tails that matched their neck hair. Their long-legged, smooth brown bodies gleamed in the sun. Jan hoped it wouldn't be too hot at the beach.

They all mounted, Dian on a separate quine this time, and the quines trotted down the slope.

Kaylyn's thoughts went to this mysterious flying object. None of the colonies on Peace had any kind of mechanical flying device. *Could there be another group of people out on the sea, or one of the line of islands offshore?*

At the beach, they all dismounted and grabbed their bags from the quines' panniers. The steeds trotted into the water and splashed around.

"They love the water," Glori told Dian. "It soothes their feet."

Dian nodded. "They are beautiful."

One end of the beach was blocked by a massive dark outcrop of cliff that extended out into the sea. Inland, the massive rock kept the mouth of the great river on the far side, except for a small stream that trickled down the side into tide pools. The other end of the beach stretched into an unfathomable distance.

They set out their sand cloths and bags and sat down. Kaylyn took off her footwear and dabbled her toes in the water. A teasing breeze toyed with her hair under the warm sun. The river, the sea was her safe place.

"Let's *reach*," Jan said. The three women joined their minds and sent them out over the sea.

"Something there. People." Glori said. "Under the sea."

"Not too far. Kay, you're the best swimmer we have. Swim out as far as you can and see if you get a better picture of the place, and if the boy is there. But be very watchful of what may be in the water." Jan smiled.

"Yes, Mama. I can sense any creature larger than my head." Kaylyn did a few stretches and waded into the water. Small waves batted her shins. When it was deep enough, she dove in and swam out along the cliff and, near the end, sensed the place where the boy from Haven had been taken.

Although the water was murky here, she thought she saw the movement of something large. Kaylyn took a deep breath and dove down under the surface. A few moments later, she yelped and gagged on a mouthful of water as a huge set of claws grabbed her out of the sea, pulled her down deeper, and stuffed her into a clear, malleable bag.

As she was drawn into an enclosed space, she *heard* her mama scream, "No! Kaylyn!"

4

KAYLYN FOUND HERSELF on her back inside a dark, moving device.

"Hey," she yelled. Fear welled. She pushed at the bag, but it only fitted itself around her hands. Heart pounding, gasping, she finally gave in, lay back and closed her eyes.

Something covered her face and pumped air to her nose. She inhaled deeply.

After a short time, the motion stopped, and she looked around. Light appeared at her feet, and the contrivance she lay on moved out of the dark into a blue, round room. A pair of pale tan-furred beings at the side of the room watched her with big black eyes.

"Let me go," Kaylyn shouted.

They shook their heads, and one spoke to the contrivance. It moved toward a doorway.

"Stop!" she cried.

The cart ignored her and continued down a hall, up a ramp, down another hall and into a pale blue room, a change from the gray halls. Kaylyn struggled again with her bonds, with no luck.

Where am I? Who are these people? How am I going to get out of this? Help!

Furious and scared, she focused on the room she was in. All she could see was the ceiling, upper half of the walls, and the tops of furnishings. No corners in this pale blue place, no odors, only machine-like sounds. *What kind of a place is this?* The cart stopped and pushed her out onto a long table. Someone moved her next to a table holding the boy in a clear, rounded box.

By turning her head as far to the left as possible, she glimpsed him. She perceived that his mind had shut down.

"What have you done to him?" Kaylyn yelled. She tried to sit up, but was held back by the clear bag that contained her body. She took a deep breath and turned her head in the other direction. A pair of little furry people stared at her, hands over their ears. *Was I too loud?*

Definitely humanoid, one had pale violet fur, wore a necklace with a lavender stone, and a brown belt with pouches hanging off it. The other had pale tan fur and a light blue necklace, with a similar belt. Large, dark eyes stared out of light brown faces. Small flaps of ears on the sides of the heads compensated for the tiny nub of a nose.

She felt something from the lavender person with the larger head and checked it. *They have mindpower. Good.*

"I need to take him home," Kaylyn said, and *sent* a mental picture of them going up a tube to the beach. The person she'd touched bobbed her head and spoke to the other. That one spoke into a device in his hand.

The waiting cart oozed back into the room, opened a side, and claws picked her up and brought her back in. The side of the box with the boy opened upward, and a flat sheet with the boy on it moved him over onto the cart next to Kaylyn. A cover came up and over them, and the cart moved to the door, through the gray corridors, back to the round blue room.

This was so unreal Kaylyn's mind could not focus on the experience.

The two brown-furred people placed the cart at the entrance to a nearby pod and the sheets the two humans lay on slipped into the pod. A hatch closed behind them with a clunk, and the pod moved. Kaylyn heard a faint clank, then a bobbing motion, as if they were in the sea. After a number of curves, turns, and rises the pod stopped, and the hatch opened. She and the boy were expelled into the water at the end of the promontory at the beach and their cocoons dissolved. The pod squirted water after them as it left.

Automatically, Kaylyn grabbed the boy and pulled him to the surface. She swam to shore, holding the boy's face above water. Several members of her clan and the boy's parents waited on the beach. His father splashed in as they approached and carried him out of the water.

Kaylyn collapsed on the soft, tan sand. Two people sat beside her, Sam and her twin, Brad, former leaders of Haven, the boy's community. Sam laid a hand on Kaylyn's shoulder.

Kaylyn's two young children came running. "Mama, Mama!" She scooped them to her.

"You did very well," Sam said. "How is he?"

"Mind closed." Kaylyn was too tired to speak.

"Your people can fix it?"

"Don't know." She dropped her head on her arm.

"Rest." Sam and Brad rose and joined the others. The children cuddled next to their mother. Jan came and sat beside them and brushed her daughter's hair back.

"Relax. We'll take care of the boy," Jan said. "So your swimming prowess finally paid off. You are a hero now."

"Mama," Kaylyn muttered. She heard the boy's mother wailing and prayed to Oneness that they could bring his mind back. Talk, both aloud and mental, told her they were tying him to a quine. She felt the cold nose of her quine and murmured, "I'm okay."

Finally, she pushed herself up, brushed back her black curls, and hugged Betsy and Barry. After a few breaths, she climbed to her feet, took the children's hands, and slogged over to the group, her mama following them.

The boy's father approached her. "Thank you for rescuing my boy. Do you think your people can help him?"

"We'll try our best." While Sam's people had no mind talent, in Kaylyn's clan many had strong mind Talents.

"Okay, folks, let's get going." Brad projected his voice. "It's getting late."

Muttering, the quines slowly walked out of the water.

The people mounted their quines and headed up the slope away from the sea. After a stretch of grass dotted with tiny blue flowers, they came to the edge of the community. Houses surrounded by rainbows of flowers and separated by tall trees lined the way to the central plaza. Paved with flat stones, it was surrounded by larger log buildings.

Jan and Kaylyn led a group to the medical clinic and introduced the parents to Susan and Della, the medics on duty.

"Bring him in here and let's have a look," Head Medic Susan said. His father laid him on a bed and stepped back. Susan checked him out and made comments to Della, who jotted notes on a clipboard. "His vital signs are fine, it's just his mind that's locked up. Janni, do you think you and Glori could help him? You have the strongest Talent."

"We can try," Jan said. "I'll call Glori." She mindlinked with her friend and *asked* her to come to the clinic.

'We need your mama, too,' Glori *sent.*

"Okay." Jan *called* Marisa, her mama.

'Yes, we should try to help this boy,' Marisa *sent* mentally, 'but first, I want to find out more about these people and what happened. Meeting in an hour at the meeting room. You two, Kaylyn, Sam and Brad, the boy's parents.'

'Okay.' Jan turned to the others. "Mama says we have a meeting in an hour. Aunt Susan, just keep an eye on him until we get back."

"I'll stay here," the boy's mother said. "You go, Tim."

•   •   •

The people gathered for the meeting in the meeting hall, on wooden benches around a large square table with a huge wooden bowl of flowers and leaves. Drawings on crude paper decorated the tan walls of the large room. An aroma of wood, flowers, and people surrounded them. Squeals of children playing on the plaza drifted through the open doorway.

"Sam, I realize it's not your fault, but I'm getting tired of rescuing your people," Marisa began.

"I know." Sam ran a hand through her auburn hair, striped with silver strands. "I must apologize for my people, but we're not a close-knit clan like you. We have the leaders, descended from leaders, the everyday people who do the everyday work, and the ones who came from Below, who only know basic labor. Some of those think you have special equipment to see into others' minds and want to come down here and take it."

Sam held up a hand. "We've told them many times your Talent is within you and has nothing to do with anything mechanical. But they won't listen, because they can't imagine anyone having that kind of Talent."

"I see." Marisa touched her silver curls.

Tim spoke up. "We have a special group of guards to watch them. If they find out you cured my boy, I don't know what these people will do."

"Maybe we should send a few of us to demonstrate our Talent," Jan said.

Sam shook her head. "They would say you used hidden equipment. I'd like to suggest you keep some kind of guard on your northern border just in case they come down."

"We'll table that for a moment." Marisa looked around. "Kaylyn, tell us about these people from the sea. Do you know how they captured the boy?"

Kaylyn sat up. "Not really. However, they do a have a mindlink something like ours. I saw in one of their minds that a flying bubble found him outside."

"He does like to wander outside in the early light," Tim said.

Kaylyn twisted her fingers. "I understood they wanted to know why he didn't have any kind of mindlink."

"What are they like?" Jan asked.

"Different. Built like us, but smaller." Kaylyn held her hand straight out from her shoulder. "Pale colored fur. Shorter legs. Tan faces and palms of hands. Small button of a nose, big dark eyes, wide slit of a mouth. The room I was in was pale blue with rounded corners. All the tables and equipment had rounded corners. I sensed they were a lot more technically advanced than we are."

"Let me see," Marisa said.

Kaylyn mentally *sent* everything she'd perceived to her grandmother. "It was very cold in there."

"So we have another group of people on our world." Marisa shook her head.

"At least they won't come here." Jan smiled at her mother and daughter.

"We hope," said Marisa. "Let me process this. Did you get any idea of the size of this place?"

"Not really, Gramisa. The room they took me to was bigger than any of our house's rooms and that was only an exam room. I sensed a lot of people, more than the clan. With everything else, it must be big."

Marisa sighed. "We'll have to keep a watch on them."

"I'd like to get to know them better," Kaylyn said. "One was kind of interesting."

"No. You're not going back there," Marisa and Jan said together.

"Oh, Mama, Gramisa."

"Absolutely not," Marisa said. "We have enough problems without more aliens. We'll discuss this later. Kaylyn, take Tim back to the clinic and arrange with Glori to be there in a half hour. I have a few things I must do, then I'll be there. Sam and Brad, stay here, please."

Kaylyn and Tim returned to the clinic, where Susan said, "No change."

"Mother, I need to go home now. Do you want to come or stay?" Tim asked.

"Could I stay?" the boy's mother asked.

"Sure," Susan said. "You can sleep here and ride up with Sam and Brad in the morning."

"Thank you." The woman touched her son's face as her husband left.

Kaylyn mentally *called* Glori and advised her to come to the clinic.

Later, when Marisa and Glori arrived, Susan said, "Still no change."

Kaylyn, Marisa, Jan, Susan, and Glori sat in a semicircle around the boy's bed and clasped hands. Their minds joined and passed into the boy's head. They found the knot of terror and started soothing it. 'Your mama is here waiting for you,' they *sent*. They continued stroking and *sending* soothing words until the boy's mind began to unfold.

Presently the boy opened his eyes. "Mommy," he cried weakly. His mother scooped him up and cradled him to her breast, weeping.

Marisa and the other women sat back, panting from the mental strain.

One problem taken care of, Kaylyn thought. *What next?*

<h1 style="text-align:center">5</h1>

PING STOOD, STARING after the two land people. They were much like citizens, except furless with pale skins. Questions piled up in her mind. She had no idea how to deal with them.

"You have assignments," Chief Eler said.

"Yes, Chief." Ping walked to her cubby in a daze.

Thoughts circled in Ping's mind as she prepared for her first assignment. How could the boy and his people not have mindpower? Every land people the Phren had encountered had it. The other groups on the land had it. She had always asked more questions than the others, and she wanted answers. Most citizens lived day to day without questioning their existence. She learned early to keep her questions to herself and find answers on her own. If she could.

Ping sensed from the fem Kay that this was not the home world of either of their communities, but they were so similar. *Could there have been something from their world of origin that prevented one of them from developing mind power?*

Ping settled in and focused on her assignment, a download of everything Chief Eler and the equipment had recovered from the boy's body and the Kay's mind. She was to scan, organize, and find everything that might pose a danger to the Phren.

"After what others did to us on home world, we must be careful," Chief Eler said when she questioned him.

Yes, Ping said to herself. When the Phren's original world had experienced global warming, the southern states pushed her ancestors' state farther north, until there was no room left and her ancestors were forced to move into undersea habitats. And then the connected habitats were moved to oceans on other worlds by a process no one in the last hundred generations could explain.

Ping found herself researching land people. Some had lived near the habitat on a few worlds. On these, drones were sent out often to keep an eye on them, to make sure they had no interest in the habitat. On other worlds, land people lived on distant parts of that world. On those, the Phren kept occasional contact to make sure they hadn't moved closer.

Stop. Why this sudden blossoming of thoughts? This not *normal.*

Ping dragged her mind back to her assignment, looking forward to her next day off.

·   ·   ·

When the day arrived, Ping traveled to Park, in Central, one of the three modules of the habitat. Besides Science, where she lived and worked, there was Maker, where items necessary for life, including energy nuggets, were created.

She made her way to the module connector tube, nodding to two other citizens that she passed. There, she touched a plate on the wall, a door slid open, and she stepped into a long, narrow room. As she moved through the pale space, the portal behind her closed and one in front opened. One of the other citizens followed her. Past the portal to Central, Ping proceeded straight ahead to Park, while the other citizen turned to the left.

This module, Central, held all the government offices, main medical facilities, the main bioputer center, and the children's living and education areas. And Park, five hundred paces in diameter and three levels high, held the greenery her people needed for mental health.

Ping walked up the ramp on the outside to the short corridor above the gardens to the portal at the top. Inside, another doorway opened to a path that spiraled down through Park to the exit on the ground level. She stepped out and tasted the fresh, sweet air. She would come here every day if she could, but citizens were only allowed to visit no more often than every fourth day. "I wish I live in place like this," she said aloud. Air outside Park tasted sour.

Among the loops of the trail, groups of lacy, long-limbed trees hung over low grasses dotted with tiny purple flowers. Tall bushes of red and yellow flowers lined the path in places, while rainbow beds of flowers lay in other areas. Wild grasses held long-stemmed yellow cup-like blossoms, and, near the bottom, an orchard bore orange fruit.

Ping stopped at an indentation into the hillside where a rill of water trickled down. The sound of the running water tickled a need deep within her. *Place like this with stream.* She didn't understand why these thoughts were coming to her now and shrugged them off.

She continued down, touching a flower here or a leaf there. All the plants were bioengineered to grow in here, and each visitor was allowed to pick and eat one fruit.

Ping could take as long as she wanted, and side paths led to wee wild areas. The one she liked best led to a tiny pond. Here, she could imagine she was far away from machines, in the wilderness of her ancestors. She watched a tiny red bug crawl up the long stem of a yellow cup. The bugs, tiny fliers in the air, climbers in the trees, and crawlers on the ground, along with a horde of microbes in the soil, processed dead plants into new soil for more plants.

This day, Ping felt uneasy. The boy had awakened her maternal instincts. She'd accepted that she would not breed, and because of that was to have no contact with children. She perceived a need to know the Kay better, to learn about her people. But, although she was allowed to go almost anywhere in the habitat, she was not allowed to leave it without permission and an escort.

Most citizens didn't even think about the rules, they had been in place forever. The Phren had lived this way for many hundreds of years. The habitat remained much as it had been built over a thousand of years before. It occurred to her that it could not last forever.

Ping wondered if she should go see the Kay. She dropped on the bench by the pond and shivered. How could she even think of such a thing? Land people were strictly off limits. But they had been brought here. *What that mean?*

She concentrated on the pond to rid her mind of such ideas. By the time she rose and reached the exit, her thoughts were on the evening's gathering of her family.

Adult members and older children of families gathered periodically to keep up to date and socialize, since each member lived in a different area. Ping's family met every other eight-day in a special room large enough to hold a group.

Ping entered the gathering room, and a rainbow of colors swirled on the blue walls to welcome her, the last arrival. She went to the grandmothers first, ensconced in their sitting nests, and touched their faces. Then to her mother and aunts and sisters and greeted them with a touch.

Finally, she took an empty sitting nest to burrow into. Long and well padded, the oval blue or green padded nests lined the longer walls. Each had a little table attached to hold the flavored water drinks, Tonight, it was dark berry.

Mater handed her a drink. "How is it with you?" she asked.

"I be well. One big thing. Drone captured land boy and brought him in. He not have mind power. One of his people came and took him away. She has mind power and touched me."

"Land person in habitat? Cannot be," the grandfather said. Few homs attended family meetings, mostly grandfathers.

"Is so. Ask Chief Eler." Ping bounced in her nest.

"This be new," Mater said. "You say they gone?"

"Yes."

"Now, Ping, you not exaggerating again?" Mater asked.

"No, Mater." Ping took a sip of her drink. *One time, and always after I get asked.*

"They come down here?" Grandfather asked.

"No, I not think so." Ping squirmed. *Why would they want to come here?* "The Kay just wanted to take boy home."

"This other," Aunt Lee, the youngest of the aunts, said, "How it find us?"

"Chief Eler said she swam out to beach tube." Ping looked at her stubby fingers.

"So land people swim in sea," Aunt Dela said. "Not good."

Silence.

Sister Bede, who lived in Maker, said, "So that what going on with travel pod. Driver all puffed up with importance."

Aunt Lee set down her cup. "I see Tola in drones and tell her keep close watch on land people."

Ping thought about asking if she could go to visit the land people, but before she could get the words out, her mother, two aunts, and one grandmother said, "No," in unison.

Ping cringed. She hated it when they read her thoughts. The talk turned to the aunts' concerns.

"My Zee scheduled to be tested for producing offspring," Aunt Dela said.

Mater and the aunts made cooing sounds.

"About time," Bede said.

"Now, Bede," Mater scolded.

Ping let the pain chase her out of the room. Not clumsy, addlepated Zee. The mere thought of her being chosen when Ping wasn't made her stomach curdle. As she made her way to her sleep pod, Ping closed her mind to that news and pondered the unexpected experiences she had had in the last few days. She had not been taught to think, but to live in the moment, day to day, do her tasks as required. Now, thoughts roiled in her mind, thoughts she could not ignore. An uneasiness about the future crept over her. She had trouble closing her mind to sleep.

6

T HE NEXT MORNING, when Ping arrived at her workplace, Chief Eler greeted her as if nothing had happened the last two days. "Your assignments await." He disappeared back onto his cubby.

Ping gaped at him. Was he ignoring what had happened, or had it all been in her mind? She went to the exam room. The place shone all neat and tidy and clean as if it had never been used. Ping returned to her cubicle wondering what was going on. She felt sure the boy and the Kay had been there, but she could find no sign of that now.

Uneasy, Ping settled into her sitnest and drew the biohelmet down. Her first assignment was to gather all information on the land people. Pleased that she didn't have to search on her own time, she went to work. She found much more than she had expected. The land people, the Kay's group, had been there a long time, and the drones had made many passes over them. Pale blue underneath, the drones went unnoticed because their bottoms blended in with the sky.

Apparently, their files had been dumped into any old Exo and other folders. The more she found and added to her files, the more positive she felt that the land people actually had been here, and perceived the need to meet these people in person.

When she reported to Chief Eler, he said, "Yes, be good to find out more about them. Us only teaching what us know, none presenting new ideas. Us need new ideas if us to continue." He smoothed tan chest fur. "Finish report and sends to Chief Adar. He send to Chief Mola."

Ping did so, and wished there was someone she could share this with besides her chief. For two days, she did her tasks and Chief Eler acted as if nothing had happened. There was nothing on the screen news about land people, coming aboard or otherwise.

"I know they here," Ping said aloud as she settled into her sleep pod the second night.

•　　　•　　　•

Two days later, Chief Eler announced that Chief Mola wished to see the two of them after midday break. They met Chief Adar on the way to Chief Mola's office. Mola was the Chief of the Science module and a Council member. His office walls were lined with curved boxes, open side out, full of papers, books and artifacts collected over the centuries. Ping saw a pink stone carving of a flying creature that could have only come from a world from three hundred years before.

"Greetings," Chief Mola said, larger than Eler and a rich cinnamon brown. He wore a necklet with a deep blue oval with three wavy lines in it.

Ping had never seen such brilliant dark blue before; it was reserved for the top chiefs. Something about the way he stared at her when she'd turned her head triggered a negative feeling.

"Tell about this boy," Chief Mola demanded of Chief Eler. The latter broke into his prepared speech, which he had tested on Ping, about how the boy had been brought in and the Kay had taken him away.

"He has no mind power. Us unable to tell whether just him, he still child, or all his people. Other groups of land people have mind power."

Chief Mola nodded and looked at Ping. His eyes were as blue as the mark on his chest. "Do you concur?"

"Yes, chief." She felt uneasy. There was an unpleasant tone to his voice, as if he were annoyed at her for upsetting the even balance of life in the habitat.

Chief Mola leaned back and closed his eyes. Ping could tell he was communicating with the other module chiefs.

Presently he opened them. "Chiefs agree. You, Ping, go to land people, find out any intentions toward us."

"Why me?" Ping's eyes widened, and her mouth stayed open. *By myself?* She didn't dare ask about having someone with her. Citizens do not question high chiefs.

"You know much of them."

"No, I need her work," Chief Eler said, "Chief."

Chief Adar nodded.

Chief Mola thumped his desk. "Us need her to do this. Ping, tomorrow, gather food and water for five days and anything else you need, and report to Pod Port C. Travel pod take you to beach. Go toward falling sun to river, up along river to land people place. Learn all you can. Look for any sign they may want to harm we."

"Gratitude, chief." Ping repeated the instructions over and over in her mind. Yet there was something off behind this she couldn't pinpoint. She would go, it was her duty after all.

Chief Mola rose. "Now we go to Park to determine how Ping sees." As he led the way to Park, he strode along, ignoring the nods of other citizens. Ping and the other chiefs nodded at them. In the upper room, he tapped a small gray square on the wall. The walls thinned to nothing, and Ping could see out over the trees to the distant walls. Chief Eler slitted his eyes, unable to handle seeing so far away, and Chief Adar closed his completely. Chief Mola focused on the floor.

Ping was the only one not affected by a distant horizon after a lifetime of only seeing across rooms. She gazed at treetops and glimpses of gardens, turning slowly to see it all. "Marvelous," she whispered. *If I could only go there now.* Ping fought to keep from running down the interior path.

Chief Mola glanced up at her. "You see well." He touched the square and the walls opaqued. "Tomorrow, early." They returned to the corridor and the outside walkway.

"Remember," Chief Mola said as they reached the bottom. "Record all on personal recorder also."

Back in Science, the other chiefs went their ways, and Ping and Chief Elar returned to their workplace. "I not like that you go out," Chief Elar said.

"I must go. Is my duty." Ping felt a tingle of emotion she couldn't identify.

"Yes. Still, tasks to be done." He went into his office cubby.

Ping settled in her sitnest, pulled down the biohelmet, and pulled up the next assignment. She briefly wondered what she would find out there, then put that thought aside for the morrow.

7

PING WOKE EARLY and fought off a sense of uneasiness. No one had gone to land for over a hundred years. She had tried to research the previous expeditions, but was only allowed to see the dates and the names of the citizens who went to the land. Researching them personally found her nothing except that one of them had huddled in the pod the whole time they were up there.

Toting her bag of provisions, she made her way to Central and Pod Port C, a bit of pleasure at doing something different wrapped around the unease. She did not allow herself to feel any further emotion.

At the station, a round, gray place with sitnests and a counter, she reported in. An aide took her to a room where a medic checked her and gave her a drink. "It protect you from many things. Not move until you feel in all your body."

Ping waited until she felt the tingle everywhere. The medic gave her a pale blue cooler wrap that covered most of her body and a strip of darkened bioplaz to wear over her eyes. "Light much warmer and brighter on surface," he said.

The aide led her to the travel pod, a one-person ovoid in pale blue. Ping shivered as she stepped inside. She was going to actually leave the habitat. The pale green, padded interior welcomed her as she settled into the nest. No windows or screens punctuated the walls, so she lay back and waited. Unidentified emotions rose.

The pod hummed, and she felt movement. Ping accessed images of the above world in her mind and reviewed her instructions. She had been given a list of what to do and what not to do. She would follow orders, it was her duty.

A modest thump and the humming stopped.

"Prepare to leave pod," a disembodied deep voice said.

The hatch opened, Ping climbed out of the nest, and stepped to the hatch. Humidity, much stronger than in Park, smacked her in the face. A mass of green, a forest of unfamiliar trees greeted her. Trees much taller than those in Park. She opened her mouth to taste their essence. There had been another sense called smell, now lost in the folds of history. The edges of these trees were much sharper than those in Park, and the air was more alive.

"Pod depart in ten sec."

"Ah," Ping said, and stepped out onto the sand. Her foot sank in, she took another step, and fell to her knees. The pod hummed behind her as it left. She dribbled the fine, soft sand through her fingers, felt the warmth of the sun on her face. This was real, not virtual reality. She felt like she had stepped outside of herself, into a new version of virtual reality, that she was someone new.

There was more. Bushes with large red flowers hunkered on the beach in front of the trees, and green grass between them held tiny blue flowers. *Real, not images on screen or projected into mind.* Ping took a deep breath and climbed to her feet. Animal noises and the whisper of the trees found her ears, along with the swish-swish of the sea behind her.

She wished she had someone with her, but she had no brothers or other close homs. Again, she wondered why Chief Mola had sent her out alone. Something about him made her fur curl.

Ping stepped toward the trees, touched an overhanging branch and a bush flower. She turned, saw the wide, tan beach and endless blue sea, and froze. Her finger touched the call button on her belt that would bring the pod back.

"No," Ping said aloud, and dropped her hand. "I must do this." Her voice sounded flat on this world. She set her bag over her shoulder and focused on her feet as they took short, careful steps along the sand toward the cliff that stuck out into the sea at a distance. Her mind could not coordinate all these new experiences. Noises in the forest barely registered.

After a while, the scene appeared to her as a backdrop painted on the wall of a room, as did the sea. Only the tongues of water licking the shore were real. Soon the trees and bushes thinned out, and the land stretched away to her right.

Must be very big room. Ping had no words for what she felt. She saw a few buildings near the forest, but no river, and plodded on.

Something brushed the fur on the left side of her head and her shoulder. Ping slapped at her head and whirled around. Air now moved past her face faster than even right at an air vent. She took a step back. The air followed her. Wind, that was it. Wind from the sea.

Ping tasted the air, a briny flavor tingled with earthiness from the trees and other plants. She recorded this and kept going. The sound of the water brushing the land and the whisper of wind in the tall grasses soothed her as she scuffled along.

Presently she came upon an outflowing of water from the land into the sea and dropped to the grass. She was not used to all this walking. Breathing deeply, she watched the water burble along, much more active than the little stream in Park. When she glanced into the distance, the world around her appeared as a view on a wall.

The path along the river drew her, and she started up the slope it marked. Although uphill, the ground was firmer and easier to walk on. Every so often, Ping had to stop and rest in the shade of a tree. *How much farther?* Her feet hurt from this hard ground, and her legs ached.

She moved on, the sun lowering in the sky to her left toward a line of trees in the distance. Shadows crept across the river from the other side. Sitting once more, Ping watched a tiny red creature climb a tall stem of grass and recorded an image of it in her mind recorder.

What other creatures are there out here?

When she rose, she startled at a tall being standing atop a rise. As Ping moved forward, the individual opened her arms wide in welcome. The Kay.

Ping stopped. "How you see me come?" She pointed to herself and back toward the sea.

Kay tapped her head covered with black curly fur. She spoke and beckoned, and Ping followed her up and across a wooden walkway over the river. The path led up the slope to log structures surrounded by flowers. *Shelters, perhaps?* Paths led among them, and they soon reached an open area paved with flat stones and surrounded by larger wood structures.

Ping plopped down on a wooden bench. This slope had been much longer than the one up to Park. She breathed heavily, mouth open, and was assailed by tastes of noncitiizens, flowers, and alien dust. Several of them awaited, all tall with the same dark mop of curly fur on their heads.

Kay pointed to them. "Marisa, Jan, Adam."

Ping understood that the words were names.

Marisa, the older fem with silver in her curls, spoke, but Ping was unable to understand the words and shook her head. Marisa looked at the others and back at Ping. This time, Ping felt a sense of welcome.

The others talked among themselves, in their minds. Ping sensed disagreement even though she could not comprehend the actual words.

Kay turned to Ping, beckoned, and said, "Kum."

Adam nodded and took off.

The three fems took Ping to a log structure. She touched the outside. *Real trees.* Inside, in a square room open to the rear, she found sitnests with little padding and square corners. Pale green walls held shelves of figurines and books. The room, the table, everything had sharp corners, so sharp it hurt to look at them.

Marisa showed her to a small room at the side of the square room. Like Ping's sleep pod, but larger, the place contained a large, flat nest, a chest with drawers, and a small table. She indicated it was Ping's to use. The Phren dropped her bag on the nest and sat beside it. *So hard. I cannot sleep on this.* Ping felt overwhelmed by all the new experiences and put off trying to assimilate them.

"Kum." Marisa moved to the doorway.

Ping rose and followed her to a little room at the rear where there were small basins, another large enough to sit in, three pitchers of water on a counter, and a pile of cloths. Marisa mimed washing.

"Ah," Ping said. *These noncitizens still use water.*

Back in her pale pink room, she lay down on the hard nest and found it uncomfortable. No matter which way she turned, lumps poked her. She sat up and tried to press them down. When she got it smooth enough for her satisfaction, she lay down again. A little better.

Ping thought about this place of shelter. Other rooms she did not see could be sleep rooms too. Perhaps a shelter for a group of people, with a gathering room and a cleaning room.

Strange way to live, others always around.

Her years of research had taught her many things beside what she had learned in her schooling, but she'd never come across something like this.

She sat up, took an energy nugget and reached for her water bottle. After a drink, she leaned her back against the wall, curled her legs in the nest, and let part of her mind focus on the local structures, especially this one. The other part of her mind focused on repairing damage to her body caused by the long trek. Her feet, especially. The sand had been soft enough to not hurt, but still wearing, and the path had been harder.

Ping found this place interesting and unnerving. She sensed no danger here, only a strangeness too vast to comprehend.

A little later, Marisa poked her head in and spoke. She mimed eating, hand to mouth.

Ping shook her head. Marisa beckoned again and left. Ping had a thought. *Perhaps I see how they eat.* She rose and plodded to the doorway.

Marisa scooped a green and brown mass onto flat plates. A brown, uneven cylinder sat on another plate. A hom with white fur reached for it, tore off a piece, and put it in his mouth.

Kay rushed in and dropped into a hard nest at the table. She rattled off something to the older fem and picked up a utensil with a rounded bowl at the end. Kay used it to scoop up some of the mass on her plate and deliver it to her mouth.

Ping could stand no more and bolted into her room. She sat and gagged, forcing herself to look at it scientifically. These people were much like her ancestors, before they learned how to process the nutrients in plants to get rid of digestive problems. The cylinder was obviously a food, but what was it?

She must rest now and see what more she could learn on the morrow. After much pummeling, she managed to make the nest almost comfortable, and curled up in it.

Later, she woke to voices beyond the curtain across her doorway. She recognized Marisa and Kay and the old hom, whose name she hadn't caught. More people came, and Ping distinguished six more voices. Two homs and four fems. She heard her name mentioned and wished she could understand what they were saying. Strange to hear so many homs in a family meeting.

8

A S SOON AS MARISA had cleaned up and settled into her chair, her mate, Old Allen, asked, "Who is that creature?"

"She's one of the people who took the boy Kaylyn rescued." Marisa glanced at the picture of Granlyn that Susan's younger sister, Ilene, had created. *I wish someone else had had room for Ping.*

"We don't need any more others. You tell anyone else?"

She met his eyes. "Mama. Jan, Kaylyn and Adam met Ping."

"Call a meeting here." He cracked his knuckles.

"Now?"

He nodded.

Probably a good idea. Marisa *called* her mama, Gramma Perri, with her mindlink. Then she *called* Jan and Willie, Susan and Glori, Susan's daughter. Kaylyn, who had left, returned upon hearing the call.

Gramma Perri, the matriarch, and her mate, Grampa Charlie, brought her twin, Peter, known as Uncle Peter because he refused to be called Grampa. Although their curls shone silver, Gramma Perri and her mate still walked upright with strong steps.

"What's up?" Susan asked as they trooped in.

"Sit down. We have a visitor, as most of you know." Marisa shifted in her seat as others found places to perch. "Ping has come from a colony whose people live in a place under the sea, not far from our beach. We are just learning each other's speech, so I'm not sure yet why she came."

"Can't you put our words into her mind?" Jan asked.

"No, her mind is different and much more complicated. I could only touch the outside areas."

"What is she like?" Gramma Perri asked.

"Smaller. Like us but with fur. Quiet." Marisa looked down at her twisted hands. "Apparently, her people do not eat food like we do."

"They must be more advanced than us." Uncle Peter crossed his legs.

"I couldn't reach her much either," Kaylyn said. "Maybe that's why her head is so big."

"Could be," Uncle Peter said.

"I got the feeling that her race has been around for a very long time." Marisa pleated her tunic.

"If they live in a habitat under the sea, they must be far in advance of us technologically." Uncle Peter leaned back. "I wouldn't be surprised if she had something in that brain that records everything she sees and hears."

"Peter!" Gramma Perri glared at him. "Don't even suggest such a thing." She pounded the arm of her chair.

Before he could respond, Grampa Charley demanded, "How long have they lived down there? How did she get here?"

"They have pods that move through the water," Kaylyn said. "One took me and the boy back out to the sea."

"Then we should close the beach." Grampa Charley bunched his fists.

"No," cried the younger people.

"Papa, that's our main recreation away from clanhome," Marisa said. "We can't close it."

Old Allen asked, "How long is she staying? Why did she come?"

"Probably not long," Adam said. "She didn't bring much."

"Good." Uncle Charley recrossed his legs. "Get her away as soon as possible."

"What's the matter with you, Charley." Gramma Perri glared at him.

"If they have a self-contained home under the water and things that can move through water and air, technology way beyond ours, how do we know they won't decide one day to come up here? Maybe this one who came is a scout." Grampa Charley sat back.

"They won't do that," Kaylyn said. "They're not like that, Grampa."

Grampa Charley looked at her. "How do you know? You met one person for a short time twice. Maybe this Ping is not interested in moving up here, but what about the other people, the leaders?"

Kaylyn sat back and pouted. She had no answer to that.

"Stop it, Papa," Marisa said.

"Charley does have a point," Uncle Peter said. "We know pretty much all about the Haven and Newamb people and what they can and can't do. We need to learn more about these sea people. Janni, you have the strongest Talent, can you see into her mind?"

"Just a little. She has most of it sealed off where I can't *reach*."

"Okay. Kaylyn, since you knew her first, spend time with her and try to learn to communicate so you can ask her questions about her life down there," Uncle Peter brushed his moustache.

"Now wait a minute." Old Allen sat up. "Are you trying to put my daughter in danger?"

"No. Do you have a better way to collect information on them?" Uncle Peter pushed his lower lip out.

Gramma Perri pushed herself up using her hand on the arm of the couch. "Boys, enough. Kaylyn will be here on her home ground. She's smart enough to stop if she senses the alien is uncomfortable with her questions." She sat down.

"Let's not get all upset about this until we know there is a problem," Susan said. "I expect she has a way to talk to us, she just hasn't got there yet. I think Kaylyn and Glori should take her around and see how she reacts to our place." She smiled at her daughter.

"Susan, the peacemaker," Marisa said. "You're right. Let's see what we can find out and then decide what to do. Kaylyn, how close to the beach did the pod come when they dropped you and the boy off? I know it was a little way out."

"At the deep end of the cliff."

"Quite a swim," Uncle Peter said.

"Swimming is what I'm best at." Kaylyn grinned. "I can hold my breath a long time, which I had to do then."

"But they could put a pod on the beach," Grampa Charley said.

"Enough." Gramma Perri climbed to her feet. "We will do what Susan suggested. Kaylyn and Glori, you two take her around the place in the morning and watch her reactions. Ask questions and see if she understands at all. It may be the details that tell us more. Also, keep your minds closed when you are around her. That goes for all of you. I'm tired and we're going home. Come along, Charley."

He grumbled something, heaved himself out of his chair, and they exchanged goodbyes.

"I'll be over in the morning," Glori said as she left.

•   •   •

Next day, the knock on the door Marisa expected to be Glori was Jan. She burst in. "Mama, I went out into space this morning." She dropped onto the couch, panting.

"I thought that was over with." Marisa came out of the kitchen, drying her hands on a pale green cloth. When Janni was in her teens, her mindtalent took her being to space, where she found the Haven and Ambaak groups and brought them to her world, Peace, through a Gate between worlds.

"I did too. But I started to wake up, I thought is it daylight yet, and then I was out in the stars."

"I see."

"But Mama, I couldn't find anything or anybody." Jan waved her arms around.

"Janni, calm down. What did you see out there?"

Jan sat back. "Stars, patches of color, and something on the edge, maybe coming this way, that gave me the shivers. Then I was back in my body." She covered her face with her hands.

"Not again," Marisa repeated. She sat beside her daughter and put an arm around her. "Not on top of everything else."

"I know, Mama. What are we going to do?"

Marisa shook her head. She was getting too old to have to deal with all this. Although Jan had the strongest Talent, she simply wasn't up to handling so many events at the same time. "Go out once a month and check on it if you can. It may just be a one- time thing."

Jan nodded.

"And keep it to yourself for now. Let me know if anything changes."

"Yes, Mama."

"Have you had breakfast?"

"Breakfast? No. Willie took the younger children over to Glori's. He does when he gets up first. He still doesn't trust me to be there in my body."

"You never liked cooking, did you?" Marisa trudged into the kitchen.

"No. All that work and gone in a few minutes."

"Stay and I'll get you something." She pulled out a pan. "They say things come in threes. Haven people, Ping's people, and now this." She banged the pan on the cooker.

9

P ING WOKE TO DARKNESS and sudden terror. Her legs and feet ached. She reached out and found only a hard wall. She jerked upright and memories opened. The pod, the long walk, the land people. Her instructions.

"Be calm," she said out loud and delved into the quiet space within herself. Once back to normal, Ping did a brief review of what she'd recorded the previous day. Next, she assessed her situation. Schooling taught citizens as children to stop and assess when a crisis occurred. *Safe here, food, water, shelter.* The call button caught her eye.

No, not yet. I must follow instructions. This day she would go out and see more of this place. But it was still dark, and she was wide awake. Ping shuffled to the window and peered out. A faint dimness in the east caught her eye. She crept out, closing the front door carefully.

Faint groups of trees greeted her. She made a sitnest under one with a view between shelters facing the hint of light so she could see the sun rise. The soft grass beneath her was more comfortable than the flat nest inside. Thoughts of the habitat mingled with wonder at this fresh world.

For a moment, Ping longed to be home, in her sleep nest thinking about the normal day ahead. The moment passed as some creature made a waking sound in the distance. She realized there was no machine humming in the background. This world was quiet. Too quiet. It made her uneasy.

However, she had her assignment here, and she must do it well. Better than well. *This day I will be prepared to ask questions through my translator. This day, I will uncover the secret these people hide.*

Ping watched the sky grow bright and narrow clouds turn purple and fade to pink. This was something she'd never forget, something she sent to her private memory to look at whenever she needed something to boost her spirits.

A small wind tousled her fur, and something clattered in the house. Ping rose and returned to the structure. Marisa and the old hom, Allen, sat at the table, so Ping slipped into her room. She made a list of questions in her mind she wanted to ask.

She listened to the conversation so her translator could pick up the words. When the words stopped, she peeped around the curtain in her doorway. The old hom shuffled into the room on the far side, and Marisa glanced toward her doorway and took plates back to the kitchen.

Ping took a step back as if she'd done something wrong.

Kay and Glori arrived. "Ping," Kay called.

"I here." Ping emerged from her room.

Kay waved her hand, said something to Marisa that Ping didn't understand.

Ping pointed to the front door. "Out?"

"Yes, we go out." Kay added a word to Marisa and led the way out the door, along flower-lined paths to the large open area. "Plaza," she said.

Ping repeated the word and pointed to a few large tables at one side. "Tables?" she asked, using their word.

"Yes. Kum." Glori and Ping followed Kay to a large building which contained counters, cabinets and shelves of dishes. Pots and bowls sat on a counter. Two fems were putting items from containers from a wall-to-wall cabinet into pots and onto plates.

"Food," Glori said, miming eating.

Like Marisa's place but much larger. "Food many?" Ping waved her arms. She gathered information from Glori's mind.

"Yes, kum."

Ping was glad to leave that place. Just thinking about eating actual plants made her queasy. The next building contained long tables where people worked at various crafts. One was making bowls out of some malleable substance, others were doing something with pieces of cloth. An older man nearby carved creatures from wood. Glori and Kay took her out before she could see more, but her recorder had captured it all.

Next, they showed her the science lab. She saw an ancient microscope and various flasks and tools. A diagram on the wall showed the outline of the community and lines Ping thought might be water or power lines. Again, they left abruptly. Again, she had recorded it all. She would study it later.

In the medical clinic Ping saw several things she didn't understand, including cloth Susan, the medic, wrapped around a boy's arm. *Didn't they have spray healer?*

At the large meeting hall, rows of small, unpadded sitnests of wood faced a narrow, tall worktable. A row of doors at the side presumably led to more rooms.

"Meeting all together?" Ping asked, gesturing toward the nests. The citizens only had small meetings, family or section. Habitat-wide information was distributed on the screens.

"Yes," Glori said, leading the way to a wooden bench on the plaza. A line of children, led by a fem in blue, erupted out of another building and marched to the tables. Ping winced, but the pain of childlessness did not come. *Maybe here ...*

"All right?" Glori asked, concern in her voice.

Ping shrugged a shoulder. She wished she could explain to them about her situation. Her translator still didn't have enough words to describe it.

After the children settled at the table, Glori took Ping and Kay between two buildings to a small, riverside park. Trees, bushes with small pink flowers, and grass adorned it. The three fems sat on a wide wooden sitnest and watched the river gurgle its way along.

"Nice." Ping opened her mouth wide to taste the area. "Good." She could stay here the rest of the day. Noticing the expressions on the women's faces, she wondered what she had done wrong.

Glori rose. "Us eat now."

Kay also stood and glanced at Ping.

"I stay here." Ping patted the bench.

Kay said something to Glori, nodded at Ping, and left.

Ping watched the river and reviewed what she'd seen that morning. They had deliberately moved her along so fast she couldn't see everything in the buildings. What did they not want her to see?

Someone, Glori, touched her mind. These people had been doing this a lot, but this was different. Words came. 'You like park. You have park at your home?'

Ping looked at the fem. This one, like Jan, had been to space. *How they do that?* She nodded. 'One Park, stream.'

'How many are you?'

Ping knew she shouldn't say. 'Many more than you. Boy's colony. How many?'

'Lots.'

"How long you here?"

'Janni, me born here. You?'

"Mater born this world."

Kay returned with two packets and gave one to Glori. Ping turned away, focused on the river as they ate. When they finished, they rose.

"Come," Glori said. Ping understood the word now.

At the plaza, two people jumped off a pair of large brown creatures who trotted away. One person was a fem with hair like a sunset streaked with gray, the other, a small grey furred humanoid somewhat like herself. Glori took her to meet them. Kaylyn greeted the red-haired one.

"Ping, this is Sam and Maxee. This is Ping, visiting from an undersea world."

"Under the sea?" the redhead asked. Her eyes widened, and she looked back and forth between Ping and the gray one.

"Yes." Glori added something Ping didn't catch, and the two fems began conversing.

"Who you?" The gray one pointed a long finger at Ping.

"Who you?" Ping repeated. She had never heard of other furred noncitizens.

Ping and Maxee stared at each other, looking each other up and down. Ping felt Maxee touch her mind and jerked away. She touched the gray alien and learned what she knew. This one had young, four of them. And some of them had young.

The personal pain came, but not as bad as usual. She perceived Maxee's hidden pain at being the only one of her kind, except for her offspring.

'You fortunate,' Ping *sent* to her. 'You have babies.'

'You not?'

'Not selected.' Ping found it easy to communicate with Maxee, they could understand each other in their minds beyond words. "Come, us sit," she said aloud. She led the way to a wide sitnest. "Walk much."

Maxee nodded and sat beside her.

'How you come here?' Ping asked.

'Spacers brought dead mother to Harmony and found tiny me in pouch. I raised with Sam and Brad.'

'Pouch. How that work?' Ping's curiosity about this new alien grew.

Maxee pulled a flap on her abdomen to make a pouch. 'Infant grow inside until big enough to go outside.'

'Ah.' Ping had seen something like this on a lesser mammal. This Maxee was the most interesting being she'd come across since the eight-armed sea creature when she first started working. This she would keep to herself. Something of her very own that no one else knew about.

'Where you from? How you here?' Maxee brushed her shoulder fur.

'I live in habitat in sea.' Ping looked down.

'Why?'

'Too hot, bright on land.' Ping patted her cooling suit.

'So why you here?'

'I was sent by chief.'

'Not tell, eh. Okee.' Maxee squirmed on the sitnest. 'What you think this place?'

'People pleasant. Kay, Marisa. Is nice they make place all together.'

They conversed in their minds until Marisa arrived. She indicated that they all come to her house.

Ping thought of the hard, flat nest and shook her head. "Park. I go to park." She pointed in that direction.

The fems talked, then nodded.

"Come to my house before dark," Marisa told her.

Ping made her way to the little park and created a nest in the grass. She snuggled into it and mused. These noncitizens seemed satisfied with the way they lived. They had plenty to eat. They appeared healthy and contented. But, still, they hid things from her. She would recommend the chiefs leave them alone.

She wanted to see the other colony, the Boy's place, where Sam and Maxee lived. She wanted to know what Kay and Glori were not showing her. Maybe she would find out when she checked her recordings.

Ping scanned the information she'd gotten from Maxee about the other colony. Those people had come from a world known as Urth, same as Marisa's people, but from a different time. They were both humans. Terrans. They had lived a long time on their other world. And they did not have mind power. *Why one and not the other?*

As the sun dipped behind the trees, Ping rose and made her way to Marisa's house. Sam and Maxee were there.

'I go where you live,' Ping *sent* to Maxee, who translated for the others.

Marisa and Sam looked at each other and went back to the kitchen to talk.

"Sam will take you tomorrow," Marisa said later. She pointed to Sam and then upslope.

•   •   •

Ping requested more padding for her sleep nest and slept better. After the people ate first meal, Marisa, Sam and Maxee took Ping to a large grove of trees upriver. Here, she was introduced to the creatures Sam and Maxee had ridden, large brown creatures with pale neck hair and tails called quines. She took them in with wide eyes and her recorders going.

"So big."

What lovely, majestic beings. She recalled reading about similar animals a while back, but seeing them in reality was amazing. A gray muzzled quine approached Ping and snuffled at her.

"She's okay." Marisa patted the old quine. "This is Ping, Qione."

The quine nodded. A young hom helped Sam and Maxee onto the backs of two of the creatures, then he boosted Ping onto another.

The sense of the movement of the creature beneath her and a connection in their minds led Ping to a feeling of ripe pleasure she never thought she could reach. A rocking nest, unlike anything she'd ever experienced, gave her a chill of delight.

They rode along a line of trees through which she could hear a great river. *Where all this water come from?*

After a stop for a meal, they arrived at Maxee's place. A number of beings like her, her size to small ones, greeted them.

"Braxi, I go up to Haven. Maybe back tonight, maybe tomorrow," Maxee called out to them. One of the larger ones nodded.

Ping heard it in her mind.

They continued on. At Haven hall, Ping saw the buildings had flatter sides and were white. As they stopped and dismounted, a tall fem with streaks of white in her long black hair approached them. "Who do we have here?" she asked.

Ping stood close to Maxee, who translated for her.

"Glenda, this is Ping from an undersea habitat in our sea. She is curious about how we live up here. Glenda is head of construction." Sam smiled.

"Welcome. This is my son, Ben. He actually runs things."

"Here's the things you requested." Sam handed over a large carrying case. "Can we show Ping around?"

"Certainly," Glenda said, heading for the nearest building. The others followed her.

Ping saw many differences. The clan was neat and tidy, everything laid out symmetrically, but here, although structures were in ragged rows, there were few flowers. Leaves and twigs littered the ground around the oddly spaced trees.

They passed Sam's house by the river, surrounded by bushes and trees. *Must be a wonderful place to live, amid the trees*, Ping thought.

Ping met more people. Except for Glenda and Ben, they were shorter and stockier than Kay's people. But she still felt things were being hidden from her. She perceived there were a lot more people here than in either her habitat or Marisa's clan.

Farther along the river, they came to a smaller one that created a corner for crop fields. Rows of almost shoulder high plants with large oval leaves filled one whole area.

"Those are loovah," Glenda said. "The large leaves make fibers for cloth and paper, the small inside leaves, the fruits, and the roots are food, and the stem,' she tapped it, "we use to make rope and cord. They grow everywhere."

"Ah." Ping said. *Very useful plant.* A field beyond held much taller plants that waved in the breeze.

They walked back along a street of houses. Some looked well built and clean, others, usually smaller, appeared thrown together, the boards mismatched and the doors uneven.

Glenda pointed to a small lopsided house. "People couldn't wait for us to build them a house, so they did it themselves. Not very well. They wouldn't listen to us."

Back at the meeting hall, Ping met with Sam, Brad, and Hal. She knew Brad was Sam's brother, but she couldn't fathom the relationship between Sam and Hal. Close friends for sure, but this was rare with citizens. Ping enjoyed the way the homs were so cheerful and laughing.

That night she stayed with Sam, in a much more comfortable nest.

"Old bones need more padding," Sam said, when Ping remarked on that.

A number of pictures of scenery adorned the walls, but the one Ping couldn't take her eyes off of was one made of stitchery, of a river, trees beyond, and mountains in the distance. "This very fine," she said, wishing she could see how it was done so she could show makers. She'd just realized how dull the walls in the habitat were.

"The view from my house on Harmony," Sam said. "Made by Hal's sister, Jan. Yes, another one. There's a few other duplicate names between our two groups, for instance, Susan. I'm ready to turn in, how about you?"

"Yes. Long day." Ping trudged into a room with a sleepnest and prepared for bed. She settled into the nest, much more comfortable than the one at Marisa's, closed her mind, and slept.

•　　　•　　　•

In the morning, Brad and Maxee rode down with Ping to Maxee's place, where the latter stopped. "We all Klocti," Maxee said, and introduced her troupe. They stared at Ping, and one of the youngest toddled over and touched Ping's leg.

"Yes, she real," Maxee said. "Ride well."

Ping and Brad left, and he showed her the big river. Ping had difficulty in comprehending so much water running along the land. He talked a lot, but Ping couldn't understand much of what he said.

Ping wondered again at this place with so much space.

10

SAM, HAL, AND HER OTHER BROTHER, Todd, met with Glenda and Ben, her son. Glenda's husband, Gus, had died from a fall a few years before, and she and Ben ran the construction department.

"What did you think of her?" Sam asked.

"I got the feeling that she thought we weren't as technologically-advanced as her people." Glenda stroked her hair.

"She certainly took in everything, looked at every little item." Ben rubbed his thumb against his forefinger.

"Marisa said she and Janni could only reach the everyday part of her mind, that a lot is hidden. Grampa Charley thinks she might have some kind of recording device in that large head," Sam said.

"What could she want from us?" Hal smiled.

"I don't know." Sam paused. "Marisa said she didn't eat real food, but she must have some way to get nourishment."

"Of course," Brad began.

"Oh, no," Sam cut in with a moan.

"What is it?" Hal patted her hand.

"I just saw something in the future." She looked at Brad, who had a sick look on his face. "A threat." Sam had a gift of foreseeing major unpleasant events, as did Brad to some extent.

"What is it, Cuddles?" Hal repeated.

After a disastrous marriage for her, and the loss of his lover in a landslide as they were leaving City, the two had found each other and formed a deep platonic relationship.

"I can't tell yet." Every time it happened, she wished her gift would be more specific. "It's not going to happen tomorrow, but in the relatively foreseeable future."

"What is this?" Glenda asked.

Sam explained to her and Ben that her mother had come from a world with traces of magic, and she had inherited one of her mother's gifts. "I foresaw the threat that caused Marisa's people to move us here, but couldn't see exactly what it was until we were over here. It was only in the last few days before that I was able to tell what it was."

"If we don't know what it is, how can we prepare for it?" Glenda asked.

"Good question," Hal said.

"We're already making our buildings as strong as possible," Ben rubbed his fingers.

Voices came from outside, and two men burst in.

"I tried to stop them," a girl said from behind them.

Hal stood. "This is a private meeting. Please leave."

The taller one stepped forward, hands on hips. "I hear there was an alien here. What did it bring us?"

Ben, a very large young man, and Todd, as tall but not as wide, stood with Hal.

"What alien?" Sam demanded, also on her feet.

"They said it had white fur."

"They who?" Sam glared at him.

"People we know. Where is it and what did it bring?"

"There is no alien here now, and it's none of your business whether it brought anything or not. Now leave." Ben stepped forward.

The tall man put his fists out.

"Out," Ben snarled.

"Come on, Fred." The smaller man moved toward the door.

"No. I want to know for my people."

"Your people?" Sam snorted.

"Get him out of here," Ben growled. He and Brad took the man's arms and marched him out, Hal pushing his back. "And stay out."

Sam sat down. "I remember him. That nick in his ear. He was a real problem as a kid when we moved out of City."

Her men returned. "We have designated that extra room in the storehouse as a jail and locked him up in it with help from security," Brad said. "We had to rough him up a little."

"He says he's the leader of his neighborhood," Hal said. "We've got someone checking it out."

"Have someone see how many there are like him," Sam said. "This is not the way it's supposed to be."

"I know." Hal sat next to her and put an arm around her shoulders. "We're also setting up security so no unauthorized people can come in here."

"I thought neighborhood leaders were allowed," Todd said.

"He's not their leader anymore." Hal squeezed Sam.

"Good," she said, leaning into him.

"We can't leave him in there forever," Glenda said. "What will happen when we let him out?"

"Have someone find out who he is, what he does, what his neighborhood is like," Hal said. "We need to know everything about this guy."

"This place has gotten too big for just us to handle," Brad said. "We need to consider a real police department, not just security."

"It's long past time for that, but nobody asked me." Ben said. "We have to set guards on our workplaces so people don't steal our materials."

"How do we do that?" Sam asked.

"First, we find a head of the department. The head of security?"

"No, Zack's too old," Brad said. "What about Yari?"

"He's younger and large enough," Hal said. "But will he do it?"

"How about Abby? She's big and tough." Sam touched her hair.

"A woman?" Ben huffed.

"Why not?" Sam asked. "As a mother figure, she can be tough, and I know she would love to tackle some of those idiots."

"Hmm." Hal looked up at the ceiling. "Would she do it?"

"Yes. She loves bossing her fellow construction workers around."

"Maybe," Ben said. "She can move those big beams like the men."

After more conversation, they decided to talk to Abby about the position.

11

A FTER A MEAL at Marisa's, Ping curled up on the long sitnest. Marisa settled in her chair and asked, "What do you think of our clanhome?"

Ping found the words in Marisa's mind. "Interesting. Very different from habitat. More open."

"How can you stand being inside all the time? Could you ever go outside?"

"No." Ping moved around. "Us have Park inside, place where us have trees and plants and water places. Like on land, but now I see this, not much like."

"How long have you people lived in that place?"

"Hundreds of years." Ping didn't want to give a closer amount. These people appeared to be honest and trustworthy, but there were things they didn't show her.

"Oh, my. Do you have any children?"

Ping winced and drew back into herself. "No. I not selected to breed. Only so much room. Must keep population at balance."

"I'm sorry, I didn't mean to intrude. Yes, that makes sense when you have a limited space."

"How your citizens come here?" Ping changed the subject.

"My grandmother, Granlyn, and others of her generation came from Old Earth when they were young. My Allen is the last of them, he was only a child then. An alien race with a spaceship took us to the world we called Harmony, with a people called Bramites. They had no mind talent and when ours grew, we were forced to move away from them.

"Some of us went exploring, and we met the quines. They'd come through a Gate from their world to ours."

"Gate?" Ping asked.

"It's a way to get from one world to another. Some people way beyond us built them. My quine, Qione, and I went exploring other worlds and found this one. Rorey, from another world, and his big black Beast was with me. He's out exploring now. We decided this was a good place, and then we had to move everyone and everything through the Gate and up here. It's in a glade back along the beach."

"Ah." Ping tried to process this. *Like moving habitat, but ...* "You go through when you want?"

"Yes. We have to wait between trips, though."

"Nice to choose."

Marisa nodded. "What do you want to do tomorrow?"

"I go home." Ping sat up. "Is nice here, I like this place, but duty says I must go home."

"Okay. I'll get Allen to ride down with you."

"Gratitude." Ping sensed a hint of relief from Marisa. So she didn't quite trust Ping either. *Makes sense, two different species, different cultures, in same place.*

•   •   •

Next morning, after Marisa and Old Allen finished eating, Ping packed her bag and went out to the main room.

"Ready to go?" Marisa asked. "The quines will be here shortly."

"Much gratitude." Ping touched her fur near her necklet. "We meet again."

"Yes. Travel mercies."

Two quines showed up. Old Allen kissed Marisa, said he'd be careful, and helped Ping onto a quine. He mounted, and they rode down over the bridge to the beach, to the beginning of the forest.

Ping noticed he continually turned his head toward her. She could not reach his thoughts.

"Riding is one thing I can still do," Old Allen said. "Getting off afterward is the problem."

Ping told the quines to stop, in her mind.

"Pod will come here. Gratitude." Ping dismounted.

"Take care." Old Allen rode off with the other quine trotting alongside.

Ping pushed the pod call button, sat in the sand, and watched the sea. *How it keep moving in and out?* She knew the sea covered almost half of the globe. Knowing it and seeing it were two different things.

When the pod finally appeared and landed near her, she jumped up and trotted to it. Ping snuggled blissfully into the nest in the pod. That hard, flat nest at Marisa's had given her little comfort.

The announcement that they were approaching the terminal woke her. She grabbed her bag, exited, and trotted out to the transport. Pale blue walls with rounded corners were a pleasant change from the land people's sharp corners and brown colors.

In the station, Ping removed her cooler vest and eye shade with a great sigh of relief, left them at the counter, and started out toward Science module. She was home, all the familiar environment wrapped around her, the harmonic hums of the habitat, the soft colors of the walls, the faintly metallic taste of the air.

And yet, something had changed in her. She had seen things, had experienced things none of her people knew. The hallway in the connector between the modules seemed narrower, and her cubby with her sleep nest, even smaller. No room for a table, no window, barely room to turn around.

So tired, her legs and feet aching, no idea of what time of day it was, she gobbled an energy nugget and crawled into her sleep nest.

12

W HEN PING AWOKE after a long, restful sleep, she checked her chrono and crawled out of her nest. Halfway through morning. She grabbed a nugget and her bag and trotted out to her workplace. After a few steps, her sore legs slowed her down. *At least, I rode one of those wonderful creatures part of way.*

Ping arrived at her workplace to find Chief Eler talking to a citizen she did not know. The citizen left, and Chief Eler stared at Ping, eyes wide. "You should not be back yet. Why you here?"

"I come because I could do no more. Very uncomfortable." Ping headed for her cubicle. "I found no danger. They primitive." She settled into her sitting nest.

Chief Elar followed her. "What you find out?" He brushed his chest.

"They appear content with life, but wary of we. They eat actual plants, prepared in special place in their shelters. Whole family live in one shelter, separate sleep rooms. They get water from river, but not see how. Power from the sun. Boy's colony about the same. They have large creatures they ride to go long distances. Places for food, makers, education, medical. They not show me all, but might be in recordings I made."

Ping paused to catch her breath.

"Ah. Download recordings first."

"Yes, Chief." Ping pulled down the biohelmet, opened a new file, and started the download. As she scanned, she did find items she did not remember seeing at the time. And something she had picked up from someone not shut down. There had been a time, when Jan was newborn, when Marisa had led all the others to rid her world of a parallel world. Ping could not determine how they did it, except it was with their mindTalent.

Parallel universe. She had learned about them but was skeptical of their reality. If this was true, could it affect her community? After midday break, Ping dug for everything she could find on parallel universes. Most of it was theory, but there was one case where a land people had experienced it.

There must be a weakness in the fabric separating two very close universes that allowed someone go through from one to another, Ping thought. *Not close as in space or time, not anything one could sense with citizens' senses.*

Later, Chief Eler called her in. "I scan your download. Land people seem safe, but why they not show you all? I sense wrongness. Keep watch on them."

"What can they do? They have little tech, no weapons."

"How you know, if they hide things." He brushed his chest fur. "Sensed only interest in us."

"Maybe they hide it too well." Chief Eler returned to his cubicle.

•　　　•　　　•

Ping returned to her usual tasks. Chief Mola sent Chief Eler a satisfactory on the report. "Archive report," the latter told Ping.

She did, with misgivings. They needed to know more about these people. Duty called and she returned to her normal routine. Whenever she had a chance, she did a little research on previous worlds' land peoples. The unease prompted her to do more.

•　　　•　　　•

At Ping's next family gathering, sister Bede had some big news. "Immense sea creature attacked Maker."

"What!" Mater and the aunts cried. Ping stared at her sister. Juni's mouth hung open. Gran sighed.

"Gray, scaly beast found collecting pod and tried to push it. Driver citizen drove pod to hatch as fast as possible, not very fast, beast followed and butted it. Pod severely damaged, they not know if can repair it, and beast tried to follow through hatch. Now hatch bent and not close properly. Inner hatch sealed and inner device push creature and water out, but hatch not usable until get fixed," Bede reported.

"Oh, my," Mater said. "Was anyone hurt?"

"Feeder citizen had upper body injuries, not life threatening, but driver citizen only minor scratches and bruises. Collector mechanism totally destroyed."

"They not know about these creatures?" Ping asked.

"They know smaller version, never anything so big. Driver said it much faster than others, so he not have time to dodge. Not that collector pods move any faster than bottom crawler."

"Ah. Now us must watch out for things in sea, as well," Mater said.

"Chiefs stopped other collectors from going out." Bede sipped her drink.

"More shortages," Aunt Dela remarked.

"Sea creatures not go on land. Masses of plants and rocks and other materials up there," Ping said. "Can collectors be remodeled to work on land?"

"Now, Ping," Mater said with a reproving look.

Ping lowered her gaze and wrinkled her tiny nose. "Us must get material for material printers from somewhere. Recycling not provide nearly enough."

"Girl is right," said one of the grandmothers. "Us must get material from wherever us can."

"Yes, Mater," Mater said.

"Enough of that. Ping, what you been up to lately?" Grandmother asked.

"Not much. Just usual. Chief Mola gave we satisfactory on my report on land people."

"Good," Mater said. "Juni?"

"Two more boys fell off climbing hill and broke limbs. Med chiefs want more and more paperwork. I heard chief wants to shut down hill."

"No," said Ping. "They need it for exercise." She took a sip of her drink. "I fell and broke my leg."

"You were only one, and a fem," Mater said.

"My Cori says plenty of handholds and footrests on hill. Maybe boys more daring," Bede said. Her son lived with his father.

Aunt Lee spoke up. "One my students had something odd happen. He worked on two-part math problem on screen, and he said he did first part correctly, but after he did second part, message said no possible answer. So he did it again, and this time got correct answer. How that happen?"

No one answered, and Ping kept her mouth shut.

After the gathering broke up and Ping headed for her sleep pod, she thought, *was that another bioputer error?* She didn't want to think about the sea monster.

13

I N THE MORNING, Ping recalled sister Bede's story about the sea creature. She looked it up on her screen and only found a basic definition. A large creature that lived partly on land and partly in the sea. She snorted and prepared for the day.

At her workplace, after she had completed a few reports, Ping looked up large sea creatures in the main bioputer. She found one reference, a few worlds back, where one had come out of the depths, nosed around the habitat, then disappeared. What other names would these creatures go by?

Ping tried 'sea serpent' and found an ancient entry. Apparently, they ate fish and were friendly to humanoids.

Chief Eler stepped in. "What this?" He stared at her screen. "How you know about serpent?"

"Sister Bede lives in Maker. She told us at family gathering last night. Infamily not forbidden."

"True. I hear from Maker chiefs. Gatherer down deep when creature came at him. Too fast to dodge, he said."

"Bede said those machines move very slow."

"Yes. The drive mechanism worked well enough for pilot to bring to habitat, but creature tried to follow into lock, and damaged hatch. That lock closed off, but who knows how long to repair."

"Ah," Ping said. She scrolled down on her screen. "They curious, too."

"Now, Ping, this Maker's problem. Leave it alone."

"Yes, chief." She didn't look at him. He went away. Ping felt a desire to go see this beast, but knew that was impossible. She accessed Maker Repairs and scrolled through until she found a notice about the creature. The image she pulled up was of a huge snout poking into the hatch, with one great green eye on one side of it. Gray and scaley, it aroused a new emotion in her.

Hearing Chief Eler moving, Ping quickly copied the image to her personal file and moved to another window. She was aware as he passed by on his way to an examining room, only glancing in at her.

Messages beeped. She found several, from her sisters and aunts, in their 'have you heard' mode about the beast. 'Yes,' she answered them. 'I have an image of it.'

Bede sent that she had got a glimpse of it in person, though the inner hatch window. This had closed automatically when the water pouring in around the beast reached the bottom of the inner hatch, swirled around and pushed the creature back out. The outer hatch wouldn't close properly, so it was sealed off.

'A device inside came out of walls and clicked together, making sheet that pushed beast and water out.' Bede added.

Ping asked, 'They going to fix?'

'They look into it, whatever that means,' Bede messaged back.

Ping shrugged a shoulder. Although she wished to learn more, she knew she would have to wait until Bede could message her again. She retreated into her normal work routine.

Two more reports finished, and still the boy, the land people, and the sea creature haunted her thoughts. It was as if she were splitting in two, the old dutifully following orders Ping, and the new Ping, with new thoughts and ideas. She focused on her tasks, and the days turned back to normal, as before all these unsettling events. Even though they faded into the background, the memories were still there and pushed into the front of her mind during her quiet time. She learned to live with it.

At the next family gathering, Bede told the others, "They working on hatch, but slow. Gatherer being repaired, only have two in use now. Second one out, in other direction, had to come in through pod port and dump materials in carts. I helped wheel them down to material printer area."

"What do chiefs say?" Ping asked.

"Us hear nothing."

"They not say," Aunt Dela said.

"Not our business." Mater moved in her nest.

Ping sipped her drink. "Habitat everyone's business who lives in it."

"Now, Ping." Mater frowned.

"Girl is right, Kati," Gran said. "Anything serious go wrong affects we all."

"What could go wrong?"

"Is creature," Aunt Dela said. "Until gatherer repaired, us short materials for nuggets and all other supplies. In Medical, possibly serious."

"What if it broke power cable?" Ping asked.

"Enough." Mater turned to Aunt Lee. "How is it in Education?"

"Well. Young children not as eager as those before them. Still learn quickly."

Ping leaned back and listened. Although she felt an attachment to them, these citizens, her female relatives, were strangers. For the first time, she felt alone in this world.

Nonsense, she thought, and focused on the conversations. When the gathering concluded, she watched as Mater helped Gran out of her nest and followed them out of the room.

Back in her sleep pod, Ping used the cleaning brush to blow dust particles out of her fur and smooth it down. She hung her belt on a hook and laid her necklet in the drawer. A last sip of water, then she curled up in her bed to think.

The meeting had brought back the memories of those bewildering events. The Kay, Marisa, the other land people seemed more real than her fellow citizens. This was not how things were supposed to be. She wanted to go back to her everyday life, where she knew what was going to happen each day, what she would be doing next.

Only, something inside her told her she couldn't. There was no way to go back.

•   •   •

One day, shortly after the habitat had passed the fifty-year mark on this world, Ping woke to a strange, brief tingle in her body. By the time she was on her feet, it was gone, and she thought no more about it as she prepared for the day.

Until, as Ping walked into her workplace, she felt movement, a slight jerk. "What that?"

Chief Eler appeared. "Not know." Another jerk, in the opposite direction. "Put on floatation device. I find out."

A slight bobbing motion caused Ping to grab a bar on the wall. When it stopped, she reached for the yellow device. Nothing could happen to the habitat. Except it was so old. And no one had made improvements in eightys of years. Her researches helped her keep up with history and current events, if any.

"Attention," came from the wall screen. "One anchor broke loose. Stow loose items. Anchor will be fixed. Continue work."

"Oh, no," Ping said. The habitat, consisting of three globular modules connected by flexible conduits, with numerous teardrop shaped sleep pods attached to the outside, was grounded to the sea floor by a dozen huge anchors.

"Keep calm," Chief Eler said. "Continue work."

Ping stepped into her cubicle. What was happening was more than just a loose anchor. She felt it in her bones and shivered. Her skin began to tingle. She found herself checking on preliminary stages of an impending transit to another world. It was way too soon, but what else could it be? The signs were there. Should she tell Chief Eler or a higher chief? *No, they know soon enough, and he tell Council and they get everyone to shut down.*

The jerks and bobbing continued. Ping tried to ignore them but knew something serious was going on.

As Ping removed her floatation device and prepared to leave, the alarm sounded. "All departments shut down and all citizens return to sleep pods and strap in."

"Go," said Chief Eler. "I shut down department."

Ping joined a stream of citizens heading for the sleep pods. The floor jittered, and her tingles continued. One old hom with a long beard mumbled, "It wasn't like this last time." Ping wondered what he meant.

In her nest, Ping watched her screen. The message continued to repeat every few minutes while a musical piece with scenery played in the background. She felt the jerks as the anchors pulled free. The light dimmed. The whole place moved sideways. Her pod swayed and she held on to the edges of her nest.

Ping's body quivered, but her mind remained calm. When she was young, her grandfather had told tales about when they'd come from the previous world to this one. Later, working with Chief Eler, she probed into the history just before and after the transit. Now, without fear, she must wait.

She ducked her head, wrapped her arms around her and pulled in her legs. Only her face remained outside the nest cover. The motion lulled her into a doze. Presently, she slept.

14

WHEN PING AWOKE in her nest, she could not focus either her vision or her thoughts. She heard a low hum, and her screen was black in the low light. "No," she howled, the noise of her voice joining and increasing the volume of the hum briefly. The harder she tried to think, the more her thoughts flew off sideways.

"Stop," she gasped, and moved a hand in front of her face. "Hand," she said, "Arm." There were her fur covered fingers and thumb, and in the tan palm, a fine dusting of hairs. On her arm, the band of tiny pink shells her pater had given her upon her adulthood shone on her silvery lavender fur. She touched the fur near her elbow, then pulled out her other hand and looked at it, concentrating on the words, 'hand', 'arm', 'hand', 'arm'.

A tinkling caught her ear. She looked up. The now pale green screen, a color she'd never seen before, displayed figures and sounds, neither of which she could understand. *What is going on? This not how it supposed to be.* She couldn't make her hands remove her cover. Fear rose.

Ping *reached* for others with her mind. Only a few nearby, in various states of panic, responded. She should be able to reach all in this section. She sent soothing vibes, but could not tell whether they were received. She concentrated on inventorying her body. This gave her a stable focus of thoughts.

On the screen, Ping saw passing glimpses of other parts of the habitat, off colors, unfamiliar shapes, never long enough to pin down anything. This was definitely not right, but she had no idea what to do about it. Although she could move her hands, she couldn't pick up anything. Unable to get out of her nest, she was stuck.

Fear crept in around the edges of her mind. Ping shrugged it off. It wouldn't help her any. The air tasted different, a hint of saltiness. She kept trying to open her cover; she needed to get up, go out, find out what was going on.

More marks and noises popped up on the screen.

"I not understand," Ping said aloud. She felt something poking about in her brain. Suddenly the words became clear.

"Habitat has transited to another locality. Wait, you allowed up shortly." The sounds became the same words.

"Where is this?" Ping asked.

"Peace."

"No." Ping had to fight to keep her respiration and heartrate down.

Presently, her cover rose to the side. She sat up. Her pod was as it had always been. She crawled out of her nest, stood and stretched. Her body and mind felt normal. She consumed her energy nugget, brushed her fur, and donned her necklet and belt. The hatch opened.

Ping stepped out into the hallway. Others were emerging from their pods. As if drawn, they all moved toward the exit to the main module. No one spoke. As they walked along the corridor, an announcement appeared on the screens on every wall.

"Report to workplace."

Ping did, but no one else was there. She sat and waited.

•   •   •

Ping was lost. The familiar walls and tastes surrounded her, but she was lost. Always aware of the outside world in the back of her mind, now she couldn't find it. The ocean was gone, the whole world had been erased. Where would the citizens get materials for nuggets and all the other things they needed? Even though everything was recycled, that was not enough.

Chief Eler trudged in. "Us are doomed," he announced. "No one know what to do. Outside is nothing, not even air. No one know where us are, not even physicists. They working on it. Drone hatches refuse to open."

"What us do?"

"I not know." Chief Eler sat down on a nearby nest with a thump.

"There must be reason. Habitat and world work to rules."

"Yes." Chief Eler sighed. "Not time for transit, but research it anyway. Start about two hundred fifty years ago."

"Yes, chief." Ping retired to her cubicle, pulled down her bioputer and went to work. In the first one, the time of transit was so short, many barely noticed. The second, one hundred fifty years ago, the citizens had just got to their sleep pods and strapped down when it was over. Fifty years back, the transit took almost a half day.

A note about a report caught her eye, dated the last transit. She told Chief Eler what she'd found. An announcement interrupted her.

"All citizens go to sleep pods immediately."

"What? No, I need to find report," Ping said.

Chief Eler scurried off and returned with a harness. "Sit in nest." He strapped the harness around her and the back of the nest. "Find it." He trotted away.

Ping returned to the delayed transit and found the report.

27th TRANSIT REPORT

Rada 12

Preparations proceeded normally.

When I regained consciousness after transit, I sensed no changes in habitat. When I pulled lever for drones to depart, I received message.

"Hatches inoperative. No air beyond."

"What?" I said, and reached for nearest sensor disc. I tapped it and sensor screen remained blank. I tried other sensors. Same result.

Chief Rida stormed in and demanded to know why the drones not launched.

I indicated message. He told me to call engineering. They put me on waiting list.

Chief Rida pulled levers and punched discs, to no avail. I recorded this report. Then I had idea, but before I could record it, everything went dark.

When I became aware again, the drones went out and the sensors showed we were at sea.

End report.

Ping found the sensor controls and saw that they showed nothing, with a blinking message: 'No data'. She could not access the drones and assumed they did not go out.

"But what was his idea?" Ping asked aloud.

15

T HE WIDE, TAN BEACH stretched from the cliff to the west that
held back the big river, to the little river to the east. The
grassy slope ended at the sand at the top. Mostly smooth, a few
rocks and tide pools lay along the cliff.

Marisa and Jan sat on the warm sand, breezes playing with
their curls, and watched as Kaylyn splashed out of the water and
ran to her. "Mama, they're gone."

"Who?" Jan asked.

"What?" Marisa spluttered.

"Ping's people. The whole habitat is gone." She plopped down
on the sand.

"Are you sure?" Marisa asked. It didn't seem possible.

"Yes. I could find no sign of them."

"Okay, calm down. We'll find them."

"Let's eat," Kaylyn's father, Willie said. "Their place may have
some way to move itself. Maybe they wanted to be farther away
from us."

"No, Papa. They didn't choose to go, they were taken. They left
bits behind."

"Janni, the food." Papa ignored her.

Marisa opened the food basket and began laying out bowls of fruit and loaves of bread. Willie grabbed a loaf and moved away.

Kaylyn rose, stomped along the beach, and sat down and closed her mind to the others.

Marisa watched her granddaughter. Janni had not been the most attentive mother, and Willie was only interested in his boys. Kaylyn, a quiet child, had played in few childhood games. The one thing she was good at was swimming. The child had been paddling around in the sea before she could run. She always could swim farther and hold her breath longer than any of the others.

Disappointment radiated off Kaylyn. Marisa went to her granddaughter. For once, the girl had produced something unique, only to have it taken away.

"Let's reach for them," she said. "Jan, over here."

"I already did and couldn't find them," Kaylyn muttered.

Jan joined them and the three women sat together and joined their minds, focusing on the area at the end of the cliff, under the sea. Traces showed Ping's people had moved along the shoreline and abruptly disappeared.

They sat back and looked at each other.

"Gramisa?" Kaylyn asked.

"I don't know." Marisa looked at Jan.

"The parallel world," Jan said.

"Oh, no." Marisa closed her eyes.

Every adult knew the story of how Marisa and Susan, with their newborn babies, had led the community in the fight to keep the other world from taking over theirs.

"If there's one place to go between universes up there," Marisa pointed inland, "and another in the sea, are there any others, and if so, where?"

"Is that one still there?" Jan asked.

"Yes. I sent Ricky up there not long ago. He said he felt something strange there."

"Uncle Ricky always feels strange things," Jan said. "But I believe you."

"You just went through by yourself," Kaylyn added. "How could a huge habitat go through?"

"I suppose a portal could be larger under the sea." Marisa pulled a curl. "It could stretch a lot more."

"So what do we do?" Jan asked.

"We stay mindful of that area and the sea." Marisa climbed to her feet, and the others followed. She was glad those people were gone. Although Ping had seemed pleasant enough, Marisa had never forgotten the terror of dealing with invaders.

16

PING SEARCHED for the reporter's idea, found nothing, then searched for more on transiting. When she took a break, she noticed how quiet it was. Everyone was curled up in their sleep pods or other safe places. The background hums of the habitat sounded louder than normal.

She turned on soft music. Not normally allowed, but who would hear her now? She continued to work, not finding anything of interest. Whenever she did find an item she wanted to look into, the bioputer would not allow her to enter.

Ping finished her assignments early in the afternoon. She couldn't just sit there, and didn't want to go to her sleep pod, so she went to Park. The emptiness of the corridors gave her the shivers. At the entrance, she looked at the ramp. Her legs ached. She found the exit hatch, but it had no handle. There must be a way to open it, in emergencies.

A pair of indentations caught her eye, and she pressed them with her hands. The door popped open. She entered and plopped down on the first sitnest she came to.

The emptiness of the habitat filled her with unease, even though she knew where the citizens were. Ping felt a strong need to see another citizen. She *reached* and found no one else in Park. She knew now they were in a transit, but for how long? She couldn't just sit here, but her legs hurt too much to go walking.

She tried to process the data in her mind. Her thoughts kept wandering to the untimely transit. Finally, she leaned back. A drowsiness stole over her. She knew she was tired, but not sleepy. She never got sleepy during the day. *Why this?* Her eyes closed.

She woke to a voice from a nearby screen saying, "Transition completed. Return to work. Verify location and status."

Is over. Ping rubbed her eyes. *Time go back to work.*

She made her way out of Park and back to Science. She saw a few citizens in the corridors. *Are us back to normal?* In Science, more people passed her, with puzzled or apprehensive expressions.

"What happened?" one asked.

"Why now?" another asked.

Chief Eler waited for her at the lab. "Where you been?" he demanded.

"Park. Where us?"

"They send out probes now." He gestured to her cubicle. "Why you at Park?"

"I finished assignments. Needed go somewhere else. I saw no one."

Chief Eler clicked his fingers. "How long since your last checkup?"

Ping stiffened, turned, and stared at him. "I fine. I must work now." She stomped to her cubicle and pulled the biohelmet down.

Chief Eler came in a little later and dropped a paper on her worktable. Another assignment. She ignored it and him. She was compiling events before and after each of their previous three transits. The bioputer worked fine now. So far, all very similar, unlike this one.

At midday break, Ping picked up the paper. Her scalp wrinkled. It was an order to go to medical for a checkup, both physical and mental. "I not need this. Made scientific statement when I said I saw no one."

Chief Eler shrugged a shoulder. "Go after break."

Ping stalked out. As ordered, she went to the medical clinic in Science. One did not disobey a chief. At the front desk, a yellow-tinted citizen wearing a pale orange necklet studied the paper and said, "You go to main clinic in Central."

Ping snatched the paper. "Where it say that?"

Yellowy pointed to a small icon at the bottom.

"How I supposed to know that," Ping demanded and stalked off. She proceeded to Central with a feeling of annoyance. More emotions coming out of hibernation. Main medical hulked on the main level of Central, with several entrances with cryptic signs. Not knowing which one she was to go to, she picked one at random.

After she was sent back and forth a few times, she found the one for checkups. It took another eighty of minims to find the testing place. Ping had never felt so unsettled in her life.

She presented her paper, and a citizen with a pale red necklet, signifying a medic, led her through a series of rooms to one with a large, square machine. An opening in the front showed a nest and many tubes and wires sprouting from the ceiling and the sides.

The medic gently pushed her into the seat. Ping settled herself, and a harness embraced her. Aware that they would test every bit of her they could, she proceeded to shut down her exobrain. The hatch closed. In the dim light of the tiny screens on the walls, she saw the tubes approach her body and closed her eyes.

She felt the tickle as they attached to her skin through her fur, and slippery pressure as tubes eased inside her various orifices. There was no pain. Ping closed her mind as best she could.

After an indeterminate time, the screens blinked, and the tubes and wires detached themselves from her body. This time she did not feel them. *Did they give me numbing ointment?* By the time the harness loosened, and the hatch opened, impatience infested her mind.

Ping climbed out. The medic took her to another room with a pedestal between two roomy nests, and she climbed into one. A head rest lifted up and covered the top and back of her head. *They going to probe my mind.* That disturbed her. She shut down the exobrain and as much of the rest of her mind as possible.

A medic entered and sat in the nest opposite. "Welcome, I am Spia." She settled herself. "I perceive you not sleep during the transit."

"I needed to work," Ping said, shifting her body. "Slept in Park."

"Ah." She pulled out a device from a pocket in her nest and twiddled with it. "How you feel when you not find anyone?"

"Puzzled at first, until remembered announcement."

The medic continued to ask questions, and Ping answered as briefly as possible. When they were done, the medic took her to another room where still another medic with a mauve necklet waited.

"Ping, you quite healthy in your body," that one said. "I see you one of ones with experimental brain upgrade. That why you so good with bioputer. You first us found who not sleep in transit."

"But I slept. In Park."

"Oh." She wrinkled her nose. "Not very long, then."

"Why us transit now?" Ping asked, pushing the other to the side to consider later.

"I not know. Us to continue our work. Perhaps after they analyze probe data us know."

She led Ping to an exit door, out of the medical complex. It took Ping a while to determine where she was. By the time she found the corridor into Science, it was too late to go back to work.

Ping turned back and went to Park.

In a haze of thoughts, Ping found her way to the bench at the pond. Her legs felt much better after the checkup. *Did they do something to them?* Annoyed at the waste of an afternoon's worth of work, her ears heard an announcement, but her brain sent it directly to her recording device. She had thought most people had the recording modules, but apparently only a few had the unusual configuration of their brains that could use it.

Why me? Was that why they not let me have young? Mater must not have been allowed to tell me.

Ping stared at the tiny golden fish swimming around and around in the pond and sorted out her thoughts. First, the habitat had transited to another world well before the time it should have, according to past events. Second, it had taken much longer than before. Third, she had learned something about herself, which she didn't fully understand.

Too much had been happening, her world had been knocked sideways and she had no idea how to deal with it. She had been taught as a child to focus on the moment, and she would do that now. Since she couldn't do anything about the first two, she would ignore them. However, the third she could check out and see what her limits were.

Another message interrupted her thoughts. "Closing time five minums."

Ping jumped up and trotted to the exit. A citizen outside asked her if she knew what was going on.

"Us transited before our time. All I know."

The citizen said, "What is transit?"

"Look it up." Ping was tired and uneasy and didn't feel like talking to anyone.

At her sleep pod, she turned on her screen, took off her belt and necklet, and curled in her nest. Unable to sleep, she poked around in the depths of her mind to find out when she first became aware she had a private recorder in her mind.

She found the memory. Shortly after she began official learning, she had been knocked off the climbing hill, a large one with ladders and various footholds around its sides. She'd woken in the main medical clinic a few days later with a healing broken leg. The medicine they'd given her for the pain had made her feel like she was in a thick fog, seeing the outlines of something every now and then.

Ping recalled that not too long after her leg healed, she'd remembered a statement her grandmother had made to her mother when Ping was an infant, that this one was going to be different. Mater had asked Ping, in her second year of schooling, whether she knew about this, and Ping did.

"I remember she said I be different. I not know what she meant."

"Neither did we."

Ping brought up other memories from her young childhood.

Her screen interrupted her wilderness program and told her to report to her workstation in the morning. She searched for information on this new world and found nothing. She settled into her nest but could not sleep. Too many questions roamed in her head.

In time, she drifted into a dreamworld and wandered amongst floating shapes she could not identify. Some were like boxes, some were round or swirly, some were long and narrow, all shades of gray. She came to a large open box in greenish gray and drifted into it. A hefty female with gray skin and long white hair sat behind a table that looked more like a rock.

"Welcome. Sit." She waved at another nest of wood with no padding and only one arm.

Ping perched on the edge. She heard the words in her mind.

"This is Peace 3, a world parallel to yours and the original Peace. We brought you here because there is danger to your Peace."

"What danger? What about land people?" Ping felt no surprise.

"They will be looked after. You have an unusual component in your head."

Ping nodded. Even in the dream, she felt the unreality of the situation.

The conversation continued, but when Ping awoke, all she could remember was the first part.

For the first time in her life, fear gripped Ping like a forceps.

17

MARISA TURNED at the tap on her door. Her brother, Ricky, barged in. Even at fifty-eight, he had the energy and vigor of his youth. "So what did you see?" Marisa asked.

"There's an outline of a bridge there." He flopped down on the couch.

"Oh, no." Marisa brought her hands to her mouth.

"I was thinking. What if the sea people went there?"

"Okay, Ricky. Thanks. You can go do whatever you're supposed to be doing. I need to think about this." She waved him away.

"Okay, sis. See you." He left as precipitously as he came.

Marisa had a little time before her afternoon class. She wiped down the kitchen area and sat in her favorite padded chair. It needed a new cover. She would get a pale green this time.

The memories returned of a time forty years ago when her mindTalent caused her to lead the clan against a parallel world that wanted to take over hers. Memories she'd hidden for a long time.

Marisa had never wanted to talk about her confusing and painful experience, and she had a new baby to take care of. But now, if the other world was back, the younger generations needed to know about it. She would have to tell Jan, Glori, and Kaylyn, at least.

I can't go through that again, even without a baby to care for.

Everything had been going so well until all this. First, Ping, and now this. Ping was different from the other aliens she knew, even Maxee. Maxee was always bubbly, eager to try new things. Ping was very quiet, of course there was the language problem, but also reserved. She'd seemed interested in how the clanhome operated, but said little about her world.

Marisa sensed this experience for Ping was a major change in her life. Something deep was going on in Ping's home and, although she felt a desire to help, Marisa knew there was nothing she could do.

That evening, she *called* the three women over for a meeting.

Allen had retired to the bedroom, and the women sat in the living area. Jan settled by Glori on the old couch and picked at a splitting seam. A cooking aroma flavored the air.

"What is it, Mama?" Jan asked.

"The bridge is back. Ricky found it today." Marisa sighed.

"The bridge?" Kaylyn asked.

"The bridge to the parallel world." Marisa shifted in her chair. "You all know about the time I led our people to rid our world of it. The bridge was gone afterwards. Now it's back."

"Meaning what?" Glori asked. She and the other two stared at the older woman.

"It means the other world is back." Marisa rubbed her eyes.

"And you do not want it back," Glori said.

"Right. The first time I saw the bridge was early on, I don't think everyone was over here yet. Qione said she sensed something strange and wanted to go up to see, but when we got there, she wouldn't go near the bridge. On the other side of the river was a meadow and forest."

"The first time?" Jan asked.

"We went up a few more times. What I remember most was the sense of strangeness, otherness. An alien took me to another world where I met Asiram, and another time Ricky went with me. That time I was pulled into the forest, into that other room, and met with Asiram again. She wanted me to have a child."

"Me," Jan said.

"Yes, you." Marisa smiled at her. "It was so strange, all black and white and gray, no colors. I had to dodge a dancing table. Even Asiram had black hair and white skin and wore gray. And everything was always moving. She said something about our worlds being stuck together and we had to separate them."

"No colors," Glori said. "Strange."

"Susan and I had to wait for you two to grow and be born. Asiram kept contacting me in dreams, telling me I must come."

"Yes," Jan agreed.

"Finally, the time came, we had to share the birthing chair. As soon as you were out, Janni, they put me on the bed and Susan went to the chair and Glori arrived. You two were only five days old, riding in snuggies on our chests, so I don't expect you to remember anything."

"I do," Jan said. "Very vague, a lot of people and quines, very important."

"All the people gathered in the plaza, and all the quines came over," Marisa continued. "We had to drag Old Art out of his science workshop, and Allen, Grampa Bay, and Papa put him on a quine."

Jan and Glori giggled.

Marisa knew they remembered him. "We rode north, camped, and the next day we saw the blue mist, which was the physical presence of the other world. All of us with Talent, including the quines and you two, joined our minds together and pushed the mist back."

"You led, not Granlyn?" Glori asked.

Granlyn was the original clan matriarch, born on Old Earth and brought to other worlds by the Watchers, nonphysical beings who looked after the galaxy. Beings who were grooming Terrans to eventually take their place.

"I had the strongest Talent. She, being the first with Talent, was only able to communicate by mind." Marisa rubbed her eyes. *It had been so long ago.* "We had to stay there overnight to rest. Qilla was a new baby still learning how to use her legs. It was a letdown when we got back and had to catch up on our various tasks."

"So now what?" Jan asked.

"I need to go up there with one of you and Ricky."

The three looked at each other. No one said anything.

"No volunteers?"

"How long will it take?" Glori asked.

"At least two days. We can arrange for you to be away from your tasks."

"I think Janni should go, she has the strongest Talent." Glori spoke up.

"Hey," Jan said.

"Good idea." Marisa looked at her hands. "We'll have a school holiday with assignments, so Janni and I won't miss much."

"Mama, I haven't said I'd go."

"You will."

"I'd like to go," Kaylyn said.

Marisa's first reaction was No. Then she thought about it for a moment. Kaylyn would be with her mother. She should learn about this, too. "All right, Kaylyn, you can go. Be ready in three days."

The three left, and Marisa thought, *I wonder what we'll find there.*

18

PING CURLED UP in her sleep nest. This was too much. She knew of parallel worlds, but this was just a dream, right? *Overlapping worlds, impossible.* That fem seemed much more real than her usual dream people.

Duty called.

She forced herself to climb out of the nest and prepare for the day. There would be information coming in from this new world, wherever they were. Information that she would have to input and organize.

Her screen showed the same forest it always had, her nugget tasted the same. She made her way through the same corridors to the same work area, nodded to the citizens she passed every day. Chief Eler greeted her the same way he did every day.

"Information from drones coming in," he added. "Your assignment is organize and make report."

"Yes, Chief." Ping settled into her sitnest. Once she became involved in her work, the dream faded into the background. That afternoon, she sent out a preliminary report, the main point being there were no noncitizens on the land.

The next day, she finalized and sent the report to the chiefs. Then, she sat back and took a deep breath. *Now I get back to my normal life?*

·   ·   ·

Three days of normalcy later, Chief Adar called her and Chief Eler to his office. Half the size of Chief Mola's, it had only a few shelves on the gray walls and one small table in a corner. Besides his desk, there were three sitnests, two for visitors, rather hard.

"I scanned your report and consulted with Chief Mola," he said, steepling his fingers. "Us need to send someone out to see land firsthand. Since you out on other world, you be selected go out to this one. Atmosphere is similar to other."

"No," Ping said under her breath.

No and yes battled within her. While Ping wanted the outdoors, this was an unknown world, with too many questions. All her thirty years, her life had been programmed for her. She always knew what to do and how to find out how to do it. In the past several eight-days, everything had been turned inside out and upside down. She barely knew whether she was coming or going. She wanted, no, needed to get back in her old routine, to find herself.

Chief Adar gave her instructions and what information they knew about this world. "Atmosphere and gravity same as other world. Water potable. You go tomorrow morning."

Ping knew that if Chief Adar said, "Go," she must go. She desperately wanted to keep her job. It was what kept her sane.

"The pod take you to place near river." Chief Adar added. "Record everything, check out people, and call for pod when you ready to return. You will have call button to put on your belt."

"The report," Chief Elar began.

"Report quite complete. She add her impressions when she returns." Chief Adar waved them away.

They returned to Exo. "Do what you can today," Chief Elar said.

"Yes, chief."

Normally Ping had no problem tucking away outside thoughts and concentrating on her work, but that day, thoughts about recent changes kept trying to push their way into her consciousness. She was of mixed minds about going out. She had enjoyed many aspects of being outside, but this place was unknown, without noncitizens to call on for help if needed.

Ping found another small computing error. That made five counting the destroyed collector. Was the hab wearing out? Since she found the problem, it was her duty to do whatever needed to be done to fix it. She sent a message to Computer Central.

She managed to finish her workday and return to her sleep pod. She put on the screen a series of outdoor scenery programs and compared them to what she had seen in reality. These were created on previous worlds, and every world was different.

After making her preparations, Ping curled up in her nest. Perhaps the experience would be better this time. Perhaps after this, she could have some time for herself. Perhaps she could get back to a normal life.

•   •   •

In the morning, Ping made her way to the Pod Port in Central. She would do this because it was necessary for citizens to know what was out there, and it was her duty. This time a medic told her she would not need a cooler or dark eyeshade. She wondered about that, but could not say anything.

The call came, she boarded, and sat back. *Why hadn't he shown her any images? Was it because this world was much the same as the other, or too different?*

The pod took her to a place inland. When the hatch opened, Ping stepped out and looked around. Overcast, she was pleased she did not need her eye shade. Trees and grass and bushes similar to the ones on the other world surrounded her, but where were the noncitizens? The tall trees along the river, shorter in small groups, the forest in the distance were as she remembered from the other world, but she saw no evidence of intelligent life.

Had Adar just assumed there be noncitizens? Had he even read report?

Which way should she go? Ping opened her mouth wide and tasted this world. Purely nature, no sentient beings. The sky was a little darker blue and not as bright as the other world. She jumped up and down and felt the difference. Slightly stronger gravity. She found no change in the air she breathed.

Ping headed for the tall trees. It wasn't as warm as the other world, and a cooling breeze swirled around her. Tiny creatures scurried in the grass, and a few flyers soared in the sky. She soaked it all in, but inside she was empty. There were no noncitizens.

When she reached the trees, she stopped to rest. The river's mighty roar soothed her, drowned out her thoughts. This river, wide as the other, showed no way to cross it here. She headed upriver. At dusk, not ready to call the pod, she made a nest of moss under a tree.

•　　　•　　　•.

In the morning, Ping continued upriver, plodding along on the thickest grass. The river's roar continued to soothe her. Definitely cooler than on Peace.

At midday, after a couple of stops to rest, Ping came to a break in the trees. A bridge crossed the river where it narrowed. A shallow arc made of some material she'd never seen before, mottled gray and stiff, it did not move in the wind. Nothing ahead except the river and the trees.

The bridge and the forest beyond drew her. After another rest, she tiptoed across.

Yellow and blue wildflowers speckled the meadow between the river and forest. When she reached the edge of the forest, the sun was still high. A narrow trail led between two large trees. She sensed only animals within.

Ping followed the trail into the dimness under the trees. Something pulled her onward. She came to a glade with high, soft grass, and fell to her knees, then sat. Exhausted and unsure of the time of day, she decided to stay there for a good, long rest. If she found nothing the next day, she would return to the bridge and call the pod.

•　　　•　　　•

Ping felt something wrong even before she opened her eyes. *What is that?* The ground sagged underneath her as she moved. Cautiously, she opened her eyes to slits. Black and white objects moved in front of her, all around her. Some darted, some moved in spirals, some up and down.

Ping gasped and closed her eyes. *What that?* She could find nothing like this in her archives. Her mind and emotions closed themselves away from this unknown, indescribable horror. Slowly, the core of the being called Ping pushed itself out of the panic until she recognized herself. She pushed the terror away.

She couldn't just lie there. *I must do something. I go back and call pod or go forward.* Duty pushed her to the latter. She needed to learn what this new thing was.

Ping opened her eyes. On one level trees surrounded her as she sat on the soft grass. On another, the black and white world seemed to spin in and around the trees. She focused on the trees.

"I must do this," she said aloud as she rose to her feet. A trail led between a wide-leafed tree and another bent to the side. As she walked, the trees faded, and the black and white world brightened. The trail remained clear. The black and white must be a vision, she mused.

At the end of the trail, the trees disappeared, and a great structure stood ahead. Many houses tall, and so wide she could barely see the ends of the sides. Gray, with a row of black doors along the front and, higher up, black shapes that might be windows. Suddenly, Ping felt a force pulling her toward the building.

She fought against it, but her weary body was no match for this phenomenon.

Her feet moved of their own volition.

A door slid aside, revealing a long, narrow room with black tables and chairs that were doing a slow dance in the dimness. Her feet stepped inside, and the door closed behind her.

Her hands curled into fists, one around the strap of her bag, and her insides curdled. A soft pressure held her, while another entity probed her mind. She allowed it to find only the day-to-day memories. Ping's whole body clenched against this unknown presence, while a bit of her recorder explored the entity.

Suddenly the entity left, and she dropped to her knees. She grabbed at a nearby table and hauled herself to her feet. She had to get out of there. Ping turned to the door. A blackness swooped over her, and she fell, unconscious.

19

PING BECAME AWARE of her surroundings, a small dark place. She lay on a hard surface, and the air was neither hot nor cold. A low hum and swishing noise found her ears. She tried to sit up, but something held her down. Panic hit her as she struggled.

"Rest," said a low, soothing voice. Light grew, and Ping saw the fem from her dream. She relaxed a little.

"Who," she began.

"I am Asiram. I am other. I am on another Peace. I have learned about the humans, now I must learn about you."

Ping stared, her mind unable to comprehend the words she heard.

The fem placed her hands on Ping's head and murmured more incomprehensible words.

Ping waited, unable to focus on her surroundings.

"Do all your people have this extra brain?" Asiram asked.

"No. Only few."

"I see. Are you a leader?"

"No. I just citizen." Ping accepted these questions with no qualms.

"Interesting." Asiram took her hands away. "You will sleep now. When you awake, you will find your way out to your world."

Before Ping could say anything, she slept.

•   •   •

This time, when Ping awoke, she was in a small glade in the forest, with no path out. After she ate pulled out and ate her nugget, she walked all the way around the place searching for an opening, a trail.

No.

She clenched her fists and closed her eyes. *Focus.* Behind her eyes she perceived an empty space beyond some shaggy bushes.

"Ah," Ping said. She pushed through the bushes and found a trail. She could not tell where it led, but it was the only way to go. Narrow and winding, the ground even and uncluttered, the trail was easy to follow.

She came to a stream but could see no trail on the other side. *Now what?* Ping wanted to scream, but citizens always kept control of themselves.

A spot of sunlight lit a rock, and then another. Something in the deep recesses of her mind told her to always follow water downhill. A third rock lit up, following the flow of the water. A narrow, grassy ridge along the stream gave her barely enough room to put her feet.

Ping walked until she came to a place where the stream disappeared under a huge boulder.

"This is nonsense," Ping said aloud. "She said there way out. Was that truth?"

She had no choice but to continue on. A bush with large thorns nestled against the side of the rock, close packed trees on the other side, so she had no choice but to go over the rock. *How?* She studied it. There were indentations where she could place her feet. She put a foot in one, reached up and grabbed another indentation, and lifted her other foot.

Slowly she climbed to the top. An open valley with a dry streambed stretched before her. A few puffy clouds hung in the sky. *Where did the forest go?* She looked around and saw it to her left.

Ping climbed down and walked through low, round-leaved plants along the edge of the forest, looking for an opening. She knew she had to be in the forest to reach the meadow. The experience with the dream fem had numbed her mind; she could only direct her body to follow the trail.

When her body tired, Ping stopped to rest, sitting against a tree with round leaves. As she mused in a half-doze, the words, 'is this real', came into her mind briefly.

A little farther on, she found a trail into the forest and took it. Something tugged at the back of her mind, but it dodged away whenever she tried to focus on it. Presently, she arrived at a mossy glade and decided to stay there for a good sleep. It finally dawned on her that the sun had not moved all the time she was traveling.

Ping made a nest and curled up in it. As her mind relaxed, the words returned. "This not real. When I awake, I be on my world," she announced.

20

MARISA MADE HER ARRANGEMENTS and gathered food. Her curiosity wanted to find out if the bridge was still there, but her fear wanted it not to be there. Her emotions battled within her for two days. She put her small cooking pot on the wrong shelf and laid her clean tunics in Allen's drawer.

On the morning of the third day, Marisa was up before dawn and dusted everything she'd dusted the day before, while waiting for the others. Jan and Kaylyn arrived together, but Ricky took his time, as usual.

"Are you ready?" Marisa asked after greetings.

"Are you?" Jan asked.

"I hope so. The quines are waiting." She collected her bags and found the creatures munching on the leaves of a large tree at the side of the house. The four humans mounted and started off, Marisa with a lump in her innards.

The group rode north along the great river. The gray sky matched Marisa's mood. She had hidden her emotions from the experience forty years before because she was playing catch up and dealing with a newborn baby who had to be cared for and fed often.

After a while, her feelings sank into her background memories, and she rarely thought about that time.

Now the memories came rushing back. The feeling of inadequacy mixed with the exultation of leading her people, the terror when the other side began gaining on her, the fear she would be unable to handle the situation, and the relief when it was all over and everyone collapsed, empty. *Was this going to happen all over again?*

"Here it is," Ricky said, as his quine stopped at a place where the trees thinned. "Hey, it's a lot more solid now."

Marisa's heart sank. The shallow, blue-gray arc of the bridge looked the same as before. Then she felt the pull from the forest. "No!" she cried out.

"Mama?" Jan asked.

"Gramisa?" Kaylyn echoed. "I feel something."

"So do I." Jan patted her quine. "I remember."

"You were too young," Marisa said. They were three or four house lengths away from the bridge, and the quines refused to go any closer.

Ricky dismounted and trotted to the bridge. "I feel something, too."

"So they are there." Marisa dismounted, walked to Ricky, closed her eyes and reached. "Nothing definite. Janni?"

Jan approached and *reached*. "I sense something, but it's not like it was before."

Marisa gathered Jan and Kaylyn to her. "Let's all try together. You too, Ricky."

They perceived an alien presence in the forest, a large creature moving toward them just inside the last row of trees.

"Hello!" a voice cried. Marisa whirled around, heart pounding. Maxee and one of her grown kubs approached from the north. "Someone come." She pointed to the forest.

"Hi, Maxee, Braxi." Marisa recognized her from the blue ribbon woven into her chest fur. She was a little taller than Maxee.

Maxee and Braxi, her oldest, joined Marisa's group.

Marisa watched as a creature with pale lavender fur stepped out into the meadow and sank to its knees. "No, it can't be."

21

P ING CAME TO in a familiar mossy nest and wondered where she was. She tried to remember what she had been doing before she slept. Her mind was blank. Other worlds. *Which one am I on?* She sat up and looked at herself.

"I am Ping," she said aloud. A pair of flyers flapped out of a nearby tree.

Trees, forest. A few things trickled back.

"I am on a mission, duty."

She touched the soft moss she sat on.

"This is real." *Why it not be?* she asked herself.

Ping saw her bag. Nuggets. Must consume nugget. She opened her bag, found the nuggets and her water bottle. She ate, drank, and climbed to her feet. A glade was open around her, and a spring gurgled at one side. This place was green, with bushes and grass decorated with red and yellow flowers. A pleasant place to stay, if it wasn't for her duty.

She tasted the air. Good, with hints of both worlds.

Both? Marisa. The other world she had visited began to come back to her.

Time to move on.

She filled her bottle. It contained a microfilter so nothing in the water could hurt her. An opening led her to a hint of a trail through a mass of trees and bushes. As she pushed through the bushes, memories began to push through into her mind.

She was Ping, a citizen of a community who lived inside, where there were only corridors and rooms. Where each citizen had his/her duties, where each had a sleep nest in a sleep pod. She recalled a device that came down over her head, but not what it was.

At a small glade, Ping followed a narrow path to her left. Trees farther apart gave her glimpses of meadow. Since the bushes were too close together to push through, she trudged along on painful feet.

Ping felt so lost she could only put one sore foot in front of the other and gaze longingly at the meadow. Why did she come into the forest to begin with? She couldn't put two thoughts together, couldn't tell if this was the same world she'd been sent to.

Presently, she come to a pair of widely spaced larger trees and a trail that led between them to the right. She stepped out into the meadow and stopped. Several figures stood at the far end of a bridge beyond. People. Ping's legs gave out, and she sat down hard.

Where I?

One of the people trotted over the bridge to her. The gray furred fem. "Maxee," Ping said. "How ..."

"Ping." Maxee squatted down beside her. "How you here?"

"Where?" Ping shifted to a more comfortable position.

"Here Peace. You here before." Maxee patted Ping's shoulder.

Marisa's Peace. But how did I get here? At least she knew where she was. Still confused, Ping stared at the line of huge trees along the river.

Maxee helped her up, looked back at the others and waved. Another like Maxee hurried over the bridge. "This Braxi, my first kub. Braxi, carry Ping."

Braxi picked up Ping, carried her over the bridge, and set her down on a clump of grass. Pleased that she didn't have to walk any farther, Ping eyed the people as they approached. She remembered Marissa, Jan, and Kay. They were accompanied by a man, tall and broad, topped with a mop of brown curls, whom Marisa introduced as her brother, Ricky.

"Why, Ping, how did you come here?" Marisa knelt beside her.

"Tired." Ping could barely move. She was only used to walking from her sleep pod to her workplace, and sometimes to Park. An exercise place was available, but she rarely went due to lack of time. Sometimes she did exercises in her sleep pod.

She stretched her feet out in front of her. Blisters covered the pads on the bottoms.

Marisa gasped. "Your feet." She grabbed her bag, pulled out a green jar and reached for one of Ping's feet. Ping drew her foot back. "This will help heal your foot," Marisa assured her. "We use it all the time for injuries."

Ping remembered Marisa's kindnesses and stuck her foot out. Marisa dabbed some of the stuff on her foot. Soothing coolness eased the pain. She wiggled her other foot. "Gratitude."

Marisa wrapped a long piece of thin cloth around the foot and did the same for the other foot. "We'll carry you to a quine so you can ride to my home. You'll need to stay off your feet for a while."

Ping nodded. Although she felt safe for now, something was wrong. She was not supposed to be here. This was a good place to be, with these noncitizens she knew. She could relax and regain her strength, plan what to do next. She had plenty of her energy nuggets. "Good. Much gratitude." Still, something was not the way it should be.

As Marisa packed up her medikit bag, Maxee turned to her.

"I come with you. I have message from Sam and Hal."

"Okay." Marisa headed for the quines. "Let's head home."

Maxee spoke to Braxi, and she strode off upriver.

Ricky and Jan helped Ping up on Qilla, Jan's quine, and Maxee rode Ricky's steed.

Ping spoke to her mount. "I Ping. I ride before."

'I Qilla. I go easy,' the quine said in Ping's mind. The latter nodded and held on to the neck hair. She found it very pleasant riding and she enjoyed being able to see all around. She could see so far in all directions. *This is the way people should live, out in the open, with nature.* She wondered at the thought and realized something inside her was changing.

Ping would think about that later, but now she would ride along and enjoy the pleasure it gave her. Exist in the moment, like she had been taught as a child. The warm sun felt a little too warm, but a breeze sent cooling waves. The forest on her screen was mostly dark green, but here there were all shades, from pale green patches of grass, bright greens of trees they passed, to the dark green of the distant forest. Multi-colored bunches of flowers sprouted around the trees and in patches in the grass.

She opened her mouth to taste and found the same earthy plant aromas she had tasted before, with a hint of home.

The quines stopped at their trees, the riders dismounted, all but Ping.

"Qilla, take her to my house and wait," Marisa said.

"Gratitude, Marisa." Ping wondered how far a quine could go in a day. They must get tired eventually.

At Marisa's, Ricky helped Ping down, carried her into the house, and set her on the sleep nest in the room she had used before. The nest contained more padding and a ridge around the open side, top and bottom. She left the door curtain open a bit on each end and curled into the nest. *Much better.*

"Gratitude," Ping said as she settled in. She closed her eyes and fell into a doze. Presently she became aware Maria and others were eating and tried to ignore the sounds.

She listened to voices. Kaylyn had gone to her home, but Jan and Ricky were still here.

"She came through the forest, but how did she get there?" Ricky asked.

"Ask her," Jan said.

"Not tonight. Let her rest." That was Marisa. "Did you see her feet? She must have walked a long way. I'll talk to her tomorrow."

"How deep is that forest?" Jan asked.

"I don't know," Marisa said. "It turned into that other world. If she came through that, how did she get there? Or is the other world only there sometimes and there's another world beyond?"

"Do you think they'll come over here?" Jan asked.

"I hope not. Maxee, what does Sam have to say?" Marisa tugged a curl.

"She want a meeting with her leaders and yours. She say people not following rules, and some boasting about coming down here. Also, grain crop not well. Not grow well and die too soon."

"Oh dear," Marisa said. "We have been missing a few things, but thought they were just misplaced. When and where?"

"Down here. She afraid if you go up there some might try to hurt you."

"Oh, no!" Jan cried.

"If your quine call, they can come down tomorrow." Maxee nodded.

"Okay. I'll have Qilla tell them to have them meet us at the plaza at midday." Marisa said.

"Okee." Maxee nodded. "I stay here?"

"No, Ping's got the room."

"You can stay with us," Jan said.

"Okee." Maxee and Jan left.

"About the other world," Ricky said. "At least we know what to expect."

"Do we?"'

22

P ING DOZED OFF and, when she awoke, the house was quiet. She replayed the conversation in her mind and sensed there was still some ambivalence toward her. All her memories and knowledge were back. She decided she would rest for a day, then return to her world. Maybe the dream fem wouldn't stop her again.

Marisa and Jan, she trusted, but Ricky was an unknown. She did not know much about the men on this world. The men on hers mainly put their interests ahead of those of the women. They raised their sons after their primary learning, and the boys lived in the barracks with their fathers.

Presently, Ping slept.

•   •   •

Ping woke refreshed, though not ready to walk anywhere. The events of the last few days crashed over her. She sighed and pulled herself together, then went over them briefly. There was no change in her plans. She waited until Old Allen left before going out into the main room.

Marisa sat at the table working on some papers. "Good morning, Ping. How did you sleep? Do you feel better?"

"Yes, more rested." Ping dropped down on the couch and put her feet up.

"Let's see how those feet are doing." Marisa fetched her salve and more bandages. She removed the old bandages. "Yes, they do look better." She put more salve on Ping's feet and bandaged them. "Why do you not have shoes?"

"Shoes?"

"Wraps for the feet." She stuck out a foot wrapped in overlapping leaves glued together.

"Us not need. Floor padded."

"How did you get here?" Marisa put the rest of the bandages and salve on a shelf. "Where did your place go?"

"You know parallel worlds?"

"Yes." Marisa sat beside Ping. "We had one whose beings attacked us when Janni was a baby."

Ping explained about transits. "Science chief Mola chose me to check new world because I out before. Some not handle distant view. Just look around and go back. No people there, so I went over bridge, like here, and into forest, which turned into black and white world." She paused. For some reason she didn't want to tell Marisa about the dream fem. "I woke up in this forest, found way out, and you."

"So it is Asiram's world. Were things always moving?"

Ping closed her eyes. "Too much."

"I see. This is not good. What do you know about parallel worlds?"

"Our physicists know how they work, but not why us move from one to another." Ping twisted a finger with her other hand. "Transits always every hundred years, this time, after only fifty years."

"Do you think it could have anything to do with us?" Marisa tugged a curl.

"No. Many worlds us go to have land people."

"Did anyone go out and visit them?" Marisa asked. Ping sensed that although the older fem couldn't understand how this could be, it still fascinated her.

"Few times."

Marisa stared at the ceiling. "I wonder. Do you suppose our mindTalent could have anything to do with it?" She looked at Ping.

Ping's eyes widened. "Possible. When I go back, I check bioputer for information on previous transits."

"Bioputer? Sam had a box she called a computer that she kept lists on."

"Yes. Our device biological. It holds much information, way more than citizen mind, and does all kinds of calculations. Must have history of transits."

"I see. Can you keep lists of things or people on it?"

"Yes."

"That would be useful." Marisa rose. "I have tasks I must do. What do you want to do today?"

"Go to little park by river." Ping looked at her feet.

"I'll get someone to carry you over."

•   •   •

Later, after Ping settled herself in the park across from the end of the plaza, she watched the river ripple by. The moving water fascinated her; the little stream in Park just oozed along. A yearning to live where she could watch this every day stole over her.

The habitat was not a natural place for citizens to live. *Why did us stay in it so long? Ancestors must move into one, thousands of years ago when others took over their land, but why they not move back on land later?* Several worlds they'd been to apparently had possible land habitat sites.

Why I thinking these thoughts?

When she heard voices in the plaza, she got up and tiptoed to the edge of the park. Marisa and several others greeted a group on the large brown creatures called quines. Ping tiptoed to the nearest bench and sat. As the group dismounted and the quines wandered off, the people moved toward the meeting hall.

Ping rose and followed.

"Oh, there you are," Marisa said. "Ricky, carry her."

Settled in one of the sitting nests in a circle, Ping looked around. Maxee and Sam sat beside her. Beyond Sam sat a hom Ping did not know.

"Maxee," Ping said.

"You here again," Maxee grinned. "Good."

"Hello, Ping," Sam said. "Nice to see you again."

Ping nodded.

When everyone was settled, Marisa stood. "Before we get to

your problems," she nodded at Sam, "I need to share something new. When we were first here, and Janni was a new baby, a parallel world tried to intrude on us. We, all of us with our minds, pushed it away. Now it's back. It's how Ping got here."

She looked at the gray furred alien. "Maxee, since you live closest to the bridge, we need you to keep a lookout for any changes in the meadow and forest beyond the bridge."

"Okee." Maxee bounced in her seat.

"Ping, what's happening with your world?"

"Habitat transit to new world way too soon. Is world like this but no citizens. I went over bridge to see if beings in forest. Found black and white place. Woke on this world."

"How," Sam began.

Old Allen sat up. "I suspect that adjacent parallel worlds are pretty much alike. You found one that we did not come to. Black and white, I don't know. Maybe Artie has an idea."

"It could be an in between place, where the worlds connect," Artie said. "We don't know enough about it."

"Okay," Marisa said. "Discuss it with your papa and other scientists. Now, Sam, what's going on up there?"

Sam stood. "Two things, Marisa. First, too many people aren't doing what they're supposed to and are making trouble. They think we owe them whatever they want. The resentment of their elders for having to move here has been passed down to their now grown children. They don't understand, and won't listen, that government has to be for all people.

"Second, our grain crops have been doing poorly. Dying off before they reach their full growth."

Marisa nodded as Sam continued.

"I'm planning to go see Liia. The Ambaak do not seem to have any problems with their people." Newamb, the third colony on Peace, whose humanoid people had come to Peace from Cityworld with Sam's group, was self-sufficient.

"I don't know what we can do about the first problem, except keep a lookout on our border," Marisa said. "We don't have that many people. The more children we have, the more people we need to provide for them."

"Did you happen to bring a sample of the grain?" Artie asked.

"Yes." The man with Sam handed it over.

"We'll check it out and see what we come up with." Artie looked at Sam. "How come you don't have police protection?"

"We never needed it in City. The Volen took care of everything."

"Until they left," the man said.

"Okay, Hal." Sam punched him lightly in the shoulder.

"The Volen?" Artie asked.

"An ancient people who no longer have physical form. They built City for the original Old Earth colony and provided everything for us. All little apartments and long corridors. Caffs where we ate, and shops, and screens in our places where we could access the main computer." Sam sighed. "Then they left, and City slowly disintegrated. We had to find a new place to live, and Brad and I were chosen to find a new place and oversee the move."

Sam looked around. "And then we had to move here. We were outgrowing our valley over there."

"You like living outside better?" Ping asked.

"Oh, yes. After I got used to it, I couldn't stand having to go back into City." Sam grinned, along with Hal. "Of course, a lot of people had a lot of trouble getting used to it. We could see all sorts of outdoor places on our screens, but actually being outside was a whole different thing."

"Yes," Ping said. "I, too, learned land and sea not being shown on walls."

"Why are your people still living inside?" Jan asked.

"Safe there. No one think different."

"How sad." Marisa twisted a curl. "Is there anyone you could talk to?"

"Perhaps. I go back tomorrow." Ping looked at the pod button. It appeared to be dead. "No." She took a deep breath and blinked. "I must go back through forest to my world."

23

MARISA PERSUADED PING to stay another day or so to make sure her feet were healed. The next two days, Ping looked at the various books and other items Marisa's grandparents, Granlyn and Grampa Larry, had brought from Earth. Marisa told her what she could remember of Earth history.

The following day, Marisa gave Ping salve, bandages and extra foot wraps, and rode with her to the bridge. The day was quiet and sunny.

"You are always welcome here," she said, as Ping slipped off her quine and shouldered her bag. Ping sensed an undercurrent of hesitancy and ignored it.

"Much gratitude for your help. I see you again someday." Ping walked carefully over the bridge toward the forest. She followed the trail to the glade where she had awakened before and rested there. Her feet barely bothered her. *A place like this would be a wonderful sleep pod.*

The next day, she continued into the forest until she came to a place where the trail split in two. Down one leg, she saw the black and white building and shivered. *Not that way.* Ping scurried down the other path. In a dim area under thick trees, a small animal crashed through the trees across the trail and tripped her. One knee landed on a small branch, and she lay there, dizzy. A second, larger creature jumped over her as it followed the other.

Ah, there are animals in this forest.

Ping shook her head, sat up, and checked her leg. Although padded by her fur, it was still painful to the touch. A *cheep* sounded above her, and she gasped. These were not the trees she'd been in before her fall. And the trail was wider.

Could this be my world?

Ping climbed to her feet. She could put some weight on that leg. She limped down the trail as fast as she could manage. Soon she came to the first glade and collapsed in a puddle of relief. This was her world. She relaxed and allowed herself to doze. Her time sense was gone. She not only did not know what time of day it was on this world, she also didn't know where she was in her circadian rhythm.

When she awoke, rested, Ping ate a nugget and headed for the trail. Soon it curved to the left and she glimpsed open space beyond the trees. She tried to go faster, but that made her knee hurt more. Presently, the trail came to the edge of the forest.

Ping limped out into the meadow and checked the pod button on her belt. Glowing green, she tapped it and moved toward the bridge. As she waited for the pod, she surveyed the area to locate a place for her nest here. It was so much like Marisa's world, except for the noncitizens.

Finally, she heard a hum, and the pod eased down to the ground. The hatch opened, Ping boarded and settled into the nest, savoring the homestyle cushiness. The journey back to the habitat seemed to take much longer than before. A closed-in sensation surrounded her by the time they arrived at the port.

She had no idea what time it was in the habitat. A pair of homs hurried by without giving her a chance to ask the time. Ping checked the chrono in the port. Midafternoon, too late to go to work, so she trudged over to Park, three levels down.

Ping entered by the exit door again, and found a place to sit, just off the main pathway. The trees in Park moved in an artificial breeze. A group of older children trooped past where she sat, ignoring her, chatting with one another.

Was I like that at that age? No, not have large circle of friends. Studied hard and worked few days of eight-day at creche with the little children. Groups of my peers like this group. They grow out of it when reach adulthood and given tasks.

Ping stayed there until closing time, then trekked back to her sleep pod. She tried to make sense of her experiences, but basically it came down to the fact that noncitizens she could relate to, lived on the land in an organized, comfortable manner.

•   •   •

Ping reported to work in the morning. Chief Eler asked, "Where you been? Eight-day too long."

Ping stared at him. "No. I measured six days. Went through forest to other world."

"Eight-day here. Download your recordings." He walked away, and Ping entered her cubicle, sat, and pulled down the bioputer over her head. She selected Outer Environment and downloaded her recordings. While that was proceeding, she opened Time. Chief Eler was right. The date here was the day she left Marisa's Peace. It made no sense.

Ping looked at the list of questions people wanted answers for and shrugged a shoulder. Most were simple, and she finished most of them by midday break. She finished up early afternoon and asked the 'puter, "What are parameters for transit?"

A complicated equation popped up, which made no sense to her. Chief Eler didn't understand it either.

"Why we not go back to land?" Ping asked.

"Not need to. Why you ask?"

"Is so much better out there, more space, better able to think. If habitat breaks, where we go, what we do, how we live?"

"Habitat fine. Us just fine here. No need to worry. Go now."

Ping left, carrying her concern with her.

•   •   •

Upon her arrival the next morning, Chief Eler told her he had looked at her download.

"More space out there. More plants, raw products for printers. But where we live? So many things." He waved his arms about. "No. Not now. Your assignments await."

As Ping worked, she pondered on how to convince him to at least look out there. She received a message from her sister, Bede, about a family gathering in a few days. Family meaning mainly female members. Homs rarely came unless invited. She decided she would share her experience with her family.

•   •   •

At the gathering room, Ping saw only one grandmother was there. Pater's mater was probably at her family meeting.

"How you been, Ping?" Mater asked.

"I been outside to land. Is beautiful out there."

"You did what?" Mater put her hands to her face.

"Mater, I sent by high chiefs. I not disobey."

"You must not do that again. It dangerous. We not know what out there. Ask for transfer to another job."

"I cannot. Exo my place. Nowhere else I want to be."

"You must not go out again," Mater repeated.

Ping could not believe how adamant her mater was about going out. "Us need to explore, find out what there. Us cannot live in habitat forever. Is old, need more repairs than ever. It not last forever."

"Girl is right," the grandmother said. "This place only meant be temporary. I die here, but younger people need find new home."

"Gran." Ping gasped.

"I may be old, but I worked in education and researched much. See way of things. Nothing changed since childhood. Lack of change lead to downfall, to death. Moving bring many changes." Gran closed her eyes, which disappeared in her wrinkled face.

Scales fell from Ping's mind. She had never thought about what Gran processed in her mind. She'd just seen her as old, retired educator who sat there and watched. An automaton. Now she saw her as real person, like herself.

Ping looked at her mater, sisters, aunts. These, too, were real now. She'd always thought of other people as props in her life, like bioputer and other machines. She did what they said because it was what she was supposed to do. She perceived a whole new vision of her world.

Must be because of this closed world. Very little touching of one another. Us learn to talk to 'puter at early age. People just mobile bioputers.

But no longer.

Ping sat back and pretended to listen to her aunts describing their work while processing this new way to look at the world. *How I be so blind?*

Her people had done the same thing for so long they had become automatons. She had been the same until she'd met the land people, but didn't realize what she was perceiving. She must find a way to get the citizens out of this overgrown seashell, out in the open, where they could grow. Especially the children. She ached for the children who were never born because there was no room for them.

24

JUST BEFORE MARISA LEFT with Ping, Sam and Hal said their goodbyes and rode over the bridge across the little river and the high grassy plain to Newamb. The quines slowed to a walk when they reached the farms on the outskirts of the community. People harvesting crops waved to them.

They proceeded on through the neatly laid-out town, small trees along the streets and in back of the houses. At the square center park, they dismounted and left the quines there to browse.

Sam and Hal found Liia in the meeting hall at one side of the park, bright with light through the large windows.

"Sam, hello. And you, too, Hal. How are you?" she greeted them.

"We have a situation we'd like to talk to you about," Sam smoothed her long, gray-streaked red hair. Even tied down, the wind blew wisps out when she rode her quine. "We left the quines in the square. I hope that's all right."

Liia nodded. "All creatures must eat. Come." She showed them to a small room. A round table with several chairs sat in the center. The only other furniture was a row of cabinets along a side wall. A good-sized window let in light filtered by a row of trees, reflected in the white walls.

In a few minutes, Liia bustled in, her gray hair tied back, her tiny nub of nose almost lost in her round face. "How can I help?"

"We are having problems with a certain group of our population," Sam said. "How do you keep your people so well-behaved?"

Hal frowned.

"Have you no police?"

The word Liia used for 'police' Sam interpreted as a combination of security and overseer.

"We have a security system, but those people ignore them." Hal touched his moustache.

"You need rules to enforce. Our children learn from a young age to respect others and obey our rules."

"We have rules," Sam said. "But not all parents can teach well."

Liia tapped the table with a stubby finger. "Ours are taught in school. They must follow school rules. Parent not always able."

"In school, huh," Hal said. "How could we do that?"

"Talk to the head of the Education Department." Sam wrinkled her nose.

"Yes." Liia nodded. "Make list of rules and punishment for breaking them. Take away things they like. We have jury of three to listen to complaints and determine punishment and make sure it is carried out."

"We could do that with young children, but these are adults. They're unhappy about the moves from City to Starview, and Starview here, even though they have a lot more room here. Some want what they had in City and don't understand that we don't have it to give them." Sam looked at Hal.

"Too many centuries of having everything provided for them," he said.

"Yes." Liia nodded. "We had much, but worked to take care of our needs ourselves."

A tall, dark and solid young man stuck his head in and grinned at Sam.

"Hi, Jim. How's little Brad?" she asked. He'd named his son after her brother, who had brought him and his sister as children to Liia during the collapse of City.

"Not so little. He's as tall as me. Liia, is there anything I can do for you? I have some free time."

"Go fetch your baton so I show it to Sam and Hal." Jim left, and Liia continued. "We do not have weapons that can seriously hurt, but sometimes this works as threat. Jim is second in command of police."

Jim returned with a long cylinder of dark wood, smoothed and polished. He handed it to Hal. "We swing these around if there is trouble. It can hurt if you are hit hard."

Hal turned it over in his hands, and Sam leaned over and peered at it.

"How do you make it?" Hal asked. Sam saw it was a smoothed tree branch.

"Find a good, straight branch, cut it to size, peel off the bark, and smooth it."

"How is your security set up?" Hal asked the young man.

"Police are chosen and trained from adolescence. They are assigned an area away from their family. They help with any kind of problem and know who to refer people to if they cannot help."

"I see." Hal nodded.

"We'll have to sit down and plan this." Sam tucked a strand of her gray hair behind her ear. "We should have done this a long time ago, but I kept hoping."

"I know." Hal patted her hand. "Thank you for your time, Liia." He rose.

"Liia, could I go with them and show them?" Jim asked.

She looked at him, counted on her fingers, and said, "Yes, you may. No more than three days. You do not mind, Sam?"

"Fine with me. Aren't you about ready to retire?"

"Yes, but I cannot. We are training Giil's grandson and his mate to take over and must make sure they are ready." Giil was her spouse.

"Giil's grandson?"

"I could not bear children, and his line must be continued."

"Okay." Sam wanted to ask who the mother was, but was wise enough to keep her mouth shut. "Take care."

"Come any time," Liia said, standing.

They all touched hands, and Sam and the men left. Her quine, Qiota, *sent,* 'Who is this? Going with us?'

Jim was much larger than Hal, so he rode Hal's quine. Sam's mount had to be talked into allowing Hal to ride with Sam.

As the trio left town, Sam's mind blanked for a moment, then her farseeing kicked in. "No, not again." She pulled Qiota to a stop.

"What is it?" Hal touched her hand.

Sam sighed and closed her eyes. "Something bad coming this way. Something affecting this whole world. Something I'd rather not have to deal with."

"We'll take care of it," Hal said, patting her arm. "Let's go, now."

25

T HE NEXT DAY AT WORK, Ping saw Chief Eler through new eyes. He was a person with his own life beyond the lab. She briefly wondered what he looked at when he went to Park, if he had sons, what he watched on the screen. He greeted her and disappeared into his own work cubicle. Ping continued to her own workplace.

Later, she received a message from someone called Nela.

Saw your download and wish to discuss it with you. I Nela, third level clerk in physiology. May us meet?

Ping was surprised and pleased as she arranged for a meeting in one of the gathering rooms.

Nela was shorter and rounder than Ping and wore a pale blue necklet. The two eyed each other. Outside of family and work, few citizens met face to face.

"You say you accessed my download. Why?" Ping asked as they settled into sit nests.

"My chief began to access it, then told me to and create summary for him."

"Ah," Ping said. "What you like to know?"

Nela picked at the edge of her nest. "You enjoy being out there?"

"Mostly. Feet got sore. Sometimes too warm. Best part, it real. Able to see all around me so far, trees moving in air, sounds of life, strong tastes."

"Wish to go back?"

"Any time." Ping paused. She knew she wouldn't get anywhere with the chiefs, but perhaps she could work up through those at her level. "I learn someday we must leave habitat and move back to land. You know, ancestors used to live on land."

"Yes. I read stories set on land. Is possible to go out there? To live out there?" Nela raised a hand.

"Perhaps. Not easy, but if citizens start thinking how to do it now, be easier later."

"Start small, just few people in pods at first."

"Yes," Ping said. "If us keep travel pod there, us stay connected with bioputer."

"Right." Nela bounced up and down, her mouth wide in her face. "They make more pods. What about food?"

"Land people grow plants to eat. Us must do that if us not get the nugget maker up there."

"Us must reprogram our bodies so us can process plants," Nela said.

"That be difficult?" Ping asked. "Land people satisfied with their lives even without computers. Plenty of space for everyone."

"If possible, I wish to go see." Nela bounced in her nest.

Ping nodded. "For now, us must talk to citizens about this. Anyone you talk to during day. Not chiefs."

"Yes."

"If opportunity comes, I let you know."

"Gratitude." Nela beamed.

•　　•　　•

Slowly the word spread. One day, a notice from above appeared on screens everywhere. Ignore rumors of doom. Habitat fine.

"Idiots," Ping muttered when she saw the message.

Chief Eler called her in. "What you know about this?" He indicated the message.

"Others contact me about my download, about problems they see. Not classified. I tell them about land world, they tell others."

"I see." Eler frowned.

"Only way to stop is delete download. Not have authority to do, or classify it. Do you?"

"I can, but they ask me why I not before." He shrugged a shoulder.

The emergency alarm went off, followed by an announcement. 'All citizens to safe pods. Breech in hull. All citizens to safe pod.'

Chief Eler and Ping took off to the safe pod in the center of the module. Large enough to hold all who worked in Science, the pod had double thick walls and a separate life support system. Chief Eler and Ping found a pair of empty nests and settled in. More citizens streamed in.

"Greetings," said Nela, settling into the nest next to Ping. "What happens?"

"Said breach in hull," Ping replied. "Not say which module."

Nela nodded. They waited.

The alarm message cut off in mid word. Cries came from several citizens. Ping squeezed the side of her nest.

"Life support continues," Eler said.

Ping probed her memories and found nothing like this.

Presently the all-clear sounded, and everyone left, muttering to their neighbors.

"So habitat in fine shape," Ping said as she and Chief Eler left the safe pod.

Chief Eler did not respond.

Ping felt uneasy. Where would something break next?

At their lab, Chief Eler said, "This not good. I find out what happened."

"Yes. Us must start planning what to do when habitat becomes unlivable." Ping saw it clearly. "As more and more of habitat closed, there be more people in smaller space. What if port goes? What if water system break? What do us do?"

"Not your worry. Go back to work." Eler trudged out of the room.

Is my worry. If not me, who will? Ping realized that another duty had found her. It was up to her to make sure citizens were safe.

She returned to her work trying not to think about this new duty and, after she completed her current project, sent messages out to citizens she knew to let her know of any problems they encountered. First, she had to collect data. To Nela, she sent, "Keep in touch."

Several replied that day, and Ping told them to access her download, in the public domain, and spread the word. She created a separate account for the responses.

Chief Eler came in while she was in that screen.

"What those?

"Messages from citizens who accessed my download and want to see for themselves."

"Ah." Chief Eler paced around the outer room, then returned to his cubicle.

•   •   •

Later, Chief Eler told Ping the two of them would be taking a pod to the land in the morning for a brief look. "Must know of land before allow anyone else go out."

Could he truly be interested? Ping hoped so. *Would be a start.*

•   •   •

The next morning, Ping met Chief Eler at the connection to Central, and they continued on to the pod station. If she could get him to listen ...

As they sat and waited for the pod, Chief Elar said, "I see problems, tell Chief Adar, he listens, does nothing. Land people coming to habitat is too different. Apparently drone thought boy small animal. Need better programing."

"Yes." Ping jumped up. "Here pod." Chief Eler joined her and went to the boarding area. They took a double pod. After they strapped in, Chief Elar asked, "No screens?"

"No. Sit and relax."

The pod landed beside a group of trees. The hatch opened, and Ping jumped out. "Come on." She took a deep breath and taste, and let the freshness of this world wash over her.

Chief Eler peered out and looked in all the directions he could see. Finally, he stepped out and held onto a handle beside the hatch.

"See how beautiful out here?" Ping danced around.

"Is different, more."

"Come out. I wish to show you some things."

He shook his head and stepped back in. "Us go back now."

"Us just arrived." Ping did not want to go back so soon to the confines of habitat.

"Come." Chief Eler returned to his nest.

Reluctantly, Ping climbed into the nest in the pod.

• • •

A few days later, Ping asked if she could take someone else up to the land. "They need to see for themselves."

"Perhaps."

26

A N EIGHT-DAY after the break, Ping had heard from almost thirty citizens. She asked again if she could take someone out, and Chief Eler granted her request. She messaged Nela and they arranged a time.

• • •

Two days later, the two fems met at the walkway to Central.

"Are us really going out there?" Nela asked.

"Yes." Ping did a little two-step as they walked. Finally, she would be outside again. The walk to the pod port seemed to take forever.

At the station with the dark counter and row of sitnests, they checked in and waited for a double nest pod to arrive. Ping picked at her fur in several places, fighting off impatience. When the pod showed up, Ping passed her green travel dot on her necklet over the patch beside the hatch and they boarded. Another change from the transit. Two nests lay side by side, with the hatch at the end.

"No screen?" Nela asked.

"No. Sit back and relax."

The pod began to hum, and Ping felt it move. She wished they had more than a few hours.

They landed near the trees along the great river. Ping jumped out. "Come on."

Nela stepped out gingerly and looked around. She took in a big taste of the world and said, "Ah, yes, I could live here in pod. Can us move them?"

"I not know. Do you know any makers of pods?"

"No. My brother drives big pods. Maybe he know."

"Good." Ping and Nela walked over to a tree. The breeze ruffled their fur and the grass at their feet.

Nela touched the trunk. "Not smooth like trees in Park."

"Natural. Alive. Real." Ping picked up a long green leaf with an orange tip that had just fallen and held it out to Nela. "Yours." She picked up another for herself.

"Ah. We show these to others, to convince them." Nela brough it near her mouth for a close taste. "This is alive. This whole world alive. Lots better than stories." She looked at Ping. "I not realize how dead habitat is. Even Park not real."

"I know. Us must tell as many citizens as possible. Then they pressure chiefs. Mine already half interested. Perhaps I get him to ask Maker to make a larger pod for more citizens. Come, show you river."

They pushed through the bushes between the trees. "Oh, fantastic!" Nela exclaimed. "So much more than in your download. When can us start moving?"

"After us convince many more citizens and chiefs to make plans."

They sat and watched the river for a while. "Where all that water come from?" Nela asked.

"Marisa said it come from mountains. Rain run down mountainside." Ping wasn't quite sure herself.

"I feel like just woke up from dream." Nela glanced around. "For first time, I feel quite alive."

"Know what you mean. Look." Ping pointed to a pod-shaped gray mass in the sky. "That cloud full of water. If get big enough, it drop water on us."

"Rain. Water from sky. Amazing." The two fems drank in the world around them.

Then Ping's pod button buzzed. "Time to go," she said, climbing to her feet.

"Must us return already?"

"Yes. I not want to leave this wonderful place." They ambled back to the pod. The hatch was open, waiting. They crawled in, the hatch shut, and they took off. The ride back seemed much too short.

At the port's waiting room, Nela gasped at the air. "This awful."

Ping nodded. A hom striding by glared at the fems.

"You find out," Ping muttered at his back.

After they walked back to Science, Nela said, "I let you know what my brother says. Be good."

"You, too."

They went their separate ways.

Back at her workplace, Ping told Chief Eler about Nela's reaction. "Younger citizens quite enjoy life out there."

"So you say. Not for long time. Too big step to move out."

Ping went back to work. *If I can only see outline, know why he can't see it.* The need to find a new home on land pressed on her. It had become her duty to lead the way, a duty she did not want.

Her next assignment was from the chemistry chief who wanted to know how many protective smocks they had in stock. Dutifully, she looked it up. He could have done it just as easily, but some citizens would rather have someone else do it for them. Chiefs had more leeway than regular citizens.

Ping was shocked at the number that came up. *500 is not possible*, she thought. She went back to previous inventories. The number should be about fifty. She told Chief Eler, who contacted the chief in charge to do a manual count. He came up with forty-two plus several being made.

Maybe chem chief just wanted me to verify what he found.

Later, the number had been corrected in the biocomputer.

When Ping asked Chief Eler, he told her not to worry about it. "Someone punched in extra zero."

Ping was not appeased. When they were told it had been corrected, Ping checked and it was. But two days later it was back to 500. She told Chief Eler. He said, "Not worry about it, just glitch."

But Ping knew what she had seen, which meant the bioputer malfunctioned. This time it could have had serious consequences.

Her duty to her fellow citizens told her they should be warned not to trust the bioputer. Everything in the habitat was connected to the bioputer. If it malfunctioned, it could disable anything and everything. Including life support.

Ping sent a message out to watch for computer errors.

Chief Eler called her in. "Why you send messages? Bioputer does not make errors."

She told him what she'd seen.

"Now you imagine things. Send message no errors."

Ping was troubled. She was required to do what he told her, but she also knew she was right. *Citizens not always forget what they told to forget.*

"Yes, chief." She sent, 'Amend previous message. Chief says there are no bioputer errors.'

At her sleep pod, on her personal screen, she sent to Nela that she could no longer send out multiple messages. 'You can.' She attached a list of addresses.

That evening, Ping met with her family at a gathering room, with blue swirls on the walls.

"What possessed you to send a message like that," Mater demanded.

"Because is true. I not recall hearing any alarms when I child. Now two in last few eight-days."

"True," Aunt Lee said. "I received two different answers to calculation, but may have spoken wrong number. I hear of other minor problems with bioputer."

"But you retracted message," Mater said.

"Chief ordered me to." Ping squirmed.

"The problem will be to get head chiefs to listen," said Gran. "I expected more of you younger females, as far as pushing changes."

"Us taught to follow rules and not question those above we," sister Juni said.

"As was I." Gran nodded. "I see much over the years. Not only little progress, but actual regression. Some things, such as energy nuggets, not giving as much nutrition. Nephew in Medical tells me they see more citizens with poor nutrition than ever before."

Ping sat up. "That why I feel better when I outside."

"Yes," Gran said. "Nephew sent report to head medical chief last eight-day but not heard anything, and no changes."

"Has anyone died?" Mater asked.

"Not that I heard." Gran settled into her nest. "It will come."

"Us must get citizens out." Ping thumped the edge of her nest.

"Council chiefs mostly very old. Why they not die?" Juni asked.

"Old when I young. Some suspect they have something they use to keep them alive." Gran muttered.

"Us must have new council when us move," Ping said.

"How you do that?" sister Bede asked.

Mater frowned. "The second message said habitat fine."

"No, just bioputer," Ping said. "Required to send that, chief ordered me. But it not true. Do any of you know of problems?"

Aunt Dela spoke up. "I heard some citizens in Energy Processing talk about materials not robust as used to be."

Ping nodded.

Others brought up items they'd heard about of poor quality of materials. Sister Bede added, "I heard they no longer teach home planet history in schooling."

"Oh, no." Ping rubbed her chest fur. "Will you help me?"

"Us must." Gran touched her face. "Us must get this information to chiefs. Section chiefs who will take it to their chiefs."

Second grandmother said, "I agree. See too much wrong."

Grandfather sat up. "Is all nonsense. Habitat last forever."

"Old man, what do you know?"

"Ping!" Mater and the grandmothers said together.

Ping huffed but did not say anything.

"This enough for tonight." Mater climbed out of her nest. The others followed.

Back at her sleep pod, Ping asked herself what possessed her to say that. Although it was true, not everything true should be said. She turned on a soothing forest scene and prepared for the night.

As Ping snuggled into her nest, a message appeared on her screen, reminding her to pick up a new supply of energy nuggets. She made note of it and closed her eyes.

Drifting down to the depths of slumber, she perceived what her brain told her were colors. Not like the ones she knew, not quite colors, on the edge of taste.

More strangeness. What more? Ping slipped into sleep.

27

KAYLYN AND HER CHILDREN, along with many of the younger clan members, enjoyed an off day on the wide, tan beach in the warm sunshine. The women sat under sunshades while the children splashed in the water. A few young men paddled in the water. Only the youngest babies stayed with their mothers.

"Mama, look," cried Barry. He ran up to Kaylyn holding out his hand.

"What is it?" she asked.

He opened his little fist to display a rusty, bent piece of metal.

"Where did you find that?" Kaylyn asked.

"In the water. What is it?"

Kaylyn looked for her mate. "Adam, come here."

A round-faced man with brown curls stumped over.

"Show Papa."

"Look what I found." Barry held out his hand.

Adam took the piece of metal and peered at it. "Looks like part of something."

"Ping's habitat?" Concern washed over Kaylyn.

"What's up?" Marisa approached.

"Barry found this," Adam said. "The only thing with metal is Ping's place."

"Oh, no." Marisa sat down in the sand.

"Looks like something on the outside." A few older children splashed toward them.

"I'll show Uncle Artie and see what he thinks," Adam continued.

"What is it?" one of the older children asked.

"Never mind. Run along." The boy peered at the thing, then ran off with the others.

"Is it a good thing?" Barry asked.

"We don't know yet. Thank you for bringing it to us. Now run along." Adam motioned to the sea.

The little boy ran off to the edge of the water.

Adam turned the ell-shaped piece in his hand. "Looks like a piece of something that something else outside attached to."

"But wouldn't they have kept it from rusting?" Marisa asked.

"You would think so."

"They must be having problems." Kaylyn rose. "We need to go see ..."

"No!" Marisa broke in. "We have new bondings coming up. Gramma Perri has already scheduled them."

Adam added, "Ping can take care of herself."

Kaylyn wrinkled her nose. "I know, but there's something wrong over there. After the bondings, I'm going, with Mama and Aunt Glori, they have the strongest Talents. You can come, too, Gramisa." *Why was Gramisa so against going to Ping?* Kaylyn sensed the older woman's distrust of the alien.

"Do you want me to come?" Adam asked.

"We can take care of ourselves."

"No," Marisa said. "Ping said everything was settling down after their move."

"If you go, I'm going," Adam said to Kaylyn. "Aunt Susan can look after the children."

"Aren't you going to ask her first?" Marisa asked.

"We could take Barry. He's old enough to see more of the world," Adam said.

"No." Kaylyn stared at him. "Not yet."

"All right, you two." Marisa looked at the lowering sun. "It's time for us to go back home."

The group gathered up their belongings, collected the quines, and mounted.

Kaylyn rode next to Marisa and sent a question to her.

'I'm too old for such a long trek,' the latter replied mentally. 'Besides, we still know very little about this alien group. Ping appears sensible, but we know nothing about the rest of her people. I don't know how they stand living inside. Some of the chiefs might be looking to move out here on our land. We just don't know.'

'Then we should go and find out.'

28

I N A PARALLEL UNIVERSE, on a third version of Peace, Asiram frowned at her interface with the other two worlds. Once again, she and her cohorts had been unable to interfere with the antigravity process being beamed on her domain by aliens. Perhaps the explorers sent to the other parts of the realm might find something.

In this universe, there were no colors, only a range of black to white. The people had no color receptacles in their eyes and projected this lack of color to visitors. The only way to keep things grounded, beside tying them down, was to use magnetic rocks.

Asiram's table was a large rock with a flat top that she had built her box of a workplace around. With not quite straight white walls and a pile of storage boxes at one side, it was the best she could get. Where there were no rocks, things floated aimlessly. She had to keep her long, white hair tied in a braid to keep it from floating in her face.

The portals to the universes of the other two worlds lay at the same location on each. One Peace had people she'd dealt with before, many years ago; the other unpopulated. If she could make a three-way portal among the worlds, perhaps she could use the other two worlds to stabilize her own universe. If she could manage it.

29

P ING WOKE FROM A DREAM of the outside world. At first, her screen showed her only the forest, then a message popped up, in a bright color for which she had no name, in letters she did not know. Only half awake, she decided to check it out later.

By the time she was ready for the day, the message had disappeared. She shrugged and trotted to her workplace. This day, her research went smoothly until she tried to look up data on the first transit between worlds. Big red letters popped up. PERMISSION DENIED.

"What?" she said aloud. She tried another transit and received the same message. After a few more tries, she found that she was locked out of anything to do with the history or function of the habitat.

"No!" Ping started to detach from the 'puter, then sat back. She had a back-door key she discovered just before the last transit. She had hesitated to use it, she didn't know how closely these things were tracked by Computer Central.

"Problems?" Chief Eler asked at her entrance.

"No, Chief. Trying to discover where all I locked out."

Chief Eler nodded. "If affects assignments, let me know. I tell Chief Adar."

"Yes, Chief." He left, and she turned back to her screen. Most of her assignments wanted history information, so she took a deep breath and spoke the key code. The bioputer let her back in, and Ping managed to get most of the data she needed to complete her reports.

A few days later, Exterior Maintenance in Maker requested a compilation of a number of drone views of the exterior of Central, theoretically the most protected of the three modules. The bioputer gave Ping a permission denied message when she tried to download the images.

She went to Chief Eler, who viewed the message. "I see no reason why that be," he said. "I call Chief Adar."

Chief Adar did not see any reason why she should be denied, and suggested she talk to the people in Computer Central.

Chief Eler made arrangements for them to meet with Chief Miki.

That afternoon, Chief Miki welcomed them at his office, where the shelves were cluttered with pieces of old bits of miscellaneous odds and ends, and piles of papers with diagrams. Taller than most, with a narrow face, he wore a necklet with a rainbow of colors.

"No problem here," he said. "Only Council Chief deny without reason."

"Mola," Ping spat. "Did Chief Adar even ask him?"

"He not say." Chief Eler moved uneasily. "I assume he did."

"Why he do that?" Chief Miki asked.

"He thinks habitat perfect and not like me showing mistakes." Ping patted her chest fur.

"You right." Chief Miki slapped his worktable. "Even bioputer must be constantly watched and corrections made. It continues to grow more memory to hold more data and becomes more and more unwieldy."

"Why you not delete old data we not need anymore?" Ping asked.

"It cannot, or will not. 'Puter deletes data from regular data banks and moves it to new storage it creates."

A citizen tapped and stuck her head in. "It ignored a command again," she said, and withdrew.

Chief Miki rolled his eyes. "This creature seems to be developing a mind of its own. Come."

They followed him down a gray corridor, to a large room full of a massive irregular growth. Branches disappeared through several places in the walls, floor, and ceiling. Just inside, a wide control station lurked. The fem sat at one of the seats before a screen. Chief Miki dropped into a sitnest at another and tapped icons on a keyboard.

Ping was fascinated by the speed of his touch and the masses of data flowing across the screen. He paused, tapped in what appeared to be a command, and hit a button at the side. A line of what she knew to be computer language popped up.

Chief Miki tapped in more digits, and another line appeared on the screen. This conversation continued for a little while.

Finally, Chief Eler said, "Pardon, but us must return to our work. Can you fix so Ping access files she needs?"

Chief Miki tapped one last button, closed the screen and opened another. "I do." He continued working. A short time later. "Ah, is fixed." He turned to them. "If any more problems with permissions, let me know."

"Gratitude, Chief," Ping said as they rose. Chief Miki showed them to the main door and nodded. Ping and her chief headed for their work area.

This time, when Ping logged in, she was able to access the files Maintenance had sent. She opened the images first. Appalled at the number of dings, scrapes and dents, especially at the bottom, Ping decided to create the report before showing Eler the images.

A sense of urgency engulfed her. The big chiefs needed to know. They needed to check the space between the double hulls. Ping looked at previous reports. Some of them showed suspicious smoothness, as if the image had been altered. Her report showed closeup images of damage, including one hole that went all the way through.

Finished, Ping sent the report to Chief Eler. He called her in. "I scanned your report. Very good, but not what they wanted. Can you find different images?"

"Big chiefs need to see these."

"True, but they reject it, perhaps even remove you from position here, move you to other department."

"No." *They wouldn't, they couldn't.*

"I not want it either. You are best I know."

Again, Ping felt warmth, this time combined with annoyance that higher chiefs didn't appreciate her skills. She refused to edit her report.

"Very well." Eler sent the report to Chief Adar, who would send it on, and to Exterior Maintenance, who had requested it.

That afternoon, Chief Adar called Chief Elar and Ping into his office. They found sitnests in a sea of clutter. One table held a pile of metal objects, round and square, long and squat, that Ping could not identify. Several shelves contained piles of paper that slopped over onto a table and nest below. A model of a creature with too many limbs stood in a corner.

"Greetings." Chief Adar sat behind a wide desk also piled with papers and gadgets. "Where you get these images?" He pointed to the large screen on the yellow wall.

"Drone footage. I told to use them." Ping rubbed her chest fur.

"There must be others, not as clear. This not acceptable. Why you send it on, Eler?"

"My duty." He shifted in his sitnest.

"High chiefs need see this." Ping stared at Chief Adar. "Might be signs of danger."

"No danger. Habitat fine." Chief Adar slapped his hand on his desk.

"Why last few alarms after none for so long? Why we sent to safe hub? Why bioputer not working as it should. It must be very old."

"Now, Ping," Eler said.

"Not 'now Ping' me. I do much research and see many things not right. Cannot make personal report, so must put what I can in other reports, hope someone sees them."

"I see." Chief Adar sat back in his sitnest. "Head chiefs and council not want to see anything negative. I send it on and try to minimize any punishment they give."

"Us need new council, younger citizens, fems. Citizens who will listen to other citizens and do what necessary to keep habitat safe. Else us be forced to move to land." Ping nodded.

"Land?" Chief Adar repeated. "How?"

"I been there. Is good, much room, big river for water." Ping nodded again. "Air much better. Many trees and green everywhere. Us can grow real food like land people eat."

"Tell me more." Chief Adar sat up.

Ping described what she had experienced on her trip. "There is download of my recordings in bioputer."

"I inspect your download and send your report to high chiefs, but not expect them to like it. You may go." He waved them off.

"Good. Gratitude, Chief." Ping rose.

"Why you say all that?" Chief Eler demanded as they made their way back to their workplaces.

"Necessary. Maybe only chance speak to higher chief." Ping nodded.

"You think this important?"

"Yes. May be life or death of citizens."

Eler stopped at the entrance to their department. "No."

"Yes." Ping was pleased that Chief Adar actually listened to her. She knew he was the youngest of three brothers, the oldest being Mola. She also knew how the youngest was treated by older siblings, from personal experience. He must be looking for something at which he could outshine his older brothers. *I do what I can, and we get those old ragbags out of council.*

30

R ODY, CHIEF OF Exterior Maintenance and Pods, stared at the report on the screen on the wall of his narrow office. Other sets of images lined the long pale green wall of his small workspace. A modest worktable, two sitting nests, and a couple of cabinets nearly filled his room.

He'd seen some of the images before they went to Ping, but not this close up. He couldn't believe the amount of damage. A long crack covered almost a third of an overall image.

Coming up the ranks following his father, he'd been taught to focus on the repair site and ignore the surroundings. It had never occurred to him to check out the big picture. It had never occurred to him to do anything but what he had been taught and told to do.

Chief Rody would have to think about this.

He knew that after the first transit between worlds, Research had produced a more impermeable material to coat the exterior. This had kept off barnacles and other sea life through the next several transits. At each transit, a bit of the coating wore off. When patches of bare hull began collecting sea life, Maintenance approved a new coating. This lasted for a few more transits. Exterior had run a scan every few years, but with no problems, it slacked off to longer and longer intervals. Now it was down to once after each transit.

Chief Rody's father had tried to get Chief Bolo, head of Maintenance, to let Chief Rody do a full scan when he took over. Chief Bolo sent out a drone and told them it was not necessary. A couple times after that, Chief Rody requested permission to do a scan and was refused. Even when the repair citizens began reporting barnacles and other stuff around the hatches and repair areas, Chief Rody could not get permission to scan the hull.

A scan right after a transit was required by law. When Chief Rody requested a complete exterior scan, he was denied. Chief Bolo did allow him to scan small areas on each of the three modules. He said they didn't have resources for a full scan.

Chief Rody curbed his annoyance as he sent his request to Drone division to scan the other two modules. The next day, he found these images showed more damage, especially on Maker, which faced into the sea current.

He called the Interior Maintenance chief and told him about what he'd seen.

"Habitat fine. Just surface damage," Chief Kolo said.

"What is protocol for puncture?" Chief Rody asked.

"Why?"

"I live here too. You must have some."

"Us have bags of patches on inner hull wall in hullway, and on inside of inner wall. Slap one on, air pressure hold it. Is that all? I have tasks."

"Yes." Chief Rody disconnected.

What else can I do? Perhaps talk to researcher who did report.

31

T HE CALL CAME as Ping finished up a report.

"Someone from Maintenance wants to talk to you," Chief Eler told her.

She connected and heard, "This Chief Rody of Exterior maintenance. I wish to discuss your report."

"You read my report?"

"Of course, always read reports. You did this well." The voice was a pleasant baritone.

"Gratitude. I do best I can. How long since last inspection?" Ping dared to ask.

"Too long." Chief Rody paused. "Last full scan done right after transit into previous world."

"Fifty years? Too long." Talking to this chief was like talking to a citizen.

"I agree. Asked Head Maintenance Chief Bolo more than once, and he said they not have resources."

Ping choked back a retort. Some things are not said to chiefs one does not know well, though she felt she was learning to know him. "I talk to others about growing problems. Habitat no longer as safe as used to be."

Another pause. "Perhaps you right. I talk to my citizens." He disconnected.

Pleased that another chief had listened to her, Ping sent messages to Nela and a few others. Next day, a barrage of requests for reports arrived.

"What is this? What you do?" Chief Eler demanded.

"Chief Rody from Maintenance called. He upset images so bad, sent to his chief, no response."

"Not surprised. "

Ping shrugged a shoulder and glanced at a list of requests. "I do these from top."

"Yes. Must do reports. But why so many? Let me see before you send them."

"Yes, chief."

Chief Eler left, and Ping turned to her tasks. The first one was simple. Chief Rody wanted a list of repairs on travel pods and drones for ten years ago and the previous year to date. She was not surprised to see many times more for the current year, and displeasure welled up within her. She sent it to Chief Eler's screen anyway.

He trotted in. "Is this correct?"

"Yes. I use their records."

"Hmf. Not good." He tugged at his chest fur.

Ping kept her mouth shut and let the figures tell the story. Unease stole over her. This was a big wrong. This was a warning.

"Send it," Chief Eler said after a few moments, and left.

Ping did so and pulled up the next item. Interior Maintenance requested a similar list of repairs. Again, all she had to do was pull up the file, make sure the items were in date order and complete, and the report was there. Again, many more repairs showed up in the current year, and more than ten years ago.

For the next report, from Medical, Ping needed to check a number of different sources and write it up. She still had many to do by midday break. She wanted to continue working, but Chief Eler insisted she get up and walk around.

After her break, Ping continued her work. The satisfaction of everything coming together in a succinct report pleased her. Most reports showed declining positive results, from fewer births to shorter lives, fewer energy nuggets in stock. Plus, conduits and wires being replaced more often, and a shortage of material for material printers causing shortage of many products.

•   •   •

Tired of doing the same reports over and over for different chiefs, Ping dreamed of Park, of her next day off. A call interrupted her thoughts. Chief Rody requested that she come with him on a trip to the land.

She gladly accepted, but Chief Eler refused to let her go.

"Need her here," he told Chief Rody.

"I agreed to go," Ping said.

"No, I not allow," Chief Eler said.

"My chief want me bring her with me," Chief Rody insisted.

Chief Eler called Chief Adar, who conferred with Chief Rody's chief and told Chief Elar to let her go. "Must see if land people there." Chief Eler gave in.

The next morning, Ping felt pleasure in the thought of going out. She packed her bag and trotted to the pod port in Central. Chief Rody was not there. She checked the chrono at the station. She was early.

She waited, thinking about what she would show him.

"Greetings." Chief Rody came up behind her.

She whirled around. "Greetings. You ready?"

"Yes. After reading report, want to see for myself," he said.

"Fine." They boarded a two-person pod and fastened their harnesses. The pod took off and Ping relaxed.

Chief Rody tensed at first, then sighed.

The pod landed at a place near a stand of trees in a wide-open area.

"This not where I was before." Ping stepped out and breathed/tasted deeply.

Like Chief Eler, Chief Rody stayed in the pod and looked out. He immediately closed his eyes. "Too much."

"You get used to it." Ping danced around. "Breathe air, so much better out here."

He took a deep breath and tasted. "Yes, is more refreshing. I have someone check air filters when I return."

Ping danced back to the pod. "Can sleep pods be detached and brought here by travel pods?"

"Sleep pods?" He opened his eyes.

"For shelter at first."

Chief Rody stepped out of the hatch, keeping his eyes on the nearby trees. "This much better than Park. But so open. Where is water?"

"In big river near where I landed first. More trees there. I not know why we came here."

"Plenty of material for material printers, much room. It take much planning. We can create new machines for land." He walked over to a tree and touched it. "Real."

"Yes." Ping plucked a small, yellow, cup-shaped flower and tucked it into her curly fur. "Plenty room for shelters."

"Shelters?" He turned and squinted.

"Multi room structures for families to live in together, like Kay's people. Sleeping rooms, gathering room, place for preparing food, and cleaning room. With openings in outer walls, called windows, to see outside without going out."

"Ahh. Many questions." He turned back to the trees.

"Is possible move all citizens out here?" Ping asked.

Chief Rody cocked his head. "Perhaps. Take much planning and changing ways us do things. Come, us must return." He turned and climbed in.

Ping shuffled her feet and took another deep breath as she moved to the pod and stepped in. *Another chief interested. Another step forward.*

32

WHEN PING RETURNED to her workplace, she pulled the bioputer down and connected. Instead of her main screen of forest and meadow, black letters on a yellow background said, "Denied. You assigned to another department. See your chief for details." The screen went gray, blank.

Ping yanked the 'puter off and stomped to Chief Elar's cubby. "What is this?" she demanded. "Why I reassigned?"

Chief Eler kept his eyes on his screen. "Chief Mola read your report and give orders. You go to Nutrition in Maker. They tell you what you do and assign new sleep pod."

"Nutrition?" She managed to keep her voice level. *What I possibly do there?* She forced herself to be calm. She must do this even though she wished otherwise. "Yes, Chief. Now?" She felt no animosity toward him, he had no choice in the matter.

"Yes." He turned to look at her. "I regret this move. Continue with your work on saving habitat. Be well."

"Gratitude, Chief." Ping stalked out, went to her sleep pod, and gathered her belongings into a large green carry bag. Her energy nuggets, grooming tools, plus a small wooden quine Marisa had given her, carved by Old Allen, all went in.

As she trekked across three modules, Ping felt something new, something she presently recognized as anger. The big chiefs could not stop her by moving her around. With two minor chiefs on her side, it would be just a matter of time. *But how much time us have?*

In Maker, Ping studied the directory screen and located Nutrition. On the far side, of course. She followed the directions and found the main office, a small brown room with a counter across it and a small citizen wearing a pale yellow-green necklet behind the barrier.

Ping announced, "I Ping. I transferred here. I do research."

"Ah, Ping," the citizen said. She called out something to another citizen in the rear and led Ping out a door at the side of the room. "I Mili." She took Ping to a new sleep pod, where Ping dumped her bag of belongings. Smaller than her old one, she could barely squeeze into the cleaning room. At least it did have a screen.

Mili showed Ping the way to a workroom, the latter memorizing the way. The room contained a series of bins containing small pieces of various types of materials. Along the parallel wall sat other sorting bins, all in light shades of brown. A single sitnest crouched in a corner. The gray walls pushed in at Ping.

On the wall screen, Mili brought up a list of items and which bin they were to go to. Ping was to use a screening device to pull out larger pieces. She found it simple.

As Ping did the mindnumbing task of screening and sorting, she tried to think of what she could do. Children were raised to follow orders without question. Now she had a lot of questions and no answers. *Is good others had concerns, but could they do anything without chief to lead them?*

Later, at her new sleep pod, she tried the screen. Instead of her usual forest screen, she saw ENTER ID CODE in black letters on a white screen. She did.

DISALLOWED

"What?" Ping cried.

Another screen appeared. CREATE NEW ID CODE.

"No." She pounded on the wall, then remembered she had Chief Elar's code, which he had given her some time before. The bioputer accepted it. A list of options appeared. Entertainment, information, connections.

She tried them all. Information provided only basic data on life in the habitat. Connections showed only her new chief and her mother and sisters. Entertainment, she would look at later.

She had thought her transfer was distressing before, but this was the bottom of the waste bin. "At least I can contact my family," she said aloud.

The anger was back. *This was not acceptable.*

After Ping calmed herself down, she called sister Juni, whom she was closest to, both in age and relationship.

"Ah, Ping," Juni said. "What goes on?"

"I transferred to Nutrition and assigned to sorting material in intake department for material printers."

"Ah, no. Why?"

"Because I concerned about safety of habitat. High chiefs not care about citizens?" Ping waved her hand around.

"I not see any sign of it. Wonder if they consider what it be like without all of we making their food and everything else they need."

"And keeping their habitat functioning," Ping added.

"Yes. Heard material printers not functioning well as they used to."

"I need your help, Juni. I can only message family and my chief here. Can you send short message for me to Nela? Her address is S3457."

"I received message not send anything on from you, but I do short one."

Ping saw her smile. "Just that I cannot contact her or anyone else and to carry on."

"For sisters, I do anything I can. Be well."

"Gratitude." Ping signed off. She sat back in her nest. At least she wasn't totally cut off. She tried sister Bede, but her line was busy. She tried entertainment, but the inane stories and silly games bored her.

●　　　●　　　●

After another long, boring day, she reached sister Bede in the evening.

"Ping. Are you well?"

"No, I transferred to Nutrition. Are you well?"

"I fine. Why they do that? I thought you doing well in Exo."

"High chiefs not like to be reminded of flaws in habitat." Ping rubbed her chest fur.

"Ah. No good, that. Low chiefs repairing hatch. Be much faster if high chiefs approve everything."

"Is creature still there?"

"No, it gone. Was swelling up from lower water pressure here." Bede rubbed her eyes. "Face torn up from hatch. I suppose it heals."

"I wish I see it. Only image." Ping closed her eyes for a moment.

"Not scary, just curious. Wonder if it come back. Should have sensor directed toward deeps."

"Yes," Ping said, "But will chiefs do it?"

Bede snorted. "Must go now. Keep well."

Ping sat back. At least, she could reach her sisters. She cleaned her teeth and curled up in her nest.

•   •   •

Next day, Ping focused on her tasks and dutifully did them best she could. She kept in touch with Juni, and Bede called her every so often. The odd events receded in her memory, but not the anger at being transferred to Nutrition. She kept open an awareness for any way she could get transferred back.

33

AFTER THE BONDING AND FEAST, Marisa prepared to go through the forest to Ping's world. She was not looking forward to the long hike, but felt she needed to go to Ping. The little furry alien had roused her maternal instincts, along with a respect for her willingness to come to a strange world all by herself. But she could not shake that warning in her innards.

As Marisa and Jan returned from the plaza kitchen after gathering food for the journey, Marisa stepped on something round, lost her balance, and fell. The bags of food spilled on the ground.

"Mama," Jan yelped. A young girl stopped to look.

Marisa sat up, took a deep breath, and looked at her right knee. Scraped and bleeding, bruising started to form around the wound. She touched it and flinched with the pain. She sighed and reached for her bag.

"Let me help." The young girl picked up the spilled packets and fruit and restored them to the bag. Jan helped her mama to her feet. Pain lanced through Marisa's knee.

"Ow, I can't stand on it." Marisa hopped to a nearby bench with Jan's help and lowered herself onto it. "Thank you," she said to the girl, who set the food on the bench and ran off.

"Stay there, I'll get Aunt Susan." Jan ran to the clinic. Marisa focused on the medical clinic building and soon saw Jan and Susan run out.

Susan arrived, panting, and dropped her tote. "What did you do now?"

"I fell." She pointed to her knee; her tunic pulled up above it.

"Nasty. It's already starting to swell." Susan gingerly felt around the knee. "I don't think anything's broken, but you probably pulled a tendon." She cleaned up the wound, slathered numgoo on it, and wrapped the joint the best she could without hurting Marisa anymore.

"Thanks," Marisa muttered. Her head ached and every muscle felt weak.

"We'll get someone to help you home, and you stay off that leg for a few days."

"I'll take her," Jan said.

"But I have to go ..." Marisa began.

"You're not going anywhere for a while," Susan ordered, grinning.

"I know the way." Jan picked up the food bag, adding it to the ones she carried. "Unless you want to wait a few weeks."

"No." Marisa looked at the trees behind the craft hall.

"There's Ricky." Susan waved at him across the plaza. He came over.

"What happened, sis?" he asked,

"I fell."

"Oh, your knee. Need any help getting home?"

"Yes, she does." Susan gathered her supplies and rose. "I'll come by this evening."

Ricky helped Marisa up, she put her arm around his shoulder, and they did a three-footed dance down the path to her house.

"I hope that wasn't your grandson's ball I stepped on," Marisa said. "The plaza is supposed to be kept clear of toys and tools."

"I know, sis. I'll find out who left that there and rattle their brains."

Jan followed and got her mama settled in her big chair. She pulled a footstool over and propped the injured leg on it.

"See you," Ricky said. "Take care." He left.

"Anything you need?" Jan asked her mama.

"Not right now." Marisa leaned back and closed her eyes.

"I'll be here for a while if you do." Jan took the foodstuffs to the kitchen.

"You go on," Marisa said without opening her eyes. "I can call Kaylyn if I need anything. I want to see you three after supper."

"Yes, Mama." Jan patted her shoulder and left.

•   •   •

That evening, Jan, Glori, and Adam arrived at Marisa's together.

"How are you doing?" Jan asked.

Marisa wrinkled her nose. "Okay. Kaylyn fixed my and Allen's supper."

"Good." They all sat down. "We've decided. We're going." Jan said. "I know the way."

Marisa sighed. "All right. Susan says it'll be at least a month before I can take any long walks. Don't rush, take breaks often, drink lots of water, and if you do contact Ping, give her my best wishes."

"Yes, Mama."

"Here's what you need to take. Seven days of food and water per person, a couple changes of clothes including footwear. Something to cut or chop with. A sewing kit and first aid kit. Personal items." Marisa counted on her fingers.

"Okay." Jan nodded. "We'll leave in the morning."

Marisa took a deep breath. "Ricky is digging out the old wheeled chair that Roroy used a long time ago when we first found this world. He'll fix it up so I can use it to get around. When you return, expect a backlog of tasks. I don't know how much I can do, and how much of your tasks can be done by others."

"Yes, Mama." Jan sighed.

"Be careful," Marisa said, an uneasiness in her gut.

"I'll take care of them," Adam said.

"I'm sure you will." Marisa nodded. "Travel mercies."

34

ONE NIGHT, PING WOKE to a great shaking and grabbed the sides of her nest. Blackness surrounded her, not even the screen glowed. The tremors went on and on until something grabbed the pod and threw it out on a straight line. Ping went numb and her body shook. She could not comprehend what was going on. All she could do was hang on to her nest and pray to Great One to stop it.

Sounds of tearing metal and the thump of the safety hatch closing came to her dimly. Her sleep pod hit something with a great thud, rolled over, and dumped her on the padded dark blue floor. She curled into a tight ball and grabbed the edge of the opening into the cleaning room. Even though it was dark, she kept her eyes squeezed shut, along with her mind.

When she was sure the pod had stopped moving, she waited a little longer and crawled back into her now slanted nest. For the second time, she felt deep fear.

After she managed to control her shaking, she pressed the light control. Nothing, not even the screen lit up. Ping huddled in her nest and tried to understand what had happened. A little later, she realized she was panting. She couldn't hear the subdued hum of the air circulator. *Line must be disconnected.* She crept to the hatch and pushed it open. The hatch groaned to a stop part way.

Ping peered out, gulping fresh air. A pale, pinkish light hovered over the swishing sound of the sea. *How I, pod, get here?* She squeezed out and struggled to stand on the soft sand. Several other pods lay along the beach, and one was out in the water. As she watched, a great gray snout poked up put of the water and pushed it up mostly onto the beach. The snout backed into the sea and let out a great spout of water.

Ping's mouth hung open. *Sea beast back?* She sent gratitude to the Great One. *Where rest of habitat? What happened? Where my family, Mater. Juni, Bede?*

Ping focused on a nearby pod. Its hatch was trying to open. *Deal with feelings later.* She shuffled over to the pod.

"Greetings?" she called into it.

"Help," came a small voice. "It not open."

"You push, I pull."

Together, they managed to get the hatch open far enough so a smaller fem could squeeze out. One of her coworkers.

"Ping," she said. "What happened? Where are us?" She looked around and shut her eyes.

"I not know, Essi. Are you well?"

"Not hurt. Pods well padded."

"Come, sit." Ping led her to the grass above the beach. "Breathe in good air. I go check the others."

Still trembling, she went to the nearest pod and opened its hatch. A fem cowered inside. "Come out."

"No," the fem whispered.

Ping nodded. "I leave hatch open. Breathe good air." She treated two more the same way. A fem crawled out of the fifth pod and Ping helped her stand and walk over to sit by Essi.

Ping turned to the pod in the water. It lay at a slant with the hatch end buried in the sand. "Essi, can you two come help?" she called to the two on the grass.

Essi rose, helped the other to her feet, and they slogged down to the water, eyes slitted.

"If we all push here, perhaps we can get it to roll over." Ping and the others pushed and strained, finally collapsing in a heap.

When she looked up, most of the hatch was uncovered. She crawled over and dug out the rest.

Essi crept to the pod and helped her pry the hatch open. The fem inside did not respond to their calls. Ping crawled in, wiggled around behind the older fem and pushed her out as Essi pulled. Together they carried her up to the grass and laid her down. She was not breathing.

Like most of the citizens, Ping knew the stimulation measures to help someone breathe, and set to work on the older fem. Soon, the fem was gasping, her chest heaving, then taking more normal breaths. "Gratitude," she whispered.

One of the other two crawled out of her pod and crept over to the group. They all sat together around the older fem, Luci, eyes closed, minds blank in shock. A few moaned.

It grew lighter as the sun rose and warmed them, with a little breeze off the sea. Ping took a deep breath. She had to do something, but what?

Essi, now in control of herself, asked, "What us do now?"

"Stay here and wait. Pod may come to see what happened." Ping felt empty and wanted to shout at the high chiefs, "Do you still think habitat perfect?"

•　　•　　•

Inside the habitat, Chief Rody was rattled awake, along with everyone else in Maker. Alarms went off, and a message in large red letters flashed on every screen. DISASTER, DISASTER, GO TO SAFE PODS IMMEDIATELY. In smaller letters, 'Group of sleep pods has broken off from Maker. Other modules in no danger.'

Chief Rody reported to his chief and checked the passageways to the sleep pods. All the hatches had been closed, and one sealed off. The way to Ping's sleep pod. An unaccustomed emotion rose in him. He knew how well the sleep pods were padded, but still. *No, Ping must be well.*

He reported to his chief, who was in the safe pod. "This pod closed, go to sleep pod," his chief told him.

Rody didn't think it would be safe, considering what had happened, so he returned to his office and buckled in. He dozed uneasily until it was time to get up.

His first task was to rearrange tasks in Nutrition since six of his workers were missing. He knew he was not going to make his quota that day. Later, he noticed the screen showed the council chambers.

After the councilors strode or shuffled in and made themselves comfortable in their sitnests, Head Chief appeared and did roll call.

Since there were only five, Rody thought this was unnecessary. He listened as Head Chief described the situation and asked for comments.

Medical, mostly alert, said, "I suggest us send pod out to see what is situation on other side of hatch, with medics in case there injuries."

Head Chief nodded.

Education mumbled something and went to sleep.

Science said they must check systems.

Government soothed, "Let we wait until things settle down."

Maker said, "I have pods ready to go."

Head Chief told him to send out a pod. "Cannot do anything until us know what out there."

"Yes," Chief Rody said aloud. "And find out what happened to fellow citizens."

•   •   •

Outside, Ping and the others waited. "Has anyone taken morning nuggets?" she asked. No one had. "Us go do that. Us need to keep up our strength. I bring one for Luci."

They straggled to their pods. Ping and Essi pushed Essi's hatch open a little further, and Essi wiggled in. Ping went to hers and retrieved two nuggets and her water bottle. She made sure everyone took their nuggets. Two fems remained in their pods.

Ping couldn't sit still. She wandered over to the line of trees at the river and looked at the flowering bushes and plants along the trees. Then, she returned to the tan beach and walked east for a little while. The end of the beach faded into distant mist. She sat and took stock.

I and five others on beach with sleep pods. Habitat gone, still under sea. There no way back. Us hope for rescue. Else us must find way to live here. Us have shelter, water in the river. Food. Must find plants us can eat.

Back with the others, they all sat and watched the sea.

It was almost midday when a pod flew over, circled around, and disappeared.

"Wait," Ping yelled, running after it, Essi following her. *No.* Ping shook her fist. *At least, someone alive in habitat, and they know us here.*

For a long afternoon, Ping and her fellow citizens waited for a pod to return. After a brief nap, Ping wandered over to the river and tall trees and looked for a place where they could get down to the river to refill their water bottles.

At dusk, Ping said, "Us retire to pods. Keep hatches open for fresh air. I see no signs of other creatures, be safe."

•   •   •

Next morning, Ping woke to light coming in the open hatchway to her sleep pod. Her first thought was, *why had screen moved.* Then she realized it was the hatch, and she and the pod were on land. She crawled out to sit and wait for the others. As they joined her, one by one, she prayed, 'Please come soon.' They had several days' worth of nuggets, but were running out of water.

Midmorning, Ping saw a pod pop up out of the water and come toward them.

"Oh, gratitude," she said under her breath.

The pod landed nearby, and the hatch slid open. A large hom with a gray necklet and grayish-brown fur peered out. After a moment, he stepped out. "Greetings. I am Gogi. How in health are you all?"

Ping approached him and introduced herself.

"The Ping?"

"I only one I know of. We all well."

Gogi opened his mouth wide and tasted the world. "This is scrumptious. I see why you and Nela want to move out here. Not be easy."

"You know Nela?"

"My sister. Are pods damaged?" Gogi peered at the nearest one.

"Not obvious." Ping's spirits rose. She was out, and here was another person who liked outside.

Gogi wandered around, inspecting the pods. "No one seems to know what to do about you out here. I bring you in one at a time, but you not have private sleep pod. How are you on nuggets?"

Ping followed him. "Us have enough for few days. Is habitat damaged?"

"Not that us see yet. Just out of balance, two more anchors pulled up."

The two fems who had stayed in their pods came out and watched. Essi followed Ping, who pointed out the pod in the water. "Any way pull it out?"

Gogi shuffled down to the water's edge. "Us need largest tow pod to get this out, perhaps possible." He inspected the broken passageway around the edge of the hatch.

"I ask Maintenance to send someone out to see if possible to reconnect. Hatch inside sealed off ways from that end."

"No problem if not," Ping said. "If move pods farther up on land, us could live here for while. Big river over there," she pointed, "If us can find way to get water up out of it." *Start of our new home.* "Good comes from bad."

Gogi nodded. "I go see." Ping followed him over to the river. "Wooow," he exclaimed. She watched him examine the edge. "I have rope. Stay here."

Ping stared at the rushing river, trying to understand how much water could come from land. If the water department could find a way to bring it up, they would never have to worry about enough water.

Gogi returned with a large, open container and a length of rope. He tied one end around a stout tree, and the other around the handle of the container. Ping watched as he dropped the container over the edge down into the water. It filled, and he drew it back up. Then he used a syphon to fill her water bottle.

"Show others how this works. Be enough in one containerful for three bottles," Gogi said.

They returned to the others.

"We have water," Ping announced. "I show you."

Gogi nodded. "I must go, but will return. Enjoy this while you can."

"Take Luci back. She was in pod in water, took longer to get her out. I enjoy this for always."

Gogi carried Luci to his pod, strapped her in, and left.

"What us do now?" one of the other fems asked.

"Come. I show you how to get water." Ping led the way to the tree, filled two bottles, and drew up another containerful for the others. "If container empty after fill bottle, let container down and draw up more. Not have to be full, if too heavy."

Essi stared at the river, but the others turned away. They returned to their place on the beach.

"Now us stay right here and wait." Ping sat down. The others joined her. "Us have energy nuggets and water and sleep pods. Us may be living out here one day, so learn way of land. Feel air?"

"Better than inside," Essi said.

The others agreed.

One asked, "What us do without screens?"

"Talk to each other. Explore area. Enjoy freedom." Ping leaned back on her forearms.

Another asked, "What if they not come back?"

35

JAN, GLORI, AND ADAM LEFT EARLY the next morning. The first day, sunny and warm, passed smoothly. Jan and Glori, happy to be going somewhere, broke out into song. Adam looked at everything. They camped at the glade and sang songs around the campfire.

The next day, the forest grew thicker and gloomier. No one felt like singing. Midday, when they stopped for a meal, Jan felt something in her mind. She began to see double, out of focus. "You have any problems seeing?" she asked Glori. "My eyes are going funny."

"Something's not right, but I can't figure out what."

"I'm seeing double. The forest and the other world."

"Me, too."

Jan and Glori looked at each other, wide-eyed.

"My eyes are okay," Adam said.

"You're younger." Glori rubbed her eyes.

Something danced in the nearby stream, but Jan could not focus on it. She closed one eye and saw no trees, but several layers of black to white objects moving around, like seed pods in the wind.

"No." She closed that eye and opened the other. Now she saw the trees with a faint overlay of the other. Jan jumped up. "Let's go."

The others joined her on the trail, which soon narrowed into a grove of large trees with thick undergrowth. They pushed through until they came to a place where the trail split into two even narrower ones.

Jan stopped. "Which way?"

"Stay here, I'll go check." Adam plunged down the left-hand trail.

"Adam, no." Jan reached for him, but he was gone.

The women waited, clutching each other.

He returned and trotted into the other. Back shortly, he said, "This place is like a maze."

"It wasn't like this before," Jan said.

"Something about mazes," Adam muttered. "Ah. Always go to the right to get through." He moved into the right-hand trail-tunnel and Jan and Glori followed. Jan no longer saw separate images with each eye, but a superimposed image of the objects moving within the forest.

The rest of the day, the trio proceeded through the maze. The farther they went, the grayer the trees and bushes became, although the overall shapes of the moving objects remained the same.

Very quiet, except for their feet slushing through the fallen leaves and an occasional cough or sneeze, the place smelled like a room shut up for too long. Finally, they reached the end and found a wide-open space between the maze and a row of umbrella-shaped trees. Even out there, the light was fading.

Jan slumped to the ground. "I'm getting too old for this. And Mama wanted to do it. Let's camp here."

The others agreed, and Glori took a loaf of bread out of her food bag.

Jan took a few bites of her share, a few sips of water, and collapsed onto her blanket. Exhausted, not only from the long hike, she was also mentally drained from fighting off the other world. *It wasn't like this last time. There must be an easier way.*

•　　•　　•

In the morning, the three of them passed between two trees and found themselves in a meadow with a line of tall trees beyond. A path led to a break in the trees where Jan thought she saw the hump of a bridge.

"Let's go." Adam strode to the bridge. Jan and Glori followed. They stopped at the top of the hump and looked down at the rushing river.

"Just like ours," Jan said. "This gray hump."

"It's not as bright." Glori looked at the sky.

"No buildings," Adam added.

The plains spread out before them, a copy of Peace, with no signs of habitation. Looking to her right, Jan thought she glimpsed the sparkle of the sea. Occasional small trees dotted the plain, many surrounded by a rainbow of flowers. In the distance, she saw the green of the forest. *Where was the small river? Where were they?*

A knot of fear grew in her stomach. Jan looked back at the forest behind her, and the path that led to it. *We can always trace our steps and go back.*

Adam stepped off the bridge, out past the trees, turned right, and the three walked under the hanging branches of the trees. They were like the ones Jan knew. At a place where a tongue of trees licked out into the plain, they sprawled on the ground and rested.

"There's the sea down there." Jan pointed.

"Let's see what else is down there," Glori said.

Jan and Glori connected their minds, *reached* and found a few sentient beings on the beach. They disconnected and looked at each other.

"What?" said Glori.

"Who?" Janni added.

"Why don't we go find out?" Adam got up.

"We have to go down there anyway." Glori rose.

"Okay." Jan scrambled to her feet.

When they reached the area where the quines' trees were on Peace, they found only a few small trees.

"This is different." Glori looked around. "Let's camp here and do the rest tomorrow. I'm beat." She sat down under a tree.

"Sure is." Jan sat beside her. "Let me check." She *reached* and recognized Ping with a few others. "Whoa, what happened here?" She *touched* the alien but could not communicate.

"What? Adam asked.

Jan explained. "It's Ping and some others. She was only out those two times when she found us, as far as I know. Why is she out now? I sense something bad happened."

"We'll find out tomorrow."

36

T HE SUN WAS PEEPING over the distant forest, when Jan and her friends headed down the slope. A ragged row of large egg shapes lined the grass above the beach, and several pale-furred people moved about among them.

As they approached, one pointed at them. Another, with a larger head, took a few steps up the slope.

"Greetings, Ping," Jan called. "We have come to visit you."

"Jan, Glori. Greetings." Her eyes were wide with surprise. "How you come?"

"What's all this?" Jan swept her hand about.

"Sleep pods. Branch broke off in shakes and came up on beach. How you here?"

"We came through the forests." Jan noticed a line of seashells and other debris up in the grass. "Water came up to here? How's the rest of your habitat?

"Gone when us came out. Gogi said it unhurt, but he only go in Maker so he not know about other modules. Come." She introduced them to Essi and the other females.

They all looked like Ping, in slightly different sizes and shapes, with varying pale colored fur. The one called Essi said, "Greeting." The others hung back and stared.

"So you're stuck out here? Didn't anybody come to get you?"

"Yes. Gogi. He said big chiefs not want us back." Ping shrugged a shoulder.

"They can't just leave you out here," Glori said as they all sat on the grass.

"Ah, they can." Ping touched her shoulder fur. "They not want us telling others how nice is out here."

"Why not?" Jan fiddled with a blade of grass.

"They say habitat fine and my warnings upset citizens."

"They don't believe you? After this?" Jan waved her hand around.

Ping shrugged a shoulder again.

"What about food?" Adam asked. He was making a little pile of dead leaves and twigs.

"Gogi bring we more. There water in river," Ping pointed to the line of trees to the west, "if us can find way to get it. We have container on rope to collect water for water bottles, but need more."

"I'll look at it." Adam added a leaf to his pile.

"This not how I plan to start colony here. You come through odd place?"

Jan nodded. "Yes. Different this time."

"You come at good time. How we make home here?" Ping looked down and twisted her fingers.

Jan was pleased to find Ping on this new world. Apparently, there were two portals between her Peace and this one, the one on land she went through, and one under the sea. If the worlds, the universes, were lined up like a row of stones, it made sense that two portals on one side would lead to the same next universe.

However, she had no idea how to build a colony from scratch.

Glori spoke up. "You will need food, water, and shelter. Storms blow water up the hill, so your place must be higher up. I didn't see the little river we have, but you have the big one over there. I don't know what you eat, you'll have to plan that. Shelter is houses like we have."

"So much." Ping looked around. "Not know how us do it, but us must."

Jan noticed a large, black mound rising above the sea a long way out. "Is that your place?" She pointed.

"That top of Maker. Our pods came from there." Ping blinked "I like being outside much better and like to live here, but top chiefs on council not see problems. Citizens see problems but those who can fix them, not."

"I do not understand how the people in charge can ignore this," Jan said.

"Are they all old?" Glori asked.

"Yes. All but Chief Mola, he still middle age. His pater die young. When they die, they replaced by younger old men."

Jan thought of Old Artie and Old Chad, two crotchety old men who ignored the younger generations. Gramma Perri, the matriarch, was old in years but not in spirit. "You need younger people, women, to be your leaders."

Ping nodded. "I wish to do that when us move out here. Hope oldest council chiefs die."

"Ping!" Both Peace women were shocked.

"They useless. Head chief and three on council ancient. Chief Mola of Science and head chief of Medical not quite old."

"Oh." Jan gasped. *How could younger people not take over?* Of course, she shouldn't judge Ping's system by her own. They were totally different.

"Us have strict rules us abide by," Essi said. "Hard to change anything."

"I see." Jan nodded. Her stomach growled. "We need to eat our midday meal, so we'll go over there. I wish there was some way we could help." She rose and led the way to the huge trees by the river. Adam sat where he could watch the river.

As they ate, Jan thought about what she and her people could do. Not with Ping's system, but to build a colony out here. Perhaps some construction people could show them how to build houses. Crops people. Water.

"The trip here and back is too long," said Glori, who had been listening to Jan's thoughts.

"Yes, we need a better way to get here."

'I'm working on that,' a voice said in Jan's mind.

"Who?"

'Asiram. Three Peaces will become one.'

"What? How?"

The voice did not answer. Jan and Glori stared at each other.

"Asiram is the person who contacted Mama about the mist," Jan said.

This, on top of being here at Ping's place, made her head ring. She had no idea what to do about it. Now, she just wanted to get back home.

37

ALTHOUGH PLEASED TO SEE JAN and the others, Ping could not shake a sense of foreboding about the future. With no screen, no tasks to do, she was bored. Unsure of what she should be doing out there, she made up names for and catalogued the different plants.

She watched as Jan, Glori, and Adam made places to sleep in the grass. They wouldn't have fit in the pods anyway.

•　　　•　　　•

Next morning, Ping crept out of her sleep pod in the purple haze of dawn. The sea slapped at the sand and a small breeze swept off the land. She trotted over to the river, found the water container empty and let it down into the water. After collecting it, she filled her bottle, returned to her pod, and consumed her morning nugget.

Ping sat on the flat step of the hatchway of her sleep pod and watched the sea beyond the long stretch of green grass, punctuated by groups of taller grass and flowers. This was her home now, her world. A feeling of joy stole over her as she felt the warmth of the rising sun and listened to morning breeze in the grass.

Later in the morning, Gogi returned with a towing pod and moved the sleep pods farther up the slope. Ping introduced him to the Peace people and told him how they got there.

"No wonder drones not go into forest," he said. "Welcome to our messed up world and may you get home safely." To Ping, "Here more nuggets. All I can do now."

"Not very many," Ping said, bouncing the small bag in her hand.

"All there is. New recruits doing your tasks, not very well. Chiefs cut down amount of nuggets citizen take at one time until Nutrition going again. At least, they still count you as part of community."

"For how long?" Ping asked.

"As long as I can come out." Gogi looked around. "Keep well. Must go now." He returned to his pod and left.

"That thing goes through water as well as air?" Jan asked.

Ping nodded. "Some only go in water." She shared out the brown and white nuggets to the other fems. "These our nourishment. Has all elements us need."

"Can you eat plants at all?"

"Never tried. Body not programmed for plants."

Jan wrinkled her nose. "I'll show you what we eat. Let your scientists look at them, see if they're safe for you to eat. If you have to live out here, what will you eat?"

"I not know."

"Come, I'll show you." Jan led Ping to a row of plants along the big trees. She picked a long seed pod off a round bush and pulled a string to open it. Several oval green objects lay along the inside.

"These are beans. They need to be cooked."

'Cooked?" Ping could not comprehend.

"Heated over a fire in a pot of water. It breaks the beans down so we can digest them."

"Ah. Maybe. Our digestive systems programmed to consume our nuggets. Not know if us can consume anything else." Ping hadn't thought much about food before. *What us do if us cannot make nuggets?*

"I guess you need to get your scientists to figure it out."

"Yes. I give one to Gogi next time he come."

They moved on. Jan found several plants she said she recognized. Ping soaked it all in. *Maybe ...* At midday, they returned to the others so Jan and her friends could eat a meal.

Ping shared what she had learned with Essi and the others.

•   •   •

The following day, Gogi returned, his pod towing another. He landed below the sleep pods, and Nela stepped out.

"Nela, how you come?" Ping rushed to greet her.

"Gogi told me. Us brought water tank and open tub to collect rainwater."

"Nela, this Jan from other world. Glori and Adam. Nela is Gogi's sister." Ping said.

"Hello," Jan said. Nela was Ping's size, with a necklet like hers, and pinkish fur. Nela nodded. "Collecting rainwater is good. What about power?"

Gogi shook his head. "Chiefs decide they cannot connect. They just leave you out here."

"I need my screen. I have reports to do." Ping stamped her foot.

Gogi shrugged. "Go back, then. I take one."

"No. How you learn this?"

"Through my chief who asked Maker chief. Head chief said you wanted to come out, so you can stay out. Do you want go back?"

Ping clenched her fists. "Anyone want go back?"

"I do," said the youngest, who stayed in her pod most of the time.

"I'm staying," Nela said.

Ping looked at her. "You can have her pod."

The young Phren packed up and huddled in Gogi's pod.

Gogi, Ping, and Adam unloaded the water tank and basin. "Gratitude," Gogi told Adam. "We homs stick together."

Adam nodded.

"Gratitude. Come when you can," Ping said as Gogi climbed into his pod and departed. She found him pleasant.

"Well, fems, seems we starting a new colony out here," Ping said. "Jan, us need your advice."

"First, water," Jan began, sitting down on the grass. The others followed suit, Ping across from her. "The river water is good. Your water tank and tub is a good start. Second, food. As long as Gogi keeps bringing you your nuggets, you'll be okay, but you need to plan for the future. Gather as many different kinds of plants as you can and have your scientists look at them, see if there's any you can use. Do you eat anything besides those nuggets?"

"Only drinks from fruit us grow in Park. Our bodies programmed for nuggets."

"Here, I made some mash from those beans. Take a taste." Jan picked up a bowl, scooped something out of it with a stick with a bowl on the end of it containing some green stuff.

Ping touched her tongue to it and breathed in a taste. It had a different flavor than the nuggets, but not unpleasant. "This be good if our bodies can use it. Us will test."

"Can you eat the solid fruit?"

"Yes. Must chew to mush before swallow. Nuggets dissolve quickly."

Jan nodded. "Power. If you can't get any from the habitat, you will have to find your own. We have a waterwheel that gives us power from the river. Maybe we can get one of our water people to show you how to make that. Also, reflective materials can produce heat."

"Good." *This becoming more and more possible.* Hope rose in Ping.

"Now, shelter." Jan looked up the slope. "You will need more than just your little pods. You will have to build houses to live in and other buildings for your workplaces and storerooms."

"Build," Ping repeated. Hope sank.

"We can help you. First thing is to plan where you want your homes and buildings. Not too close to the sea, because bad wind can blow the water up the slope."

Ping looked up the slope. "How high?"

Jan rose. "We'll show you." She led the way up to the tide line. "The water came to here. See all this along?"

"Ah," Ping said. She looked down at the shoreline and back at the line of debris at her feet. "Came all this way?"

"Yes."

Too far from habitat.

Jan continued on. At the little group of trees, she stopped. "Should be safe here. This is about where our town starts."

"How us put places?" Ping asked. *How could us live way up here far from sea?*

"Adam, you know construction."

Adam stepped up. "Put your work buildings in one place, around an open plaza, then houses around that and up and down the slope. Make a plan how you want them, how far apart. Mark out the plaza first, then the buildings around it."

Adam continued but Ping was lost and only saw how far above the shore they were. She closed her eyes. Who of her fellow citizens would understand this? Someone in Maker, most likely. She had no idea it would be this complicated.

She heard something about cutting down trees. "Hurt trees?" Ping's eyes widened.

"Others will grow in their place," Glori said. "When we find little trees growing where we don't want trees, we move them to where we do want trees."

"Ah." Ping was able to process this. She had never thought about how the trees in Park had come to be there.

"Do your people have any tools for building?" Adam asked.

"I not know. If any, chiefs won't let us have them." Ping's shoulders sagged.

"I guess we can bring some. You can start by making your planning diagram, where you want your plaza, buildings, and houses." Adam looked around. "Nice here, like ours."

"Yes." Ping puffed out a breath and started down the slope. She had no idea how they were going to make this plan.

Back at the pods, Jan and Glori and Adam went off to sit together.

Ping settled in her pod and looked around at this green world. Green grasses covered it, some clumps almost waist high, others low to the ground, easy to walk on. A line of low plants with colorful flowers along the row of tall trees by the river pleased her. Out to sea, beyond the line of flat green islands, an orange glow flickered for a moment, and she also glimpsed it in front of the islands.

What was that? What did it mean? Was it a foreshadowing of something to come?

38

T HE NEXT MORNING, Ping watched as Jan, Glori, and Adam prepared to leave. She sensed Jan taking in the grassy slope, tall river trees and rippling sea as she slowly turned in a circle. She faced Ping. "We, or someone from our clan, will return in a while. Marisa will determine when. I hope everything goes well with you."

"Gratitude," Ping said. "Safe trip." She watched them walk up the slope, then turned to Nela. "Tell what happens in hab."

"Not well." Nela sat on the grass next to Ping's pod. "Chiefs say anchors moved, and cannot fix them. Habitat rocks in big waves. Scientists say something going on way out in sea. Maker in sand, other modules float. Some of we concerned constant motion may damage connectors."

Ping shuddered. *Severe damage could break water, air, power lines.*

Nela nodded. "I continue network of citizens in Science and Maker. Gogi leads in Maker. Some relatives in Education and Medical with us. Our two chiefs definitely concerned, and Chief Adar interested. Forget council, except Chief Mola. Energy nuggets in short supply. Gogi says new people slow, and they running low on material for material printers."

"They not think about that before leaving we out here."

"True. Like most citizens, chiefs not think either."

•   •   •

The next two days, Ping, Nela, and Essi made plans for their new community. Ping kept her many questions to herself. How to process food and water, how to make homes and places for science labs, hospital, schooling, makers, where to keep pods and drones. The more she thought about the new place, the more the project overwhelmed her, and it felt more and more impossible.

One day Gogi brought Kile of Medical along with a measuring device and a travelling nest. Smaller than a sleep pod, one end open to crawl into, they were used by pod drivers and citizens who wished to camp out in Park.

Kile stepped out, glanced around, then down. He inhaled a taste of the air. "This is great. Us need this."

"Yes, but how us move everyone and everything out?" Gogi asked. "How us make power and water and bioputer?"

Kile shrugged a shoulder. "I told to check all you fems." He brought out a medical tool kit.

"We well." Ping backed away.

"Where I set up." Kile glanced around again and went to a group of trees. "It not hurt."

Ping thought of her checkup not too long ago and wondered.

Nela went first. "He says I well, and lot easier without big machines."

"You not here as long as rest of we." Ping went next. Kile poked and prodded and ran a silvery diagnostic device over her that beeped occasionally.

Kile pronounced her well, as was Essi who followed her. The other three were not well.

"These fems have weaknesses in backs, hips, and thigh muscles, and lessening lung function. All you, especially you three, must do exercises. Even just walking up and down the slope be good," Kile announced. "Without exercise equipment in habitat, you must do much walking, every day. I return in three eight-days to see how you are."

"Gratitude," Ping said. She had not thought of the exercise room, since she rarely went there. She did her own exercises in her sleep pod.

She showed the two homs where their new place would be, and answered many of their questions with, "I not know."

Gogi and Kile stayed the night and gawped at the stars.

"Other suns," Ping said.

"Other worlds?" Gogi asked.

"Maybe other people." Ping widened her mouth.

In the morning, Gogi said, "Us continue to talk to citizens. All us can do."

"Yes." Ping nodded.

"Only talk in small groups, but word spreads."

After Ping watched the pod sail off and dive behind the top of Maker, she turned to the others. "Exercise time." She, Nela, and Essi each chose one of the others and walked with them until the latter tired. "We do this every morning and evening."

The other three groaned, but did not protest.

•   •   •

The next day, Ping and Nela took the measuring device up to a level area below the place Adam had shown them and marked off a circle for the plaza. Neither of them could visualize buildings around it. They returned to the pods and met Essi with another fem. "I with them today, you have your walk."

"Gratitude," Ping said, and trotted on down to the sea and sat on the edge of the grass. A light breeze tickled her face and her fur. Every situation led to more questions. *How in habitat are us going to accomplish this?* The new colony seemed to move further away every day. But they couldn't stay in the habitat much longer.

The sea sloshed up to her feet and the ground seemed to move uneasily beneath her. *Now what?* Whitecaps lined the incoming waves, larger than she'd seen before. One of the fems yelped as the ground shook. Ping looked around. Nela was attending to her. *Good.* Ping wanted nothing more than to go to Park and get away from everything, only there was no way to get there. The sea, which began to quiet down, would have to do.

39

Two DAYS LATER, Gogi returned, and Chief Rody stepped out of the pod onto the long grass under cloudy skies.

"Chief." Ping jumped up. "Greetings. Why you come?"

"Need you back inside to do tasks." He looked around and took a few steps toward the trees along the big river.

"No!" Pings insides clenched. "I not go back."

"Is order, Ping," Chief Rody said softly, turning to her. "Is your duty. Wish not, but is my duty to bring you."

"Then I must. But our pods, they stay here?" *Anything to keep a link with the outside.*

"Yes. You sleep in barracks. Move citizens to other areas. Get your belongings, I cannot stay long."

Ping heard him think, *'but I would very much like to'*. She and the other fems proceeded to pack up their possessions. She left the little wooden quine that Old Allen had made for her in her pod. She would be back.

They all bundled into the big travel pod. At the habitat, Nela said farewell and trudged off to Science, where she lived and worked, and the others followed Chief Rody to the barracks. A line of six tan sleep nests with white vertical dividers between faced a pair of cupboards and a pair of cleaning rooms. A single screen hung on the gray end wall.

I will find a way out, Ping thought fiercely as she dumped her bundle on a nest.

After they all dropped their bags and looked around, Chief Rody said, "Come, fems." He led them to the workroom where they were to do their tasks. Each was matched with a new recruit.

Ping had to redo everything her assistant did, leaving little time for her own tasks. *What is wrong with young people, why they not taught to work quickly and efficiently? Why they not think?*

When Ping returned to the barracks after her shift, she intended to check the screen, but two other fems were using it.

"Pardon, but might I check something quickly?" she asked.

"Us using it," one said, not looking at her.

"Only few moments," Ping said, louder.

The two ignored her. They were playing some sort of game.

Ping clenched her fists. Only the barracks residents controlled the screen; there was no one she could go to for assistance. She sat in her sleep nest and thought. *Inside, no privacy, no screen either here or at her workplace. What more could happen?*

Later, after the fems were finished with their game, Ping strode over to the screen and clicked it on. She found only news about how well the habitat was doing, and simple entertainments. No way to connect with anyone, not even her family.

Ping curled up in her nest and fumed. The anger was back, along with something else she couldn't name. She had learned as a child to ignore her emotions; they were just a waste of time. If a problem arose, she was to consider it. If she could deal with it, do so. If not, refer it to someone who could handle it.

I cannot control going outside, and I cannot get more on the bioputer. But I can control training recruits.

The next morning, Ping told Cura, her recruit, to work faster. "Us take out rocks and metal, anything too big. This is good." She held up a strand of seaweed. "This good for food. Why you throw away?"

"He said discard all big stuff. How this muck become food?"

"Is pumped in from sea. Us take out big stuff and creatures here. Then goes through screens and more sorting into vats." Ping had learned this from her screen in her sleep pod. "Then greens and nutritionals come from Hydroponics, added and mixed. They take samples, adjust and form into nuggets."

"Oh. How you know that?"

"All information in bioputer, in screen. Look it up." *Have these youngsters no interest in how their habitat worked?* Ping pushed the thought aside.

"I play games." Cura twisted her hands together.

Ping shook her head.

"Now creatures like this," she held up a large seashell, "us put aside here." Ping dropped it into a green bin at the end of the line. "Others remove shell and put creature in food mix."

"Yuk." Cura wrinkled her upper lip.

"Is protein, which us need for strength."

Essie and her recruit moved closer to listen to Ping, who explained everything she had learned about nutrition. They shared with the other fems in the sorting room, and the recruits improved.

Ping withdrew into herself, doing her tasks properly, answering questions but otherwise not speaking. She dug into all the corners and cul-de-sacs of her brains to find a solution to her dilemma. She could do no good for the habitat stuck in here.

•   •   •

One day Chief Rody called her in to his office. Larger than Chief Elar's, the wide screen on the pale green wall shone down on his worktable and two large sitting nests, one occupied by him. The pale blue bioputer hung over his head.

"You doing good, Ping," he said as she settled into the other nest. "Recruits doing better."

"They not know how to think." Ping glanced at the screen. Three separate lists, each with the same lists of names beside each, stared at her. "Why you not just put name first, only once. Columns across show matches. Save room."

"Eh, Ah, I see." He erased the second column of names and moved over the column of items. He nodded. "How you know this?"

"I researcher. I had access to most of bioputer." She looked at the screen again.

Chief Rody clicked to another screen full of random geometrical figures in various colors. "Sort by shape, then color." He handed her the activator.

Ping took the device, looked at the screen and went to work. Soon it was all neat rows from yellow triangles to green circles.

"Excellent. I not told you did research. I put you there."

"I accept. I also wish to go outside."

"Not yet. Catch up on research, maybe later. Other researchers too slow."

Ping smirked inside. No one was as fast as she.

She had no choice but to accept his words. *At least, I have bioputer.* Chief Rody took her to a cubicle with a screen and gave her a list of projects. Her ID worked, and she clicked on messages. Among the ones asking questions was a call from Juni about an upcoming family gathering.

She sighed with relief and picked up the first assignment.

When Ping checked out with Chief Rody at the end of the day, she asked, "May I have permission go to my family gathering in Central?"

"When?" He laid down his computer activator.

"In two days, in evening."

"You may go. Not stay too late." He picked up his device.

"I not." Ping took a big breath as she left.

•   •   •

On the day, let off from work early, Ping made the trek across Maker into Central. She saw no damage there. At the pale, oval gathering room filled with soothing music and a taste of flowery scent, Juni hugged her. Ping found an empty sitnest and settled in. All her sisters, aunts, and grandmothers sat around her.

"Where you been?" Mater demanded. "Us not able to access you."

"I assigned to Nutrition and in group of sleep pods that broke off. They not want bring me back."

"Why Nutrition? You are researcher." Mater rubbed a finger over her other hand.

Ping shrugged a shoulder. "I was given order, so I went." She noticed sister Bede's daughter hiding in a corner. "Hello, niece Cori."

"She old enough to come to gathering now," Bede patted the girl, who was at the beginning of adolescence.

"What you study in schooling?" Ping asked the child. "History?"

"They not teach that anymore," Bede said. "No point. All same."

Ping was speechless for a moment, then snapped her mouth shut. *How could citizens think this way? It was given in her schooling that one must know history to learn from it, to do better.*

"From my researches, history not all the same. Many changes, even from hundred years ago. Us must know what us did, so us not make same mistakes over and over." Ping pounded the edge of her nest.

"Now, Ping, stop that," Mater said.

"Without history, no progress," Gran added.

Ping nodded at the old fem. "Ignoring problems not progress." She waved her arms. "Chiefs not listen."

"Not your problem," Mater said. "Just do your duty."

"Chiefs not listen," Ping repeated. "They just let habitat die." She wiped away spittle at the edge of her mouth.

"Now, Ping," Aunt Dela said. "Calm down. Problems being taken care of."

"No, they not." Ping pounded on the edge of her nest. "Problems growing. I see everywhere. Nugget machine down twice in last eight-day. More rationing."

"Ping right," sister Bede said. "In supply, many items short. I want Cori to have good life. If habitat die, where my Cori live? Juni's Peni? Other children?"

"Bede, you with me." Ping smiled at her. Bede, the eldest, usually ignored Ping, the youngest.

"Of course, little sister. Juni has young, too, still in nursery. Us must give them what us have."

"Chiefs take care of things," Mater said. "Now, Juni, how young Peni doing?"

Ping sat back, mumbling to herself, half listening to Juni praising her daughter. The pain of childlessness resurfaced. Finally, Ping pulled herself up. "Must go now. My place on far side of Maker."

"Be good and behave," Mater said. "And not worry."

"Keep on," Juni added.

Bede nodded.

Ping left, wondering what she was doing trying to change habitat. *This not my duty. I to do and go where I assigned.* She thought of what she had been taught as a child. When everyone did their assigned duties, the community would prosper, and everyone would have plenty of whatever they needed.

The habitat not prospering. Who not performing their duties?

40

MARISA WAS MENDING a tunic when she *heard*, 'We're back, Mama.'

'Welcome home,' she *sent*. 'Come to my house.' Then she *called* Qilla to send three quines up. As she worked, she followed them in her mind until they crossed the bridge. She knew Glori would call her mama.

That evening, Kaylyn had just helped Marisa to her big chair and propped her leg on a wooden box, when someone pounded on the door, and the three travelers burst in. She welcomed them all with hugs, and the women collapsed on the green couch.

Adam turned to Kaylyn and gave her a big hug. "Missed you." To Marisa, "Do you need me?'

"Just a quick summary."

"Mama Jan can tell you about the trip. Ping and several others and their sleep pods were out on the land. They're all okay."

"Good," Marisa said.

Adam shrugged. "We'd like to go now." His arm was still around Kaylyn. "The kids are with Aunt Susan."

"Please," Kaylyn looked up at him.

"Very well. You two go on." They ran out the door.

"Have you eaten?" Marisa asked.

"No," Jan said.

Glori shot to her feet. "Brian."

"Relax. Susan is taking care of them. There's a casserole in the kitchen and you know where the breadbox is. I've eaten."

"Good." Glori sank back into her seat. "I don't think I could walk another step."

Jan rose, shuffled back to the kitchen and brought back two bowls of casserole with hunks of bread, and handed one to Glori.

"How is Ping?" Marisa asked.

"Well," Jan swallowed a bite and settled in between lumps on the couch. "She and several other Phren women were out on the hillside. Their sleep pods broke off one night in a storm and were washed ashore. They weren't hurt, those things are well padded inside. She calls them nests."

"Oh, my. Do they have food and water?"

"Yes." Jan took another bite. "She said the big chiefs don't want them back inside."

"What!" Glori sat up straight. "Why didn't you tell me?"

"I thought you knew. It was clear to me." Jan glared at Glori.

"Girls, girls," Marisa said.

The two sat back, facing her.

Marisa shook her head. The little tug of caution inside her subsided beneath the concern about Ping's situation. "How can they do that? How do they expect them to live?"

"Ping wants to build a colony on the land but has no idea how to do it," Glori said.

"I told Ping we could send some people to help them build their homes and buildings," Jan added.

"No." Marisa pulled a curl. "It's one thing to give her our hospitality when she comes here, but we can't send our people there when we need them here."

"Mama," Jan cried, "We can't just let them die."

"They are not dying. They can take care of themselves. If they ask for help, we will consider it." Marisa paused. "Sorry if I sound harsh, but I remember the Bramites who chased us out of our first place on Harmony."

"Ping wasn't anything like what my mama told me about the Bramites." Glori swallowed a bite of bread. "They are even on another world now, Peace in a different universe."

Marisa looked around at her house's pale green walls. "It really hurt when I found out we had to move away because of me, my Talent. At seven, I didn't yet understand how we were supposed to use our Talents, and mine was strongest even then."

"Not your fault you could see where the other children were hiding." Jan smiled.

"Mama told me later I was always a handful when I was little." Marisa smiled back. "You were a handful, too."

"Oh, Mama." Jan took a sporkful of stew. "What about Sam's people? They have a lot more than we do."

"Perhaps. That's Sam's choice."

"So what are we going to do?" Jan asked.

"I'll ask Sam for a meeting. See what she thinks. You two better get home. Your mates will be waiting. I'm surprised they haven't broken the door down yet."

Jan rose. "Okay, Mama, I'll see you tomorrow. Thanks for the meal."

"Take care, Aunt Marisa." Glori followed her out.

Marisa sat back. The unease she'd felt for the past several days was still there. Nothing she could pinpoint. The clan was doing well, growing. The coming harvest looked to be plentiful, the weather had been fine, most everyone was doing what they were supposed to be doing. *Janni had noticed the unease too.* She wasn't sure about Glori, that woman kept things too well hidden.

She would ask Sam if there was anything new in her farseeing. The next morning, she *called* Maxee and asked her to tell Sam that Marisa needed to see her. 'She'll have to come down, I hurt my knee and can't ride.'

'Be well. I tell her.'

Old Allen stumped out of the bedroom. "They're gone," he said, settling into his chair.

"Did you hear what they said about Ping?"

"Yeah. Glad you said no. We don't need any more problems."

•　　　•　　　•

Two days later, Sam and Maxee arrived, along with Hal and Ben. Jan greeted them at Marisa's front door and ushered them in. Gloria, Brian, and Adam were already there, sitting at the table. Marisa sat in her chair, leg propped up.

Sam went to Marisa and took her hand. "What happened? How are you managing? How bad is it?"

"I fell. It's not broken, just sprained. I can get around on crutches," Marisa indicated the pair against the wall next to her chair. "How are you?"

"Problems, always problems." Sam found a seat on the couch.

As Marisa was about to speak, Kaylyn rushed in. "Sorry, Paul's boy just had to show me his drawing." She ran into the bedroom and dragged out the sea blue padded chair Marisa sat on to comb her hair.

"Okay, are we all ready?"

Nods.

"Janni, tell them what you found."

Jan sat up. "We went through the forest, which was different, and Adam led us through a maze to a place like ours. Glori and I saw an overlay of the black-and-white world, but nothing bothered us. There was no little river. We found Ping and five other women out on the land, where their sleep pods had landed, after a storm broke them off."

"Off what?" Hal asked.

"Their habitat. Ping said they used to all sleep inside, but when they needed the space for workrooms, schoolrooms and labs, they made these padded pods with a bed, storage area and cleaning room. They put them together in groups and attached them through a main corridor to the habitat."

"Were they all right?" Sam asked.

"They weren't injured, but the only shelter they have is their sleep pods."

"Their people not come get them?" Maxee asked.

Jan shook her head. "Ping said the head chiefs didn't want them back."

"No." Sam clenched a fist. "How can they leave Ping and her friends out there to die?"

Jan explained how the chiefs saw no problems in spite of all Ping had found. "Ping wants to start a colony on the land, for the people when the habitat is no longer livable. They need builders, engineers, someone who can build a water wheel, food preparers and crop people."

"And you want us to provide them?" Hal frowned.

"You have far more people than we do," Jan said.

"We need more people, because we have more people to provide for, to keep under control." Hal crossed his arms.

"And we need them all," Ben said. "A careless cook let a fire get away and a dozen houses burned. They're still clearing the rubble, and we will have to build new ones. Some moved in with others, a couple families are camping out, and the rest are in the meeting hall."

"No." Marisa sank into her chair. "I'm so sorry to hear that. Was anyone hurt?"

"The cook had severe burns, and a few others had smaller burns helping people get out." Sam moved in her seat. "Several lost everything and we're having to resupply them. It was a shock. Some lost precious family keepsakes."

"Those poor people," Glori said. "Is there any way we can help?"

"Thank you, but no. There are some saying your people came up and started the fire."

"What!" Marisa sat up straight.

"No way," Jan said.

"Why would they think that?" Glori shook her head.

"They're the ones who think you have magic up here," Hal said. "There's no question it was a cooking fire out of control."

"So you see, I need all of our people here to rebuild." Ben patted his moustache.

Silence.

"Kaylyn, do you have anything to say?" Marisa asked her granddaughter.

"Why does Ping want to move outside?"

"Their habitat is dying." Jan looked at her daughter.

"I didn't see any problems when I was there," Kaylyn said.

"You only saw a very small part which may not have had anything obvious yet." Brian rubbed his right thumb against his middle finger. "And you said it was over a thousand years old."

Kaylyn nodded.

"Okay," Jan said. "If we can't send people, can we send plans and instructions?"

"That might be possible," Ben said. "What exactly are they wanting to build?"

"A place similar to ours, with buildings around a plaza and houses beyond."

"When I get back, I'll see what we have. We can make copies of it for you."

"Thank you, Ben." Jan smiled at him.

After a pause, Marisa asked, "Anything else?" Marisa touched her knee. "That's all for now, folks. Sam and Maxee, you stay with me. Brian, find a place for the men to sleep."

"Certainly," he said. The men left.

'You fall on knee?" Maxee asked, frowning.

"Yes. It's getting better. I don't feel old, but my body keeps telling I'm a great grandmother."

"I know what you mean. My brother's oldest son is about to become a grandfather." Sam looked around at the pale walls dotted with pictures and drawings of Old Earth mountains and beaches, and the people of Peace among the shelves of books and carvings. "This is such a warm, homey place to come to." She sniffed. "Are you baking something?"

"Just bread. Kaylyn prepared it for me. It's done. Would you like some?

"Yes, thank you."

Marisa pulled herself up out of her chair, with Maxee's help, grabbed her crutches and stumped to the kitchen. Maxee followed her and carried the large loaf out to the table. Sam joined them.

While they ate, they discussed Sam's problems.

"We have a chief of police, a gal who worked in construction, called Abby," Sam said. "She's getting a group together and having meetings in the neighborhoods. We've also started classes in the schools about how communities get along and why it's important to follow rules. Especially, treat other people the way they want to be treated."

"Yes, that's our basic rule. Artie says to try growing your grain in a different, untouched field. We alternate fields every year. You have plenty of room up there."

Sam nodded. "We'll try that, thanks."

Marisa agreed to let one of her engineers go with Sam to help figure out how keep fires contained and collect plans for Ping's people.

Poor Sam. We are so careful about fire here, with all these wooden buildings, but then, she has so many more people to look after.

Suddenly, Sam's face went white and wide eyed.

"Sam?" Marisa's heart clenched.

Sam shook her head and reached for the table. "I saw something coming. My farseeing. I don't know, it was too strange. Part physical, in the world, part something else. I can't describe it." She caught her breath in a half sob.

Marisa saw it in Sam's mind without even trying. "Asiram's world. Is it coming here again?"

"I don't know. It was as if someone was trying to contact me." Sam shook her head again. "Something about a big change, worlds coming together."

"No," Marisa said. She had barely escaped them before. Now the clan had more people, but fewer with the strong Talent needed to deal with the situation. She looked at Sam. "When Janni and Glori were just newborns, the other universe tried to take over ours. We had to use everyone's Talents to keep them out, even the babies'. We did it then, but I don't know whether we could do it again."

Sam looked up. "Where did they come from?"

"The forest beyond the bridge."

"Maybe we could help. Why do they want this world?"

"I don't know." Marisa shook her head. "Her world was all black and white and grays, everything moving on their own. Asiram said she wanted to stabilize hers. Maybe she's just checking you out."

Sam nodded, color beginning to creep back into her cheeks.

"Don't worry." Marisa patted her arm. "We'll handle this together."

41

ASIRAM STARED AT the drawings pinned to the pearl-gray walls of her workplace. At least they stayed in place. Everything not tied down wandered with the movement of air. She cursed the aliens who were using her domain as a test place for their antigravity technology. Unable to communicate with them, the only way out was to attach her world to a solid parallel world.

She had done this before, when she was young, but it had not lasted. That world had had one group of beings who called themselves humans, now it had three colonies. A third parallel world had a small group of sentient beings. Portals between hers and theirs sat near one another; if she could get the three of them together into one solid world, it might become permanent. Her domain lay on a different continent than theirs so they could remain separate.

Her adult niece broke into her thoughts. "Hello, Aunt Asiram. Yes, it should work."

"Nanj. You know better than to snoop in other's minds." Asiram's voice softened. "What have you found?"

"Nooj is back from the northern realm and says he can't jump near as high up there. When he lets go of a small branch, it falls slowly and stays on the ground." Nanj dropped into a wide chair with three legs in a triangle and a sloping back.

"I see. Aliens are not perfect. What does he think is causing this?"

"The only major difference, he said, was that it's much colder up there. I didn't know temperature would make any difference to gravity."

Asiram pushed an errant strand behind her ear. "I don't think it does, but this is artificial antigravity so it could be possible, I suppose. Did he find any more of these magnetic rocks?" She indicated the lumpy table between them with a smooth, flat top.

"A few, but they were too big to bring back." Nanj held on to the one arm of her chair as she bobbed up and down.

"You need to wear more metal to stay in place," her aunt said. The metal kept people close to the large magnetic rocks scattered about her realm and in the ground. She had built her workplace around this one. "Very well. Tell Nooj to keep looking for smaller ones that can be moved. What is your latest project?"

"I am working with Boro. He found a new kind of plant and we are analyzing it. It is similar to pofruit, but does not have the bad odor."

"Very good. That is all." Asiram waved her away.

Nanj bounded up from her chair, floated along the handhold on the wall to the door and out.

Too bad Nooj refused to see me in person, second hand loses much in translation. Asiram knew she couldn't do this herself, she needed the aid of the Keepers in no-space/no-time.

42

I N HER CUBICLE, Ping prowled the infonet for missing data for her report on all the positive things in the habitat. Chief Mola had provided a short list for her to start with, including Park. She listed it first and researched its history. Several gaps in upkeep and maintenance became apparent. She found something else. Up to about the last sixty years, all data was neat and organized. Since then, especially in the last twenty years, bits of data had been plugged in wherever it was convenient.

Did Chief Mola know about that? Is that why he assigned me this report?

It took Ping several days to complete the report, around a few other high priority assignments. Since she was not allowed to move data from file to file, she made note of where each datum came from.

Finally, her report was complete. Almost. She needed something extra to encourage the council to act. Statistics rattled in her mind and came up with a question. *Dare I? What they do to me worse than where I am now?*

"What is percentage of habitat becoming unlivable in ten years?" She gasped when she saw the answer.

Ping added, *Nothing Lasts Forever*, to her report. Below that, 'According to bioputer calculations, Computer Center predicts an 83% chance of the habitat experiencing unrepairable damage within five years.' Although the actual prediction was for ten years, she altered the timeline on purpose to prod the chiefs and sent it to Chief Rody.

He called her in. "What this?"

"Truth from bioputer." She stood straight.

"I cannot accept this."

"Is true according to bioputer." Ping projected sincerity.

"How you know factors are correct?" He thumped his worktable.

"Is in bioputer. Bioputer always correct."

"Yes." Chief Rody stared at his screen in silence for a moment. "If so, either truth and us all die, or bioputer malfunction, which cannot be."

"So what us do? I verify figures." Ping waved a hand.

"Very well. Bioputer is truth. I send report on without those figures."

"No, must show it." Ping bounced on her feet.

"They refuse it."

Ping sighed loudly.

"Very well. I send it to chiefs and also to Eler and Chief Adar."

"Gratitude, chief."

"You do very well. Too well to be stuck in Maker. I send you back to Chief Eler in Exo."

"Gratitude." *Easier to get permission to go outside from Chief Eler.*

"You may go."

Ping returned to her cubicle and watched as Chief Rody sent the report with the amendment to the higher chiefs. Now she must wait for the chiefs' reactions. Only a tinge of curiosity touched her calm mind. It was done. She turned to the next assignment.

Later that day, Chief Elar called Ping. "Your report very good, but Chief Adar refused it, said 'Your calculation incorrect and to redo it.' He told Chief Mola who called me to reassign you to refuse cleanup. I declined, saying your gift too good to waste on that. He insists bioputer correct."

Ping cursed under her breath.

"But what if it not?"

"Ping, enough. I must think about this. You must have assignments. Go."

"Yes, Chief." Ping returned to her cubicle. The only thing she could do now was work and wait.

Two days later, when Ping signed in, she found a message that she was being transferred back to Exo. She sighed with relief, showed it to Chief Rody.

"Go. Be well."

Ping trotted to the barracks, packed her bag, and marched out of Maker and through Central to Exo in Science. Chief Eler greeted her and put her to work.

The movements of the habitat quieted. Ping worked dutifully and yearned to go out. She heard nothing from any of the chiefs, and the unease within her stirred. She did hear that another pair had been sent out to collect plants. Most of the stuff they brought in was no good. A nub of pleasure rose in her at the news.

Some days later, the power went out. The bioputer stations in Exo shut down along with the lights. When backup lights came on. Ping wondered how long their auxiliary power would last, and if there were any other backup power sources. Before all this, she would have shrugged and thought, *they'll fix it.*

Air movement continued, so there was power somewhere.

"What I do now?" Ping asked herself. She stared at the blank screen. *They fix soon.* She hoped. A message popped up on her screen. "Bioputer unavailable. Check back later.'

How much later? How I work without bioputer?

Chief Eler stopped at her cubicle. "I go see whether it just here or all over. Do what you can."

Ping went through her pile of assignments on paper and made a few notes on how to do the reports. If and when she got the use of the bioputer back. Maybe now the chiefs would listen and do something.

A little while later Chief Eler returned. "Just bottom half of Science," he told her. "Take break."

Ping wandered the darkened halls, with only tiny lights in the corners to light her way. Other citizens sat in their cubicles, waiting. Lights flickered on, then off again. She returned to her workspace, collected paper and organized each assignment, noting where to look for information.

Just before the end of the workday, the lights came on, dimly, but the bioputer screen still stared blankly at her. Ping left for the night, hoping for better news in the morning.

•   •   •

Some power was up next day, but devices worked sporadically. Ping found she could access current information since the last transit, but nothing earlier. All she found was a message saying data not available.

Ping's uneasiness grew. Then, as she tried to access a certain file, the computer burped, and she was in a completely different program. Files labeled, 'water', 'food', power', 'construction', and others displayed on her screen.

This was the information she and the habitat needed. She found an empty memory module and proceeded to download everything to it. She noted the folder's address, but when she tried to enter it later, a message said no such folder existed. She hid the module in her personal bag within her carry bag. *What next?*

43

THEN PING RECEIVED A MESSAGE that it was time for another family gathering. She hoped someone had good news. The next evening, she trotted to the oval gathering room. After everyone had settled into the wide, padded sitnests and had their nutrition drinks, Aunt Dela announced, "Daughter Zee approved to bear children."

No. Ping thought. *Not her.* Her cousin Zee had the body, but Ping thought she was a bit scatterbrained and did only average in schooling. She taught young children, and sometimes had trouble keeping order in class. She was also on evening shift with the children, so unable to be at meetings.

"Wonderful," Mater exclaimed, echoed by the other aunts and sisters.

"Good for her," Ping said, trying to hide the pain. She would have made a much better caregiver.

"Ping, you not pleased?" Mater asked, sounding annoyed at her reaction.

"Yes, Mater, but do us have room for more people?"

"Now, Ping, not our concern. Lee, you speak?"

"Yes. Medical finally allowed do checkups on Council members. I participated. I not permitted to tell you this, but you need to know." Aunt Lee looked at Ping. "Chief Mola and Chief Akoi in good health, with minor problems. Other three chiefs on edge of or in dementia with physical problems. High Chief unstable physically. Us not heard anything since us sent in report two eight-days ago."

"What?" Mater said.

"You mean us being ruled by men who not only ancient, but also brain dead?" Ping squawked.

"Looks like it," Gran rubbed her fingers together.

"No wonder us not get anything done," Bede said.

"Is there any way us can get rid of them?" Ping asked.

"Ping. That's enough." Mater glared at her.

Ping sat up, knocking over her drink. "No more." She grabbed a cloth from the shelf above her nest and mopped at the liquid.

"Mater, us cannot go on like this," Bede said.

"Yes, Kati, us cannot keep ignoring it." Aunt Lee sat up.

The others agreed.

Mater looked everywhere except at Ping. "What you think, Mater," she said to Gran, her mother.

"Ping is right. Do any of you know if there rules for removing disabled councilman?"

Blank silence, then Ping said, "I research it."

"Do so." Gran leaned back. "Only way those old men listen is if something directly affects them."

"Ah," said Ping. Mater looked at her but didn't say anything. "Gratitude, Gran." Ping climbed out of her sitnest. "I must go now."

On the way back to her sleep pod, a thought came. *Disrupt something vital. Air, water, food, if they even eat any more. In their section only.* She decided to talk to Gogi.

The next day, she sent him a message to meet somewhere. He suggested Park, and she told him when her next free day would be.

'I can manage be free in morning that day,' he replied.

When they met, found a bench, and she offered her suggestion, he widened his mouth.

"Not water or air, we cannot limit them to their area. Cut down nuggets maybe, if Nutrition agree to send fewer. But waste ..."

Phren produced little bodily waste, as their digestive system was very efficient, but continually shed fur. That, and other waste, such as items at the end of their useful life, were recycled.

"Yes." Ping bounced up and down. "Even waste smell after while."

"I know someone in recycling." Gogi bent over, plucked a blade of grass, and nibbled on it.

"You eat grass?" Ping demanded. "It not upset your insides?"

"No. Not eat too much, though I can eat more now than before."

"Ah." Ping tucked the information away. Pod drivers who went out often learned different ways.

"You think it possible to live out there?" Gogi asked.

"Yes, but not easy. Need food, shelter, power. Jan says us get power from river."

"Yes. River current like sea current. Should be possible." Gogi dropped the end of his grass blade. "This nice," he waved his arm around, "but I must go. I arrange for waste pickup shut off at council center. Be well."

He trotted down the path and Ping leaned back. *Gogi pleasant to be with.* She let her thoughts wander around the early transit. If transit time program not accurate, how many other programs failing?

She wondered why she had been chosen to discover these problems. Why was she given the extra brain to begin with? Mater was smart working with things. Pater worked in maintenance, but she understood he was very good at finding solutions to problems. Gran had been a top-rated educator, and Grandmother had been a top researcher. The grandfathers, she didn't know well.

However, she had been selected for the duty, and she would do it to the best of her ability. She wasn't sure exactly which one of the higher chiefs had chosen her.

She prayed to the Great One to help Gogi find someone who could shut off pickup of recycled waste to the council area. *That should get their attention.*

44

P ING CONTINUED TO DO her assignments even though she thought most of them were worthless. She could not find anything on the succession of the council members, except that the senior chief in his department would be appointed to take the diseased council member's place, and lesser chiefs promoted.

"But how does one become chief?" Ping asked aloud.

Again, she could find nothing on it.

Days passed, Ping continued to do her assignments, and longed for outdoors. Her concern about the habitat grew. She felt more movement of the habitat, and occasionally, little jerks. She and Chief Eler received no word from the council chiefs.

One day, Chief Eler told Ping that Chief Mola, wanted to meet with them.

"Why?"

"He not say."

Ping wondered if the council was actually listening. Chief Mola, as head chief of Science, was on the council.

On the way to Chief Mola's office, Chief Elar said, "Not say anything unless he asks you question."

Although Chief Mola lived in one of the suites off the council hall in Central, he also had an office in Science. Lines of shelves attached to the blue walls held books, artifacts, and papers. He greeted Ping and Chief Eler and they sat.

"Eler, why you let this citizen send out ridiculous report?" Chief Mola sat with his hands folded on his massive desk.

"Is what in the bioputer, Chief." Chief Eler did not look at Ping.

"Statistics can be manipulated. Redo it correctly." Chief Mola glared at Ping.

Ping stared back at him.

"I want it tomorrow."

"Yes, Chief," Chief Eler said. "Is that all?"

"Yes. Go."

Ping and her chief rose and left.

"How he say that," Ping exploded once they left his premises.

"He believes habitat perfect. He cannot see problems."

"How he not see what before his eyes." Ping was flabbergasted.

"Council chiefs see what they choose to see. Go through report and add citations where you found information in bioputer." Chief Eler took several steps and added, "Once, many years ago, I found error and told my chief. He told me I wrong and do it over. I did and changed answer to be right. But I know what I saw, and is not good if bioputer gives wrong answer."

They returned to Exo, and Ping edited her report to show where she accessed data. She added a note. 'This is what entered. Perhaps entered incorrectly.'

Chief Eler looked at it, approved it, and sent it out. They heard nothing from Chief Mola or anyone else.

Ping continued with her tasks and research, tucking away her concerns about the habitat. Although she could keep them out of her conscious thoughts, they kept appearing in her dreams. She had never dreamed much, but now it was almost every night.

One day Chief Mola called Ping and Chief Eler to his office. The same piles sat on the same shelves. They settled on the hard sitnests.

"Council setting up a new department to determine what needs be done and oversee restorations. Ping, you to head it." Chief Mola stared at them.

"Me?" Ping squeaked, touching her chest. *Not right, something akilter about this.*

"No," Chief Eler said.

"Yes, you, Ping. You have organizational skills us need. Eler, only take up part of her time. She work for you when she can."

"Ah." Chief Eler sat back.

"What I do?" Ping asked. She had trouble seeing herself leading a department.

"Will be eight citizens, three from Science, including you, one from Education, one from Medical, and three from Maker, including Nutritional. You tell them to list problems in their areas. You discuss each problem with all, then in detail with two citizens most concerned, and brainstorm for solutions. You keep master list of problems and solutions, subchief Ping."

"What? No!" *I not want to be a chief, just a worker.* Ping was appalled.

"You be good at it," Chief Mola said with what Ping saw as a snarky smile. "Tomorrow morning at second hour, meet in gathering room next to my office. Bioputer screen be available in room. I be there." He stood. "You do well."

"Come, Ping." Chief Eler moved toward the door.

"Gratitude, Chief Mola," Ping said as she followed Chief Eler out.

"I not expect that," Chief Eler said as they returned to their workplaces.

"Nor I. Me, a subchief?"

"Totally unexpected."

"Yes," said Ping. "At least, somebody doing something about this mess." *Maybe.* A warning tingle ran down her spine. Chief Mola was up to something. It was not like him to recognize any problems.

"Yes." They arrived at their workplace. "Meanwhile, do what you can."

"Yes, Chief." Ping trotted to her cubicle and pulled down the helmet. She had trouble concentrating on her work. *Is this for real? Would they actually let me do anything after I drew up lists?*

•   •   •

Next morning, Ping reported early and tried to work on a report, but other thoughts kept sliding in. Who were other citizens?

Would they have anything useful to say? Would she be allowed to work in her own way?

Finally, she shut down. "Time for me to go," she told Chief Eler.

"Yes. Come back when you done."

"Yes, Chief."

Ping found her way to the room. A table and round sitnests for eight nearly filled it. The bluegray walls were bare. Chief Mola stood at the screen at the end of the room, and Nela sat in one of the sitting nests.

"Nela," she said, thankful that there would be at least one person she knew.

"Greetings, Ping. What this all about?"

"Wait until others arrive, and I explain to all you," Chief Mola said. Taller than most, he wore the very dark blue necklet of the council members and a wide belt with many pouches hanging from it.

Aunt Dela and a hom from Education arrived.

"Aunt Dela," Ping greeted. Another I know.

Next, Gogi and a hom she did not know arrived from Maker. Gogi shook his head at her slightly and Ping said nothing. Behind them, sister Bede hobbled in.

"And sister Bede." Ping was even more pleased. "What happened?'

"Greetings, Ping. Twisted my foot in doorway. Why they not make them level?"

After everyone was seated, Chief Mola addressed them. "For those of you who not know me, I Mola, chief of Science module and council member. You now department of rehabilitation, led by subchief Ping." He nodded at her.

Ping bobbed her head, uncomfortable with her role.

Aunt Dela raised her eyebrows.

"Now introduce yourselves," Chief Mola ordered.

The others nodded.

"Nela, physiology."

"Cale, Physics." His light brown fur was overly long.

"Mang, education overseer." A narrow face with splotchy fur.

"Dela, supply nurse in Medical." Her round face beamed.

"Gogi, pod driver and caretaker." He grinned.

"Bede, manager of material printers in Maker." Pinkish fur covered her body.

"Otre, nutrition manager under Chief Rody." Smaller than the others, his fur was a darker brown.

Chief Mola passed out personal pads. "Today, list all problems in your area, and that you hear about. Be detailed as you can. When you finish, give pad to Ping. She may have questions."

Ping tried not to roll her eyes.

"After that, you may leave. Meet again in three days, same time, right here. I not be here; Ping lead meeting."

Ping felt Nela looking at her.

"Gratitude to you all for participating." He walked out of the room.

Everyone looked at Ping. "This new to me as to you." She picked up her pad. "Sooner we start, sooner we finish and leave."

They all bent over their pods. Nela gave Ping a nudge, which Ping returned.

For a while all was quiet as everyone scribbled away.

Ping gathered the pads. Gogi was the last to leave. He scrawled a last note and handed her his pad.

Ping stuffed the pads in her bag and returned to her workstation to set up a spreadsheet. The first item was computer problems. Everyone had at least one. Shortage/lack of materials was on all except physiology. She was appalled at the sheer number of problems.

She still couldn't understand why Chief Mola was doing this. He'd always refused to acknowledge problems. But it was a task given to her by a high chief, so she must do it.

The next two days Ping worked on problems, squeezing in other assignments as she could. When she had a comprehensive list, she broke it down into departments, and entered the relevant items into the department pads.

At the next meeting, she passed out the pads. "Here lists of problems that involve your department. Think about them, what to do to correct them. What you need. Today, Bioputer. Nela, what is main problem you have with it?"

"Calculations not same," Nela said. "Have to do many at least three times to get matching result." Others nodded. Some said they were losing data. Otre said the computer told him they were low on calcium, but when he checked, there was plenty.

Aunt Dela said, "Us find same thing. Also dropping items on lists of procedures."

"Gogi?" Ping asked.

"It tells me pods due for maintenance when they not. Even one checked out only two eight-days ago."

"Not good," Ping said. She remembered a meeting. "I know Chief Miki of Computer Central. I send problems and see what he says."

They continued. Each was given a list of problems in their sector and told to do what they can to fix them.

At the next meeting, a few minor issues had been resolved, things they could do themselves without involving chiefs, but no approvals from chiefs for major problems.

Chief Miki sent a message that he was checking on bioputer problems. The entity was still trying to do its own thing.

Frustrated, Ping went over everything with the others and found a few workarounds. Meanwhile, the habitat started making little movements again.

45

PING WAS ASTONISHED when Chief Mola strode into their next meeting and announced, "I make arrangements for you eight go to land."

"Why?" Ping asked as her heart thumped. *What Mola up to? Does he see problems now?*

"If, as you say, us may need move out, us need citizens experience the outdoors first. You been chosen. Prepare to leave in three days. I rearrange schedules to complete your tasks." Chief Mola strode out.

"Nobody can replace me," Ping said. She sensed something wrong. *This not like Mola. What he up to?*

"I think they just trying to get rid of we," Nela said.

"I not mind seeing outside," Aunt Dela said. "I let Kati know."

"She not be happy about it." Sister Bede rubbed her ear.

Ping was glad she wouldn't have to face Mater for a while.

"Did he say how long us be out?" Gogi asked.

"No." Ping rubbed her chest fur. "Back to problems now."

The next two days, thoughts of the pleasure of being outdoors rubbed against the big question. *What Chief Mola up to? What he really want? Was it like Nela said, to get rid of we?*

•   •   •

Three days later, it took two trips to get all of them up to the land. Chief Mola came too, in his personal pod. Ping made sure she and Nela were in the first group. She jumped out, and Nela stepped out gingerly and looked around. She took in a big taste of air and said, "Oh, yes, I can live here, in pod. Can us move them?"

"Yes. Gogi has pod mover."

Sister Bede stepped out and held on to the handle by the door. Aunt Dela stayed inside.

"You must come out, Aunt," Ping said. "Here, you sit in this pod." She led the older fem to one of the sleep pods. Bede went to another sleep pod and sat in the hatchway.

When the second pod arrived, Gogi jumped out. The other three came out timidly, and Cale and Mang, eyes on the ground, headed for the nearest sleep pods.

Ping noticed the high tide marks on the grass, a line of shells and seaweed. "Gogi, us need move sleep pods higher."

"I must go back and get two more anyway. Is Chief Mola staying?"

"I not know."

A little later, Chief Mola arrived in his personal pod, followed by a large tow pod pulling another sleep pod. Ping ran to the latter and told the pilot to take it farther up.

"Greetings, all." Chief Mola said, stepping out of his pod. He took a brief glance around, shuddered, and looked down. "Any problems?"

"Most need get used to distance viewing," Ping said, approaching him. "Few days, maybe. Us need move all pods much higher. See where water came."

"Do whatever you need to. Here are supplies of nuggets and drink mixes. Someone bring more in eight-day. You have water?"

"Yes." Ping indicated the water tank and collector. "What you want us to do here?" She sensed his discomfort at being outside.

"Build shelter. You can do. I go back now." He stepped back into his pod and left. The two transport pods followed. Ping and Nela found their pods and the other two fems took the other two.

Build shelter. How? Ping remembered what Adam had told them. It seemed impossible. The tow pod returned. "Take mine first," she told the pilot, and she rode up in it. When her sleep pod settled, she stepped out. Higher, but not close to the place Adam had indicated they should put the new colony.

She walked back down to the others, passing the tow pod as it brought up another. Bede sat on the grass. "I not ride in that thing," she said.

"Not as smooth as travel pod, but not bad. Now you must walk up." Ping sat beside her. "How is Mater?"

"Quite displeased. She tried to talk me out of coming, but I said Council Chief told me to and I not disobey him."

"Of course." Ping scooched around to a more comfortable position. "You have any idea why she so against us going out? Besides possible dangers?"

Bede rubbed the fur on her thigh. "I think Gran said or did something that scared Mater when she small. I remember I barely into learning when she told me to not listen to anyone talking about outside. She told me all sorts of stories about monsters and awful creatures that would eat me, and poisonous plants."

Ping nodded. "I remember some stories. Looked up one she described and could not find anything on it. I thought if they that bad, there should be something in bioputer on them."

Bede widened her mouth. "You always poking about on your screen."

"Everything so interesting, and always want to know."

"That why you so good in research." Bede patted Ping's hand. They watched as the tow pod came down and picked up another pod.

Aunt Dela tottered over and sat beside them. "Kati is all in twist," she said. "She imagining all sorts of dangers."

"I told Mater after first time I went out there no monsters, no dangers," Ping said.

"I know, but us three fems so programmed by our mater, and Kati oldest and most sensitive of we. By time Lee came along, she not pay much attention to Mater." Aunt Dela touched her pink necklet.

"How you two doing out here?" Ping asked.

"Well, if not look too far," Bede said.

"Passable if keep looking down," Aunt Dela added.

"You get used it. I saw distance as painted on large wall of long room my first time. Took me most of day to get used to it." Ping took a deep breath. "Is so nice for you be out here with me."

Bede chuckled. "I think I like out here, once get used to it, and figure how to bring Cori."

Nela joined them as the tow pod took her sleep pod. "Ping, you lucky you have sisters with you."

"Do you have sisters?" Bede asked.

"One. She thinks I out of my mind to come here."

"There's Gogi," Ping said.

Nela nodded. "But he brother and stays with other men."

When the last pod was carried up, Ping got to her feet. "Come, fems. We must go to our pods." Amid groaning, everyone rose. Ping took Bede's and Aunt Dela's hands and led them up the slope. She went slowly and stopped for rests often. Nela trudged along beside them.

"Look," Nela said once. "Are those flowers?"

Tiny purple and white buttons poked out of the grass. "Yes," said Ping.

"Wonderful," Aunt Dela gasped, bending over.

"Us almost there." Ping led them up to the pods and found hers. The little wooden quine stood in its niche, waiting. She assigned two to her sister and aunt, and Nela went to her pod.

"Well, here us are," Gogi said. Cale and Mang sat in the hatchways of their pods. Otie wandered around, looking at everything. "What us do now, Chief?"

"I not chief." Ping stuck her head in her pod for a moment. "Not much room in these. Us must make place to store things."

"With what?" Gogi asked.

"I not know." Ping looked down at the sea. On the blurry blue she saw what appeared to be a giant flower sprout out of the sea into a great orange ball. She blinked and it was gone. *Did I really see that, or was put in my mind?*

A little later, a pod flew over and dropped a large parcel, then buzzed away. Ping and Gogi trotted to the bundle, followed by the others. They tore it open and found more nuggets, cleaning supplies, extra cloth bags of various sizes, paper and writing materials, an assortment of tools, and several large sheets of stiff fabric.

Ping laid everything out on the grass. She put the nuggets and paper aside. Others looked and touched.

"Where us put all this?" Nela asked.

Gogi picked up one of the sheets of fabric and stretched it out.

"This works," he said. "Need prop." He went over to the trees and returned with a handful of sticks. He laid out the empty bag on the ground, pushed sticks into the ground at each end, and laid a long stick over the top, sitting in forks of the vertical sticks.

Ping saw what he was doing and moved the items onto the bag. She and Gogi stretched the cloth over the sticks to make a tent.

"Very good," Aunt Dela said. She walked all the way around it. "How you know how to make it?"

"Pod drivers must take survival class to get permit. Us learn to make shelter from what available. Us always keep extra nuggets and water in pod."

"Good." Ping studied the tent. "If you make it taller and not all the way down on one side, us have shelter to sit in." She picked up and counted the pieces of fabric. "Is nine. One for each of we and one for other use."

"Yes," said Gogi. "Come, Otie." The two homs and Ping headed for the trees. They collected downed branches and Ping gathered long streamers of moss.

Everyone helped build sit tents except Mang, who refused to come out of his pod. Ping and the other fems gathered more moss to make pads to sit on, using the extra cloth bags.

When they were done, they had a semi-circle of sit tents facing the sea. A little lopsided, the men couldn't always find branches the same length, but nobody cared. As the sun slid down behind the river trees, Ping and her group shared thoughts.

Ping asked, "How you all feel about living out here. I plan to."

"I want to," Nela said. "It's so much nicer out here."

"Yes," Bede said. "If us can create what us had in habitat."

Aunt Dela shook her head. "Not safe out here. Too many unknowns."

Cale and Mang just shook their heads.

Gogi and Otie said they'd stay.

That night the wind blew, slightly rocking the sleep pods. In the morning, Ping found the sit tents blown away and scattered, some of the supports down. Usually the first one up, Ping started gathering the tent cloths.

Nela emerged from her pod and helped. "Us need something to hold down edges."

"River stones. Many lay along little river in Jan's world."

Gogi appeared. "Afraid of that. Yes, stones. Bigger than ones around pond in Park. Otie, Cale and I go collect some after us consume nuggets."

After the homs left, Ping asked, "Who wants go exploring with me?"

"I will," Nela said.

Bede and Aunt Dela looked at each other. "We go." Aunt Dela rose, followed by the others.

Ping led them over to the big river where her sister and aunt goggled at the size of it. Nela had seen it before and sat beside Ping.

"How we manage this?" Aunt Dela said.

"Problem for water department." Ping touched a yellow starflower nearby. She rose, and they moved on, along the line of trees.

A grove well away from the river drew Ping's eyes, and she turned in its direction. A wide, flat space with tiny, round-leafed plants covering it caught her attention.

"Here is nice place for plaza. Open space among structures for workplaces and medical building. Pods and shelters beyond."

Ping had discussed a new colony with Nela, but the other two wore blank faces.

"Explain," Aunt Dela demanded.

"This where new community be." Ping waved an arm around. "When us no longer live in hab."

"Ah," said Bede. "Much room for young. Maybe real park."

"Not for long time." Aunt Dela plucked at her ear.

"Yes, long time to build." Ping walked around the edge of the plaza area. "Need to start soon."

They headed back down to the pods.

•　　•　　•

Midafternoon saw the homs return with heavy bags. Everyone except Mang, who huddled in his pod, helped spread stones around the bottom of the tent cloths.

222

"That should hold it," Gogi said.

"While you gone, us went exploring," Ping said. "Little farther up is flat place for plaza."

Suddenly, the ground shook hard. The homs dropped to their knees, and the fems, sitting, fell over. Pods rolled in their hollows and some tents jerked down. Ping pushed herself back into a sitting position and shivered.

A sense of catastrophe overwhelmed her. Holding her hands together so they wouldn't shake, she said, "Well, citizens, us may not have as much time as us need."

46

ONE DAY, MARISA received a message from Maxee. She and Sam were coming down to discuss something very important to both communities. *Now what?* She didn't need any more problems.

The next day Sam and Maxee arrived. Sam moaned and rubbed her knees after she slipped off her quine. "This ride is getting to be too much,"

Marisa saw her as she opened her front door. "I know what you mean. What's up?"

"The sea." Sam plopped down on the couch. "The menace I've been foreseeing is coming from the sea. "

"Something out of the sea?" Marisa asked. "Do you want anything to drink?"

"No, thank you. I'm not sure about that. Maybe the sea itself. Something's going on out there." Sam let Marisa look in her mind to see what she saw.

"Not very clear."

"I hate this," Sam said. "Seeing these things, but no details as to what and when, so I can't prepare for it."

"That must be awful. Have you always been able to do this?"

Sam shook her head. "Only since we left City. I think the Volen were blocking it. Brad has it too, but not as strong. I think we got it from our mother. She came from another planet where they have some magic,"

"How'd that happen?"

"Dad met her someplace where she'd been stranded, when he was in the Space Service, and brought her home. Somehow, she was able to allow his sperm to fertilize her eggs."

"You never mentioned your parents before. Are they still living?"

Sam winced. "Dad died before we left City. Mother left to return to her native world when we were five. She was sick, and the only way she could be cured was to go home. She wanted to take us, but the City council wouldn't let her. We were born in City, so we had to stay there."

Marisa noticed the wince, but decided to not ask about it. "Oh, my. That must have been hard on you and your papa."

"He had a close friend with a boy a little older than us, and his wife took us in and raised us. Dad was always there, too. We had a brother and two fathers, although Todd's dad only disciplined us if Dad wasn't available."

"You were fortunate to have Brad. Do his children have this talent?"

"Only Felicia, the older girl, has a little. Brad and I did everything together until we started growing up." Sam paused. "But back to our problem. I'm not positive, but I think this menace has to do with the sea rising. You're pretty far up, I don't think it'd come this far, but keep an eye on it."

"Will it be gradual or all at once?"

"Probably all at once."

"Okay." Marisa sighed. *Something else to worry about.* "How is everyone up there?"

"Good except for Hal. He fell off his quine and broke his leg. The quine spooked at something. Hal couldn't figure out what it was."

Icicles crept down Marisa's spine. She knew sometimes quines saw things that humans couldn't. "How is he doing?"

"He's on crutches now, but I think he'll aways have a limp."

"Tell him I'll send healing wishes."

"Will do." Sam leaned back and closed her eyes.

Jan came by. "Oh, hi, Sam, Maxee. I just came to check on Mama."

"I'm fine, dear. We are discussing something Sam has foreseen, the rising of the sea."

"Oh," Jan plopped in her papa's chair. She closed her eyes. "Yes, I see. Something big is going on under the sea way out past the horizon, but I can't tell what it is."

Marisa noticed the circles under Sam's eyes and the lines in her face. "Sam, would you like to lie down and rest for a while?" "Yes. It's a long ride down here. I can't do as much as I used to."

"I understand. Maxee, how are you?"

"I rest here on couch. I not young either."

Marisa led Sam to the front bedroom. "Stay as long as you like. I'm going to ask Artie if he can come up with some sort of message system between our communities that anyone can use. The girls who mated with your boys can send messages to their families, but not to me."

"Good." Sam settled on the bed. "I don't know if I'll be able to do this ride any more. Unless someone rigs up a cart or something, I may not be able to come down again."

"Oh." Marisa sat down hard in a nearby chair. "You don't think about things coming to an end. I don't go down to the beach much anymore. Did you ever miss having children?"

"No." Sam closed her eyes, took a deep breath, opened them. "I had Brad's children. They were as close as I wanted." She paused. "Although lately, I sometimes wish I had a grown daughter."

"When I was pregnant with Janni, I wasn't sure I was ready to be a mother. It helped that I had Mama and all the aunts."

"Aunt Linda, Todd's mother, was good to us, but she wasn't Mother. Maybe if she had stayed, definitely; if we'd gone with her ... But then, I would have missed Dad." Sam rolled over facing the wall.

Marisa rose. "Rest." She left and drew the curtain across the doorway. She limped to her chair, sat and picked up a small, pale green garment. With the latest bonding, soon there would be more babies. She looked at Janni in Allen's chair and put the garment down.

Allen was very old, he couldn't live much longer, even though he was in good health. When they were first bonded, it didn't matter that he was older than Mama. Now, she would see Kaylyn's children grown and bonded and with children of their own. And Allen wouldn't be there.

Marisa shook her head. It had been hard enough losing Granlyn, she had been the first matriarch and the one who held everything together. Allen was the only one of the first generation left, and he had been much younger than the others.

Now, Sam.

A knock on the door, and Kaylyn stuck her head in. "Just checking. Hi, Mama."

"I'm okay. Thanks for stopping by." Marisa waved and Kaylyn left.

She picked up the garment. *A lot of young ones in the clan now. Life will go on.*

"Why so sad?" Jan asked.

"Thinking about mortality. Allen ..."

Jan jumped up and kissed her mama. "We will carry on. Bye."

47

P ING DREAMED she was being rolled down a hill in a barrel and woke to find herself on the floor of her sleep pod with the nest above her. A loud noise echoed in her ears. The hatch had swung shut. Stunned, she fought her way out of the coverlet and pushed at the hatch. Just as it opened, she caught a glimpse of a bright light over the sea.

Over the low roar, she heard yelps, and Gogi's voice saying, "Hey."

Ping crawled out. Something sharp hurt her hand. The quine Allan had made her. Its legs had broken off. She stuffed it in her belt pouch. The ground rocked. Gogi on his knees, and Otie gawked at the sea. The other fems crept from their pods.

"What going on?" Aunt Dela demanded, her normally brown face a pale tan.

"Something not good." Ping, on her feet, looked around.

Bede emerged. "My Cori," she cried, fists clenched.

"The childcare fems are looking after the children," Aunt Dela said.

"Look at sea," Gogi said. The water was moving away from the land as if the ocean was being drained.

"No," Ping said. She slammed her hatch shut and yelled, "Everyone out and up slope. Close hatches. Now."

Gogi and the other fems did so. Otie looked at her, at the receding sea, and trotted to his pod and closed the hatch. Then he went to Mang, dragged him out and closed his hatch.

"No, leave me alone," Mang cried, trying to yank away.

Otie pulled him up the slope. "If our chief says to run, we run."

Cale took Mang's other arm, and together they trotted up the slope.

When Ping stopped to catch her breath, the others did so too. She and Gogi looked back. The rising sun sparkled off a rising wall of water far out to sea and moving toward them. It towered over the top of Maker, crashed down, and swept up the slope. The sea curled around the pods and Ping backed up, then trotted up the hill. "Come. Not know how far …"

The others followed. Finally, Ping's feet ceased moving and she bent over, gasping. Farther down, Aunt Dela, on her knees, shook her head. Bede and Nela stumbled up to Ping and Gogi. Otie sat on the ground, Cale sprawled beside him, with Mang curled in a ball.

Up past the pods, the water slowed to a stop, appeared to ponder for a moment, then rushed back down, taking the pods with them. Ping could only watch. The sea left the land, leaving the pods and a glistening seabed behind.

Maker, firmly embedded in the sand, had not moved, but Central and Science had been thrown up on the beach grass, and separated, surrounded by a mess of sleep pods, mostly detached.

"Hatches automatically close if connectors are breached," Gogi said.

Ping sucked in her breath. Bede and Aunt Dela latched on to her. She could feel them shaking. Ping shivered, not just from the chill of the morning.

"Gogi?" She asked.

"I not know. There are pods." He started down.

"Stop," Ping cried.

He turned.

"Wave come back, like sloshing on beach."

Gogi stopped. "You right."

Ping glanced around. Otie sat with one arm around Nela, Cale held Mang.

"What," Aunt Dela began, and could go no further. Ping squeezed her hand.

The sea returned, but just short of where the pods had been. None of their pods moved this time, but several sleep pods bobbed on the water below.

"Sleep pods …" Ping began. *Broken off, citizens inside, need to help.*

She trotted down the slope. Gogi and the rest followed. When they came to the place where they had settled, some of the tents had been rolled into the mud by the pods, which were scattered down the slope. Ping automatically picked up a couple of muddy cloths and laid them over a bush.

"Now what us do?" Nela said. The others were speechless.

"Get citizens out of sleep pods before they suffocate."

"Wait." Gogi laid a hand on her arm. "Look." The sea was returning, but only as far as their sleep pods.

Ping felt herself split in two, one in a network of unreality, the other perceiving her world being destroyed.

After the sea sucked itself back in, the need to help others drew her down the slope. At her sleep pod, she checked briefly. It was dry inside. She continued down to the first of the other sleep pods. It appeared undamaged. She and Gogi opened the hatch; it also was dry. A young fem huddled in her nest and refused to come out. Ping left her there, with the hatch open.

At the next one, they found an adolescent boy. He crept out and sat in the hatchway. "Where …" He pulled in deep breaths.

"You safe. Wait here," Ping said. *We must get them all out, but there are so many.* "Bede, you and Cale open hatches. If they not come out, leave hatches open. Aunt Dela, you and Etie go together. Nela, can you manage by yourself?"

"Yes. This is so …"

The pairs went their separate ways. By midmorning, Ping was running to each pod, yanking the hatch open and calling, "Come out," then running to the next without seeing whether they responded. A few were empty, the inhabitants inside one of the modules.

Gogi broke off to do his own, and another pair split up. The pods were all dry, except the one buried in the ground behind a small ridge that had caught the pod in a pool of water.

Ping had seen Science and Central on the lower slope, but her mind had refused to make sense of it. She mushed through the wet grass and mud littered with sea debris to Science. Uprooted trees and mangled plants dotted the slope. A few scaley creatures flopped listlessly, and one long black slithery thing caused her to miss a step.

The Science hab towered over her at a slant. No obvious great damage, but some sensors had broken off. Ping looked for hatches. She knew there were four, one in each quadrant, plus the connector hatch and pod port hatch. She saw one up high, so she went around to the other side and found one down low, open, with someone's head sticking out. She waved, and the head pulled back in.

Gogi arrived with the others, except Mang, who escaped into a vacant pod.

"Help me, us must get citizens out," Ping said.

"Modules all have backup power," he said. "Otie, take citizens and check Central. I go to Maker."

Someone threw a rope out of the hatch. Ping could not reach the hanging end. A male wearing a dark blue necklet climbed and slid down the rope and fell in a huddle at the bottom.

Ping stepped to him. "Chief Mola." A feeling of elation crept over her. He was out here, on her territory, where he looked extremely uncomfortable.

He opened his eyes. "Ping. You, here," he growled.

"Of course. You sent me out. You?" This was her world; she did not fear chiefs here.

"I feel no pain." He looked up, got to his feet, and leaned against a nearby sleep pod. More citizens descended, including a couple more chiefs, followed by Aunt Lee, who mostly slid down.

"Your arm," Ping said, leading her away. Bandages from wrist to elbow decorated her right arm, which was in a sling. "What happened?"

"I sent to medical in Science to get new set of learning sheets and almost there, when whole thing started rolling and bouncing. I tossed around, and my arm hit wall. After it stopped, I crawled to nearby medical office. The fem there hurt, also, and us took care of each other."

"Great One, help we." Ping twisted her hands together. "Much damage inside?"

"Mostly things tossed everywhere. Power off, air bad." Aunt Lee gulped a breath and her eyes widened at the taste. "Fresh air. Good thing everything big bolted to walls or floors. Chief came in and told we go to the nearest exit, so us did and here am I. What us do now?"

"Do you have any food and water with you?"

"Yes, in bag." It hung around her neck. "How are Bede and Dela? Juni in childcare."

"They well. There room for two in sleep pod, so you can stay in mine. Help anyone you can." Ping was relieved that her aunt was not badly injured.

She moved citizens along, told them to find their sleep pods and a roommate. Presently Chief Eler showed up.

He limped to her. "Ping, you well?"

"Yes. Your foot?"

"No, knee. I thrown into wall. No time for harness." He took a step and winced. "Chief Mola gathers all chiefs to determine what to do. I keep you informed."

"Gratitude, Chief. Us can put two in sleep pod, so everyone has place to shelter."

"Good. I go now." Chief Eler limped to the group around Chief Mola.

Surely now the chiefs will see the problem, Ping thought.

Otie returned, leading a group of citizens from Central, including Council Chief Akoi from Medical and a large group of fems with young children. Ping looked for Juni. When she saw her sister carrying her baby and leading Cori, she waved. Juni trotted over to Ping, little Peni in her arms, Cori with her.

"Greetings. How you?" Ping widened her mouth.

"Good. Zee in Maker." Juni's eyes were slits. "How you see out here?"

"You get used to it," Ping said, relief welling up in her.

Several citizens with Chief Akoi carried medical supplies out of Central. "All other council chiefs dead," Akoi said.

"Chief Mola over there." Ping pointed. "He gathering chiefs."

"Good." Chief Akoi collected a few lower chiefs and headed that way.

Ping looked around. Citizens wandered around or stood by pods, mostly looking at their feet. She watched as Cale led a pair of huddled homs to a sleep pod. The sun slipped down behind the trees and a cool wind picked up.

Gogi trudged over with a group from Maker, including Chief Rody. Ping greeted him and told him about Chief Mola's gathering. He and another chief trudged over to the group.

"Find your pod or someone to share with," Ping told the citizens milling around. "We know more soon." She wished there was somewhere dry to sit.

A little later, Chief Mola stepped away from the pod and rang the council gong. When he had everyone's attention, he spoke in a carrying voice. "Citizens, take heed. Habitat has suffered major damage. I now Head Chief. Tonight, find place to sleep, in sleep pod or inside module. Tomorrow, us begin assessing damage and plan how to make habitat livable. Anyone with ideas about how to accomplish this, report them to your chief. He report to me. Us need help of every one of you. May the Great One be with we."

He turned away.

"No," Ping cried under her breath. *He can't mean that. Habitat is dead. Us must make new place out here. He did bring we out here to get rid of we.* Ping took two steps to the nearest pod and leaned against it. *If he think he get me back in there, he has his mind on inside out. Enough. Focus on now.*

Citizens wandered aimlessly, seeking a center. Ping banged on the pod and raised her arms. "Here," she called. As citizens approached, she assigned them to groups of three. "Check sleep pods. If you find yours, stand in front of it. If you find one you know who it belongs to, call out. If you hear your name, go to caller and stand by your pod. Caller move on to next pod."

Citizens looked at her, then to the huddle of chiefs by the science module. An older fem in the first group of three said, "Come," and led the other two to a nearby pod. A sign above the hatch said, Luby. The fem called out the name and a young fem came running. She peered in.

"Yes, this mine." She sat in the open hatchway, and the trio moved on.

"Good," Ping said. "This working." She watched as the citizens scrambled around until most of the pods had someone standing or sitting at them. Then she gathered her group and headed for their own pods. Aunt Dela had found Aunt Lee, and Nela, someone from her department.

As Ping settled in her nest, the reality of the situation hit her. Unless they could get all the modules and systems hooked up, the community would be living out here, in sleep pods with no power or water.

How in habitat are us going to do this?

"It's not your problem, Ping. Let the chiefs handle it. You're only a subchief," a voice from her past said in her mind.

Is everyone's problem, including mine.

"Do what you can for your group and family, and let the chiefs take care of the rest," the voice said.

Quiet. I need to sleep.

The voice went silent, and Ping rolled over, aware of Juni and Peni breathing next to her. Thoughts of how to acquire water and food and power muddled in her mind as she delved for information in her extra brain. After what seemed hours, mentally searching for foodstuffs, she found a bush with little blue flowers and focused on one perfect five-petaled blossom. Forcing all thoughts of the future away, she let the bloom draw her into sleep.

Tomorrow would take care of itself.

48

PING AWOKE TO A SNORE from Juni, for the fourth or fifth time. The child in her arms did not stir. Ping grabbed her bag and a nugget from the recess in the wall above the nest and crawled out of the sleep pod. A pink strip hovered above the line of forest to the east.

She walked east and tripped over a sit cushion. It felt dry, so she carried it up to the top of a ridge and sat on it, facing the sunrise. She fluffed up her fur; it was cool out here. Yesterday's events rushed back. The force of the sea, moving not only sleep pods, but the habitat modules themselves. Water, food, power, the big three.

Head Chief Mola was everything the old world stood for. She'd thought for a time he understood the habitat was dying, but apparently he was only pretending. *Why would he want to stay in there?* She wondered how much help, if any, she would get from the other chiefs.

Ping had no idea whether the habitat power could be restored. Science and Control and their connector hatches were close enough together so that they could be rejoined, but Maker's hatch was on the water side. They could create more connectors if they had power, but they needed to get power first.

Ping sighed and ate her nugget.

She would have to let the power department handle that, and Maker the connector. She needed to talk to Chief Rody.

"Hey," said Gogi, dropping down beside her. "Planning your day?"

"Thinking. So many questions. Gogi, is pod mover functioning?"

"Why? I check." He leaned back on his forearms.

"Pods must be arranged higher up."

"Not too far if us want to use anything in hab."

Ping nodded. The pink in the sky grew and turned orange just above the trees where a line of narrow clouds hung.

"Do you know how power machine works?"

"Some. I talk to many citizens since I found out what happening."

"Us not do much without power," Ping said. "Is anything us can do using citizen power?"

Gogi shook his head. "Leave for chiefs to figure out."

"You too?" Ping looked at him.

Aunt Dela came up next to Ping, carrying a sit pad. "Pretty morning," she said, settling on her pad.

"Not for long," Ping said.

Aunt Dela looked at her foot. "Us need something to wear on our feet."

"Yes." Ping's feet had toughened enough she hadn't thought of that. Later, she showed Aunt Dela how to make coverings with big, thick leaves.

"Greetings, citizens," said Bede, Nela, Juni with Peni, and Otie as they joined Ping's group. "Us ready for another day?" Bede added.

"Mang not," Otie said. "Cale trying to get him to come out."

Ping recalled the sun dimmers she wore over her eyes on her first trip out. "Could us make eye covering for him to wear?"

"Good idea," Gogi said. "I do."

The pink had faded out and a bright patch shone just above the far forest.

Gogi rose. "Come, citizens, time go down and see what us can do."

Ping and the others followed. Bede coaxed Cori out of her pod and joined them. They collected Cale and Mang and headed toward the group of citizens below. Closer, Ping saw a panel down off the side of the science module, and citizens swarming in. Lower chiefs were trying to stop them. Head Chief Mola pounded on the gong until most citizens quieted down and looked at him. Chief Rody stood next to him.

"Listen to Rody," Head Chief Mola yelled.

"My citizens have supply of nuggets." Chief Rody pointed to a group of citizens nearby. "Form a line there." One of the citizens held up his hand as several ran to him.

"Ah," Ping said from her viewpoint. "They came out from workplaces, not have nuggets with them. If none last night, must be needy."

"Yes," Aunt Dela replied. They moved toward the others.

Obedient to a chief's orders, the citizens formed a line. Others stood and watched. *They must have supplies in their sleep pods,* Ping thought.

The chiefs huddled around Head Chief Mola. Other citizens wandered around, and one fem scraped debris off her sleep pod.

"Ah, there you are," Chief Mola said, waving at Ping's group. After all the nuggets were passed out, he rang the gong and citizens gathered around him.

"We go in to assess damage now. Each chief, choose underling to accompany you. List damage and bring out anything important and easy to carry. No, Ping, as sub-chief, you in charge here and start arranging for shelters."

"With what, Chief?"

He glanced around. "There trees."

"How?"

"Your problem. Chiefs, select your helpers."

Despite planning to keep an even disposition, anger rose in Ping. "Bring we some tools," she said, but Chief Mola ignored her. She watched as the chiefs dispersed and selected citizens. None of the people in her group were chosen.

Chief Miki approached Chief Mola with the saddest face Ping had ever seen. After he spoke to Chief Mola, the latter announced, "Miki say bioputer dead. Too many connections broken. All chiefs set up information sheets for their departments."

No! Ping couldn't believe it. What were they going to do without bioputer? Bioputer was her life. *There must be some way to fix it.* Ping looked around aimlessly. The chiefs wore expressions of disbelief, as did those who did most of their work on the bioputer.

"My exobrain," she said aloud. No one paid attention to her. *Is there any way to hook the memory module to it? Chief Miki might know.*

Ping found him standing by himself, except for his assistant, staring into space.

"Greetings, chief," she said.

He looked at her. "Ping."

"Unfortunate about bioputer. I have exobrain and memory module of how to set up colony. Any way to plug module into my exobrain?"

"Ah," he said, eyes widening. "Let me see." He poked at her head. "Here something just under skin. Show me module."

Ping dug the module out of her bag and handed it to him. She had retrieved it before she left.

He felt her head and the module's plug. "Is possible. Are you willing to have skin cut on head? By top medic."

"Yes." She realized she must do this. Duty still lingered.

"Stay here. I arrange." Chief Miki strode off, followed by his assistant.

Ping shivered. She did not want to become computer. Other citizens had exobrains. Others must have memory modules. She sighed and looked around. The grassy places were dry enough to sit on, but long streaks of mud fouled the slope. She started for the trees along the river, and Chief Miki called her back.

The chief of surgery accompanied him. "This Chief Dano. He check your head and module."

"Yes." Ping followed them into an enclave surrounded by three sleep pods, turned around and bent her head forward. Chief Dano poked around in her head fur.

"Must remove fur here. Not much." She heard a rustle, then something cold on a spot over the exobrain. A humming sound and brushing. Something touched the bare spot and Ping jerked. "Yes, it should fit. Does Chief Mola approve?"

"Must he?" Ping asked. She was sure he would not allow it.

"Not for minor surgery." Chief Dano smirked. "Although anything on head not minor, since it just skin cut, I say it is."

"I like that," Ping said, feeling relieved.

Chief Miki touched her arm, and she straightened up. She felt the bare spot on her head, felt a round ridge underneath.

"Well?" Chief Miki asked.

"Yes. Where us do it?"

"Inside. I prepare surgery." Chief Dano trotted off.

"Inside? Upside down?" Ping shivered. "Must us?" She glanced at the up-side-down Central module.

"Equipment on new floor. Operation must be sterile. Operating and recovery rooms in Medical have their own air. Only cut skin. You be well." Chief Miki widened his mouth. "I show you way."

"Us do now?"

"Soonest done, soonest over. Come." To his assistant, he added, "Find others with exobrain, see if any have extra memory modules."

She nodded and trotted off.

Ping followed Chief Miki into Central, to medical. She was not happy at having her head cut open, but if she could access the colony information, she would be in charge. There was no way anyone could make her give it to them. They passed through corridors with emergency lights along the floor, and open rooms showed beds and tables hanging from the ceiling. Citizens were still cleaning up the messes on the new floor.

Chief Dano greeted them at the operating room. "Chief Miki, wait here." A young fem medic led Ping into a little room with a cleaning apparatus. The fixture, three arrow nozzles on hooks, halfway between floor and ceiling, worked upside down. Labeled water, air, sanitizer, Ping saw they were similar to those in her sleep pod cleaning room. The once ceiling/now floor was getting soggy; it was not tiled like the regular floor.

The medic blew the air all around her head and shoulders, followed by the sanitizer. Her bare skin tingled.

She led Ping into a larger room with gleaming white walls. A long table with a half circle cut out of one end sat in the middle surrounded by several small tables holding various equipment and tools. "This operating table not fastened well. Us removed it from floor/ceiling," the medic said. Ping lay prone with her face in the cutout. Her forehead rested on the upper padded rim, her chin on the lower, and a belt held down her shoulders.

Chief Dano came in. "You ready?"

"Yes," Ping mumbled. She was aware of him standing next to her head.

The other medic put a mask over Ping's face, and Ping remembered no more.

49

P ING CAME TO lying on her side, a strange feeling in her head she couldn't put words to. She reached up and felt a large pad on the back of the top of her head.

"Good, you awake," someone said. "Stay still. Breathe deep. How you feel?" The medic moved around so Ping could see her,

"Aunt Dela," Ping whispered.

"I am nurse medic. I stay here with you."

"How long …"

"Not long. You rest."

Relieved, Ping sent thanks to the Great One. Aunt Dela would not let anything happen to her. She closed her eyes. All she wanted was to get back to a normal life, helping her fellow citizens to live well. The ache of not being chosen for motherhood stirred inside her.

Later, when Aunt Dela checked the surgery site and replaced the pad, she had Ping sit, then stand, and asked how she felt.

"My head, strange. Like much bigger. Foggy." She shook her head and the room whirled. She lay back down.

Next time, in the afternoon, she was able to sit up with a clear head and stand. Medic Dela had her walk around.

"I feel well," Ping said. "Us go out?" Although the air was breathable, it was nowhere as fresh as outside.

"Us go to entrance and see." Medic Dela held Ping's arm as they walked to a different entrance to Medical and found the exit hatch next to it. Ping moved to the hatch and stuck her head out.

After several deep breaths, she said, "Much better."

"Good, us go out."

They stepped out and headed upslope, Medic Dela still holding Ping's arm. Citizens wandered here and there among the scattered sleep pods on the hillside.

"My head." Ping put her hand to the covering on it.

Aunt Dela stopped. "Does it hurt?"

"No."

"Many citizens have bandages somewhere. You fit right in."

Bede came up to them. "I been looking for you, Ping. Where you been? What happened to your head?"

"Little surgery so I plug memory module into my exo brain." Ping felt safe confiding in her sister. "What happens out here?"

"Not much. No one knows what to do without chiefs. Cale and Otie went up to our pod place and gathered tent cloths, and us fems washed them in sea. Gogi and some others collected sticks. They make tents now." Bede pointed. One large tent and a couple of small ones stood near Central. "Water tub is missing, and tank tipped over. Us righted that, and water department citizens trying to figure how to get water up from river."

"Ah. Good. Plenty water in river. Water department can do."

Ping watched a group from Medical come out of Central carrying containers and bundles. Head Chief Mola dropped down from Science module as Chief Akoi and his helper set a large tub in front of the big tent.

"What that?" Head Chief Mola demanded.

"Medical supplies," Chief Akoi said. "Citizens out here, need supplies here."

"Ah." Head Chief Mola turned to Ping. "Where you get tent cloths?'

"Pod brought them to we before water came."

"Who?"

"Not know. Not see driver." Ping did see Aunt Dela directing others to put bundles in the big tent.

"What happened to your head?"

"I fell. Not bad. I well." *He not need real reason.*

Head Chief Mola stared at her.

Ping turned away. "I go help make tents."

•   •   •

A little while later, Head Chief Mola called a gathering.

"Damage repairable," he began. Ping stifled a snort. "Most damage in connectors. Once us have power, they be repaired. In Science, most equipment secured, some damage from flying objects. Science chiefs checking what can be fixed. Bioputer dead. Backup power only for air and pumps. Module at slant, but is workable.

"In Central, upside down, everything not bolted down thrown around. Walls damaged, but repaired easily. In Medical, patients strapped down are well, others, many injuries. Make new nests on ceiling-floor. Medical staff take care of them. Most supplies stayed in containers. One fem giving birth, medic said they would be well. In schooling and elsewhere, moderate damage and loose items all over, many more than other areas because they not believe in putting tools away. In Government, Head Chief and three chiefs found dead. Us must plan ceremony for them and replace with new chiefs. I put important papers in waterproof storage in my room in safe."

Chief Mola paused to take a breath. A muttering grew in the crowd. "In Maker, little damage except for connector to Central. Outside sensors broken off. Pod ports appear undamaged. Science and Central disconnected, but Central torn from Maker. Our primary task now is proceed with repairs. Chiefs, list what needs to be done or replaced in your departments. Tomorrow us begin."

"Well," Ping huffed quietly. Gogi approached and she turned to him. "What you find?"

"Pod mover appears undamaged, but I need permission to use it. I dodged others." He grinned. "Power collector no longer reaches deep-sea current, although still connected to Maker. Us can make more connector materials ..."

"If us have power," Ping finished. They chuckled.

"Chief Mola, how long us must stay out here?" someone asked.

"Until repairs completed," the chief said. "Not long. Maybe one eight-day."

Ping snorted again.

Head Chief Mola swiveled his head toward her. "Enough. You will come tomorrow and help carry bodies out."

"What! I needed out here." If Ping had been able to, she would have turned purple. She couldn't decide whether to tell him about the bioputer and her memory module or not.

"Gogi do as citizen leader." Head Chief Mola turned away and stalked off. The citizens watched with various expressions of disbelief. Citizens did not talk back to chiefs, especially the head chief.

Ping stomped off up the slope. Bede appeared at her side. "I heard. You will do it?"

"No."

Aunt Dela, Gogi and the others showed up and surrounded her.

"I handle things," Gogi said. "You go do your duty."

"Duty," Ping exploded. "Not. I do what I wish to do." She stomped on.

"Ping, you must do your duty," Aunt Bede scolded. "Is how community prospers."

"You call this prospering?" Ping swung around and stared at her aunt. "This mess?" Patches of grass dotted the muddy slope, a pile of downed trees lay at the inner edge of the cliff, branches and sleep pods were strewn across the lower slope.

"Yes, when us get habitat fixed. Perhaps us can build larger park out here, and other facilities be used out here. Much more room." Bede said.

"Calm down," Ping told herself. She drew a deep breath. "Very well. I say no more. But I not move bodies." She stomped on up the slope.

"Ping, what gotten into you?" Bede asked.

"I woke to reality. I want best for citizens, and I believe this is best out here, not in habitat. Many things changed. We need new council. More citizens waking up to reality of world."

"You be well now?" Gogi asked.

"Yes." *Maybe.*

"We go back. Come when you ready." Gogi motioned to the others and started down the slope.

Bede patted her little sister and followed the others.

Ping sat on a grassy place and stared down at the community below. *How I get through to citizens? And Mola, who not even listen to me. He not like that I upset his perfect habitat, even though I only point out problems caused by others.*

Who would lead if he was gone?

Ping rose and continued up to her sleep pod. There, she was alone with her thoughts.

50

IN THE MORNING, Ping felt like her old self, with a discomfort in her head she could not pinpoint. Under a clear sky, she tasted the freshness of the morning. A slight breeze brushed her face. She stayed at her sleep pod until she saw citizens going inside the main modules below. When she started down the slope, she met Aunt Dela and Bede plodding toward her.

"Good, you up," Aunt Dela said, taking her hand. "How you feel?"

"Well. Is Mola around?"

"No, Head Chief Mola is inside." She emphasized his titles. "He come out this afternoon and make announcement."

"Ah. You find any other citizens with exo brain?" Ping asked.

The three continued down to the colony site. "Two," said Bede. "Neither have memory modules."

"When I access mine?"

"Come to Medical first and let head medic check you." Aunt Dela let go of her hand.

More medics. Ping was getting quite tired of them.

They made their way through a sea of greetings to Central. They had to wait for a chief and several citizens from Medical bearing pieces of movable walls to come out. As they made their way to the chief's office, it was strange to see several beds in one big room hanging from the ceiling. Little tables on rollers lay piled in a corner.

Chief Dano greeted her and had her sit on a high sitnest, padded with edges around three sides. He checked her vitals and the area of surgery.

"Looks fine," he said. "How you feel?"

"Good. Bit tender at site."

"To be expected. You may try your module this evening."

"Gratitude, chief."

He left and Ping hopped off the table. The others waited outside. "He say I fine. Where others with exobrain?"

"One inside Science, with Head Chief Mola. Other over here." Aunt Dela led the way out and to the one. Vana, a wrinkled old fem, curled up in a sitnest in front of her sleep pod, greeted them wearily. Her head, while larger than most, was still smaller than Ping's, and her fur all white.

"Greetings," Aunt Dela said. "This Ping. She top researcher, has large exobrain and now has way to plug in memory module."

Vana nodded. "Is good, mostly, sometimes pain."

"Yes," Ping said. "What you have in your exobrain?"

"Mostly history. I worked in Education. You wish to share?"

"If us can. I need to find Chief Miki of Computer Central."

"I be here," old Vana said as Ping left.

Ping found Chief Eler first. He was looking for her. "I go in. You have anything in your cubby you need?"

Curiosity struck Ping. "No, but would like to see how it is."

"Come."

They climbed up the rope ladder to Science. After a few steps down the hall away from the hatch Ping found the air stale and musty. The main room of Exo seemed much smaller than before. Ping stepped into her cubby and sat in the sitnest. The walls closed in around her. There was no way she could go back to working here. She dropped a few styluses and other items from her drawer into her bag.

Out in the main room, she gasped and felt a slight flow of air. Chief Eler came out of his cubby and they left. "I not go back in there again," Ping said.

"Is your workspace, your duty."

"Not anymore. Habitat is dead. I live outside."

Chief Eler was silent. As they reach the outer hatch, he said, "Everything changes."

Back on the ground, she saw more people carrying movable wall panels from Central and Maker. Two groups of citizens were building enclosures over by the big trees, and a third group working near Central. She hadn't realized the panels could be completely detached, but thought it was a good idea. *Somebody was thinking.*

She found a sitnest someone had brought out and sank into it. Her brain wasn't totally clear. She wanted to go around and see what everybody was doing, but knew she had to rest after the trip inside. What an awful place. No way would she go back in there.

Bede and Cori came by, and Bede perched on a corner of the sitnest. "How you doing?"

"Been inside to see."

"Ah. Have you tried your memory module yet?

"Not allowed until tonight." Ping moved uneasily.

"What memory module?" Cori asked.

"Is device bioputer uses to store much data." Ping fished out the ovoid device with a plug in one end.

"What on it?"

"Information on how to build colony."

"Yes, us can use that," Bede said. "How you access it?"

"After this," Ping indicated her head, "I plug it into my exobrain."

"Ah." Bede rose. "Come. Cori." They walked away.

Ping wandered around, checking things out, although her brain still seemed foggy around the edges. A citizen she did not know stopped her and told her that Head Chief Mola wanted to see her at the Science hatch. Her stomach lurched, but she went.

Head Chief Mola sat on the edge of the hatch. "Why you not show up for body detail?" he demanded.

Ping had to crane her neck to look up at him. She wasn't about to go up there. "I not know which chief to go to, or where to meet him."

"Why you not ask every chief you see?"

"I not see any. I looked. I suppose they all inside."

Head Chief Mola grunted. "One more misstep and you be banished."

"No." Ping stepped back. The head chief disappeared inside. Ping turned away, walking blindly. Banishment meant being taken to a far corner of the world and left there alone, with an eight-day's worth of supplies.

She could stay here and be very careful or go to Marisa's. *There, I be safe, but maybe I never see family again. I want to watch Peni and Cori grow up.*

Finally, she came to an empty sleep pod and sat in the hatchway. She watched citizens putting together structures of the wallboard panels and wondered if they were weatherproof.

A little later, Chief Miki found her.

"Ah, there you are, Ping." Chief Miki stood in front of her. "I want to show you something. I need your assistance."

"Yes." Clouds darkened the sky. *Not now, not yet.* A faint rumble touched her ears.

He led her to a structure made of panels from the habitat. Tied together by cords through the fastener openings, the place looked solid. Inside, she saw bracing poles at every other panel. A wide, slightly curved panel stood at the back, with narrower interior panels as sides and part of the front. Another set lay over the top as a roof. The panels were different pale colors, as they had come from different rooms.

Ping thought they made a delightful picture.

Inside, two large tables nailed together against the rear wall with edges about a hand width high, contained a square box the length of her arm with a flat tray on top. In the latter lay a rounded mass with a cover over it. A contraption with a handle was attached to the side of the box, and a keypad was connected to the front of the box.

"This what I saved of bioputer," Chief Miki said. "Core in box."

Rumbles came from above. "What that?" he asked.

"Rain is coming. Is your place sealed from water?"

"Water from sky?" Chief Miki looked puzzled.

Big drops splatted on the roof. Ping heard yells as citizens scrambled for their sleep pods. The cooling taste of rain swept over her. A drop slipped through the ceiling and landed on Chief Miki's nose.

"Hey." He wiped it away and looked up. More drops slithered through, and he threw a cloth over the bioputer.

"Can you get stuff they put on outside of habitat?" she asked.

"I ask my brother. Does this happen often?"

"Sometimes rain every day for eight-days, sometimes many eight-days with no rain." Ping looked up. *Us need to discover pattern of rains.* "How this bioputer work?

He showed her. The core processor was functional, and he had collected enough memory for bioputer to do simple tasks. "I can make it grow more once us get more power. This," he tapped the keypad, "is like your inputter, only you must touch each key for each letter."

"Not spoken?"

"No. Letters show on this little screen here. Type in your information, name, duty, age, family, education, anything special."

Ping sat down and looked for a key with 'P' on it. She tapped it and a 'P' appeared at the left side of the screen. *This is going to take all day,* she thought as she hunted for an 'I'. She studied the keyboard and picked up some speed.

As she was finishing up, Head Chief Mola walked in. "What this?" he demanded.

"What there is of bioputer. I may be able to regrow it, if us can get power to it," Chief Miki said.

Ping kept her mouth shut.

Head Chief Mola demanded, "This works? You take from habitat? Us need it in habitat. Take bioputer back in. Now."

"Yes, chief. I must shut it down first." Chief Miki showed a blank face.

"Us need it out here." The words slipped out before Ping could stop them.

"No more disruptions. Go to sleep pod and stay there."

Head Chief Mola stalked away.

Ping felt as if her breath had been squeezed out of her.

Chief Miki's face showed pale tan.

"He cannot do that," Ping mumbled.

"Yes, he can." Chief Miki snapped his fingers. "I make dummy and take it in. Put cupboard here around real thing."

Ping perked up. "You can do that?"

"Yes. You best go."

Aunt Dela arrived. "I heard. Come, us go to our pods." She gathered her sisters, Gogi, and Nela. They surrounded Ping and led her up the slope, avoiding the muddy places.

"He not like you much, does he," Nela said.

"I not think he ever did." Ping shrugged, still boiling inside.

"Now that he Head Chief, everything run his way," Gogi said. "Maybe us find way to live out here."

"I need be here. Have information on building colony." Ping tapped her head. "Have memory module I plug in. Any of you know anyone with separate memory modules?"

"Us check around," Gogi said.

"Now you must be plugged in?" Juni asked,

Ping nodded. "I must go to my sleep pod. I must think."

"Ah," Gogi said. They all led her up to her pod.

"Stay here rest of day," Aunt Dela said. "Us do what us can."

After they left, Ping pondered. All she could comprehend was that the bioputer might be rebuilt, and she had more in her head than anyone else. How on Phren was she going to get Mola to let her use it? Or anyone? If one of the others with exobrains had the plug she could give the module to them. Vana didn't, but there must be others.

She tried to plug in her module, but couldn't reach it. She went searching in her exobrain for items having to do with colonies and found very little. She was wakened from a doze by Bede.

"How you doing?"

"I well." Ping pulled out her memory module and held it out to Bede. She pointed to her head with her other hand. "Plug in."

Bede looked at the module, then at Ping's head. "Cannot. Aunt Dela says not until tonight."

"I beg you."

Bede shook her head. "No, little sister. Is for best."

Ping put the module back in her bag and looked at her feet.

"Is dark soon. Go in and rest." Bede patted Ping's shoulder and left.

Ping crawled into her sleep pod and tried to sleep.

51

T HE NEXT DAY, Ping noticed two travel pods and the big tow
pod parked to the east of the colony. *Gogi must been busy.*

Ping took the spyglass out of her bag and used it to watch as
some of the chiefs gathered more people and took them inside the
Central module. Pod Port C, normally at the top of the module, lay
near the ground on one side. Gogi followed them, drove out a travel
pod, and parked it nearby.

The citizens who had gone with the chiefs the day before sat in
their sleep pods, resting. A few went to the structures, while others
wandered around aimlessly, muttering, "What I do, what I do." Some
went down to the beach, others toward the river.

Ping wished to help them, but was not sure what to do
without instructions from a chief. Her duty called her to go back
down, but she was getting good at ignoring duty calls. Looking
around, she saw a flat round object as wide as her forearm was
long. She rose, walked over to it and picked it up. Not heavy, it
appeared to be some kind of sensor. A stem on the back of the dish
was broken, with wires hanging out.

She carried the thing down to the others and looked for a chief she knew. Or any chief; there didn't seem to be any around. She laid it on the ground next to the pod port.

"Ah, there you are," Gogi said behind her. "What that?" He pointed to the thing on the ground.

"Found on ground upslope." Ping turned around. "I see pod out. Can you tow sleep pods with that?"

"No. Not use it now. Only enough fuel to get out. Sun charge it. Maybe tomorrow be ready." He picked up the object. "I take this. Possible someone can reattach it."

Ping nodded. She saw the rows of solar patches along the top of the pod.

"Have you task?"

Ping shook her head.

"Come with me."

Ping followed him to Maker and in through a low hatch. They passed a workroom with tables. "Can us take tables out?"

"No. They fastened to floor."

They took a corridor along the inside of the hull and, in one space between rooms, Ping saw a small hatch. "What that?"

"That goes to hullway, passageway between inner and outer hulls. It goes all way around, like spiral."

"Ah," Ping said. Now she understood what it was. She had read about the hullway, but had not been able to picture it before.

They came to a wide corridor heading toward the center of the module and turned into it. Even this one narrowed and closed in on her. At a warren of tiny rooms, Gogi led her into one. "My office." He laid the sensor on his desk and pulled down a carry bag hanging on a hook on the pale wall. The hook caught on the bag strap and part of the wall pulled away.

"Look." Ping pointed.

"Usual," Gogi said. He indicated patches on the wall. After dropping a few books from a shelf into the bag, he added a handful of items from a drawer. "No chance to come here earlier."

He unplugged a couple of devices from the bioputer control board and dropped them into his bag. "This all I need here." They retraced their steps and left the module.

Ping breathed deeply of the fresh air. Then she saw the line for nuggets. She went over and asked a fem why she didn't have a supply in her sleep pod.

"Work in filing. They give we two nuggets each evening when us leave."

"Ah. Do what you can."

The fem nodded and moved a few steps forward.

Ping looked around at the sleep pods and enclosures dotting the green and brown slope. The sun played peekaboo among the clouds, warming those citizens wandering around. As always, the sound of the sea slapping the sand.

The river drew her. Here, Water Department citizens were trying to fill bottles by dunking them in the water, a Phren-height below the edge of the land.. The large container Gogi had brought sat in a clearing at the side. He had found it in the water and dragged it out. "No, use this container," she said.

"Too heavy. Us need power to use it." A thin hom waved his arms about.

"Lost two already." A fem sighed.

Ping closed her eyes for a moment. "Not be full to top. Two can lift together if full. Been done."

"Who you?" the hom asked.

"Sub-chief Ping." *Now the title was useful.*

"Ah. We try." He turned away.

Next, Ping went to Nutrition. One machine was set up to use a hand crank. A young hom dripping sweat through his fur stopped cranking.

"Too hard to do long." He wiped his face.

"Yes," Ping said. "Must be better way."

"Need something, when I move handle this far, mixer move farther."

"I ask about that. Keep going." Ping left and headed for the schooling compound. There, she found two enclosures, one for the little children, and one for older children. "How it going?" she asked Aunt Lee, who was in charge.

The latter said, "Hard to learn without materials." She pointed to a big bundle. "Need citizens to sort them."

Ping saw the children were mostly fems. "Have children sort them."

Next, she checked out the medical compound. She found it full of patients the medics had brought out, including the fem and her new baby. Clouds covered more of the sky, and Ping grew concerned. She wandered over. "What you do when it rains?" she asked a fem medic.

"Rain?" the medic asked.

"Water from the sky." Ping pointed up. "When clouds form, they drop water. Is how all plants survive." She swung her arm around.

"Ah. I ask chief."

After Ping left Medical, Chief Rody found her. "I need help with nugget materials. Running out of everything."

"Use plants scientists say okay. Plenty out here. How is hydroponic?"

"Dying."

"Find place to plant out here. Bring nutrients you feed them."

"You wise, Ping. Gratitude."

Ping nodded. She continued to talk to people, keeping an eye out for Mola.

Later, Head Chief Mola came out and called a meeting. "Us making progress. Citizens, be patient. Us need more information. Miki, what you get out of piece of bioputer?"

"Only have core processor and basic procedure files. All other gone, except for Ping and others with exobrains."

"Find others and collect."

"Yes, chief. Information on separate memory modules can be plugged into Ping's brain, but not bioputer. Bioputer must grow many more cells."

"Find one not Ping and use that citizen."

"Yes, chief."

Ping spluttered. "I have most in my brain. What if module not plug into anyone else's brain? Has much information on building colony."

"Us not need colony out here. All be back in habitat." Head Chief Mola stared at her.

"Not me." Ping couldn't help saying it.

Head Chief Mola glared at Ping. "Resume duties," he pronounced, stepped to Ping, took her arm, and led her to Science module. "Up ladder." He gave her a push.

"No." Ping felt an urge to fight back, but quelled it. It wouldn't do any good. She climbed up to the hatch. After he reached the top, he took her arm and led her to a small, dingy washroom on the bottom level. Two bins held a number of necklets of various colors, and belts, all a gooey mess, with bits of fur sticking to them.

"Retrieved from dead. Wash them." Chief Mola shoved her into the room.

Ping opened her mouth to say something, and the taste overwhelmed her. She gasped and choked and tried to leave the room.

Head Chief Mola grabbed her arm, turned her around, and pointed. Boxes of masks and gloves lay on the counter. "Use mask." He pushed her back in, closed the door and locked it.

"No!" Ping howled, then clamped her mouth shut. *I must get away from that chief.* She looked around, picked up the mask and put it on. *Away from this duty.* After a moment to gather herself and don a pair of gloves, she plucked a necklet with a pink stone from the bin, placed it in the wash machine, and rinsed her hands under the faucet next to it.

One button let in a measure of washing material, another, water to rinse. Then she tapped the start disc. A short time later the washer stopped and opened, revealing a shiny clean necklet. Ping placed it on a tray on a counter at the side and wondered where they acquired the water. Direct from the sea?

She discovered she could place three necklets in the washer at one time and they came out clean. Fuming thoughts ran through her head. *When I get out of here, I never return. Never. I find way to live outside, help others who wish to do so. But I never, ever, come back inside habitat.*

Ping washed all of the necklets and turned to the belts. They took longer because she had to take the pouches and tools off and wash them separately.

Suddenly, the door slid open, slamming into its pocket.

"Time to go. Be here tomorrow at sunrise." Head Chief Mola checked the items in the trays.

She dropped the belt she had just picked up back into the bin, pulled off her gloves and left them fall to the floor, and tiptoed around him to the door.

He picked up the tray of clean necklets and turned. "Not bad. Go."

"Yes, chief," Ping said, boiling inside. She trotted for the exit hatch. He put the tray in another room and followed. When they were back on the ground, she added, "If I am well enough. I must go to medical."

Gogi approached.

"No. You look well, you breathe well." Head Chief Mola stared at her.

Rage welled up. "No. I cannot and will not endure that atmosphere in there again." Ping coughed.

"That is enough. Collect belongings. Gogi, take her to other side of world. You not cause any more problems."

Ping felt like she'd been punched in the gut. She looked at Gogi. His face was three shades paler than normal, and his mouth hung open.

Finally, he muttered, "Yes, Chief." He took Ping's arm and led her away. She heard her aunts and sisters speaking.

"Only Ping has information we need to go forward," Aunt Dela said. "Whether in habitat or out here."

The others agreed.

"Quiet!" Head Chief Mola shouted. "Is done. Go to tasks or sleep pods."

Aunt Dela and the others turned away, and Gogi led Ping to the travel pod.

After they entered and strapped in, Gogi said, "I not do it." He took them up to her sleep pod and followed her out. "You stay here in pod. I go up and out of sight and wait, then return. Here some nuggets and drink. I return tomorrow."

"Much gratitude."

Ping stood inside her sleep pod and watched him dive into the travel pod to head north, up the slope. Anger engulfed Ping.

If thoughts could kill, Mola would be dead.

52

IN THE COOL PREDAWN, Ping gathered up her things, wrapped her coverlet around her and left Juni and her baby sleeping. She headed upslope and only stopped when she came to the place where Adam had laid out the site for her community. Looking back down the green and gray mottled slope with the mess of pods near the bottom, she said aloud, "If he not want me there, I leave. I not want to live there anyway."

Thought roiled in her mind as she marched along the river. She refused to go back, but couldn't see what else to do. Breezes nibbled at her fur.

Ping reached the bridge by midafternoon, walking faster in clean grass. She sat and rested. *What I doing? Where I going? What I do?* She closed her eyes and dozed, trying to relax. A warm sun soothed her.

When she opened her eyes, the sun hung behind the tops of the trees. A small brown creature with big black eyes stared at her from a Phren body-length away. Sitting on its haunches, it slowly swished a large furry tail.

"Greetings," Ping whispered, not moving. The animal chirped, turned, and ran up a nearby tree.

Slowly, Ping sat up. She must not go back. Gogi would tell her family. Only one place left for her. Marisa's Peace, if she could get there.

She lifted her water bottle. It was empty.

Near the bridge, a path lined with low bushes led to the water below. She eased down it and sampled the liquid. Clear, clean, fresher than that in the habitat. She dipped her bottle in and filled it. The bottle's filter should work. *Only drink sip and watch body.* When she climbed back up, she saw Gogi plodding up the slope.

"Gogi," she exclaimed. "Why you here?"

"Head Chief Mola told me check your sleep pod, to see you not hiding in it. He not trust me. I went there and you gone. Saw fresh prints going upslope and followed. Here I am."

"You tell him where I am?"

"No. You like sister. I not betray sisters." He sat down. "Where you go?"

"I go to Marisa. Tell family I need to do this. Cannot stay there."

"How you get there?" He plucked a long blade of grass.

"I know way." Ping felt a calling she couldn't hear pulling her to the forest.

"Must return today. If not back until tomorrow, Head Chief Mola put me on body duty." Gogi held out his hands.

"Go with me. I stay here tonight."

"Then I stay with you."

They settled for the night.

•   •   •

In the morning, Ping fought warring urges. While she was drawn to her family and desired to make a new home for them, even though she couldn't go back, the forest pulled her by something vital she needed to do there.

"I go to Marisa's," she told Gogi. It was the only choice. She no longer owed her duty to the Phren community.

"I go with you. Only Nela ..." Gogi looked down at the habitat modules, then at the bridge.

They trotted over the bridge and into the cool forest. Ping noticed that the trail led away from the meadow, not along it as before. She shrugged a shoulder. It was the only way. The large-leaved trees grew thick and the light dim. Plants with long, drooping leaves, larger than bushes and shorter than trees, lurked between the trees. The trail narrowed, so that Gogi had to walk behind Ping. Faint creature noises and chirps followed them.

After a sharp turn, Ping stepped into a small clearing, a little brighter than on the trail. She saw no other way out.

Gogi sat down against a tree. "Not used to all this walking."

Ping sat beside him. "Yes. This not like when I came before."

"How you know?"

"I remember." Ping glanced at him.

"Do us go back?" Gogi asked.

"No. Us must find way. Rest now." Ping closed her eyes and inhaled deeply. This place tasted different than places she knew, more earthy with a tang of a spice she did not know. She let the atmosphere infuse her. Something touched her, not unpleasant, not familiar. She felt it closing in around her and jumped up and pushed it away.

She looked around the glade, saw a bit of an opening on the far side, and tapped Gogi. "You ready to go?"

"No, but can if us must." He grumbled to his feet.

Something chirped as Ping pushed through the small space and found a way through the trees so narrow, they brushed her on both sides. A dim light ahead of her showed the way. They pushed through for hours, following the chirps.

"Can't go any more," Gogi gasped.

Ping managed to turn. He crouched in a ball. The chirps came closer together and louder. "Come," she said softly, "us almost there."

She drew him to his feet and, after a few steps, they pushed through to a brightly lit glade open to the sky. Ping blinked. There was the little spring, and the mossy bed she'd made before. She staggered to it and dropped.

Gogi crumpled just inside and gasped. After a while, after he caught his breath and opened his mouth wide, he said, "This taste free."

"Yes." Ping gazed at the trees on the far side and saw a further trail. "Us camp here."

"Good," Gogi muttered. "Water?" He held up his empty bottle.

Ping took it, filled it at the spring, and brought it back to him. "Drink all you want."

He emptied it and fell asleep where he was.

Ping returned to her nest and lay back. *This not same glade as before. Took five steps to spring before, only four now. Bush with purple leaves and pink flowers not there before. Not taste like other.* Ping relaxed her muscles, closed down her mind, and slept.

•   •   •

Ping woke to dim light, sound of chirping, and an urge to move on. She ate a nugget, poured out the river water, and refilled her bottle from the spring.

Gogi uncurled and stretched. "Where us?"

"Somewhere between Peace and Peace 3."

"What?"

"There three worlds of Peace in different universes," Ping explained. "Before transit, us on Peace One. After, on Peace Three. Two is weird world between."

Gogi shook his head.

"You not know about parallel universes?"

"No."

"Explain later. Us go now," Ping said.

They moved out onto the trail, pushing through vines hanging from the round-leaved trees, until they came to a large open area full of a bluish mist with patches of red and yellow. The chirps followed. Ping recalled a dream about a third Peace and three worlds into one. She could not make sense of it.

"Us go through or around?" Gogi asked.

Ping looked up at the chirping creature on a branch in the tree above. It faced right. "Gratitude," she said to it. "This way." A narrow space between the trees and the foggy meadow led them along one side of the mist. Ping reached out to touch this mist and felt nothing. She jerked her hand back and hugged herself.

Soon, a tree with long orange fruit partially blocked their way. Ping touched a fruit hanging in front of her and found it soft and squishy, as it popped off in her hand.

The stem and part of the skin on the side peeled off. Giving it a quick taste, her eyes widened. She took a small bite. "This very good. Like fruit drink."

"You sure it safe?" Gogi picked one.

Taking several deep breaths and waiting for a short time, Ping said, "My body does not complain." She collected several and stowed them in her bag. Again, the closing-in sensation surrounded her.

A little farther on, they came to a structure. Its red-brown tendrils appeared to extend into the sky, mist, forest and ground. The structure flickered in and out, in a variety of colors.

Ping looked for a way into or around it. Darkness oozed out of the meadow, the structure, and the forest, drawing a ring around them. Ping stepped back and bounced against the darkness behind her. She grabbed Gogi's arm.

As she fought terror, something deep inside her sent reassurance. They slipped to the ground, her mind filling with swirls of words and concepts she could not grasp.

The swirls faded, and she slept.

53

M ARISA AWOKE ABRUPTLY from a dream of Asiram. She was to collect Jan, Kaylyn, Glori, and the two men with strongest Talent and muscles, and go into the forest across the bridge.

Why? Why now? She sensed the world closing in on her for a few moments, then the feeling was gone. *What was that?*

Marisa rose and shook it off. Allen rolled over on the bed and snored. She dressed and stepped out to the kitchen. As she proceeded through her day, the dream nagged at the back of her mind. Every time it popped up, she pushed it away. She was too old to go through that again.

That night, she dreamed again of Asiram, stronger. The squeezing sensation in the morning also felt stronger and lasted longer. She limped to her kitchen.

"All right, all right," she said aloud. She called Jan, Glori and Kaylyn by mindlink.

'What's up, Mama?' Jan asked.

'Asiram came to me in dreams the last two nights. She wants me, the three of you, and two of the strongest men with strongest Talent, to go across the bridge into the forest.'

'Why?' Glori *sent.*

'She didn't say. Have any of you felt a sensation of the world closing in around you?'

'I have, a little, now and then,' Jan *sent.*

'No, but I had a strange dream the other night that I can't remember,' Glori a*dded.*

'Something's going on. Perhaps we'd better go see what it is.' Marisa sighed.

'Can you walk that far?'

Marisa felt Jan's concern. 'Ricky got me a strong walking stick. I'll manage. Do you have any suggestions for the men?'

'Brian,' Glori *sent.*

'Loren,' Kaylyn *added.* 'My brother can see thoughts below the surface.'

Marisa nodded. 'Good. We will go tomorrow. I'll get your tasks covered.'

She received a 'satisfactory' from Asiram. She did not understand how Asiram could reach her from another universe, just accepted it. First, she *called* the two men and told them to be ready in the morning.

Brian protested, he had too much to do.

'Your son can handle it. We need you for this.'

Loren responded, 'Sure. What time? I hate moving muck from outhouses to the fields.'

'You'll still get your turn.'

Marisa talked with others, rearranging schedules. When she told Susan at the clinic, the latter asked, "How serious is this?"

"I don't know, but Asiram does, and she'll keep pestering me until I come."

"Do you have to go?"

"Yes."

"Okay. Take care. Brian will take care of the girls." Susan hugged Marisa.

Back at home, Marisa packed her go bag, with food she'd collected from the plaza kitchen, and other necessaries. After lunch, she dozed in her big chair. Excitement to be going somewhere partially overrode the worry that she couldn't walk that far. A strong inner conviction told her she must go.

Later, she called Qilla and arranged for quines to be available in the morning.

•   •   •

Marisa's group rode up to the bridge in silence. She suspected Janni and Glori were communicating by mind. The quines walked slowly, and Marisa felt their unease. Thin clouds striped the sky, and the air was warm and still.

Halfway there, someone *called* her to ask a question. Marisa answered shortly. 'I'm not going to be available for a few days. Figure it out yourself.'

When they reached the bridge and dismounted, the older women groaned. "Can we rest here?"

"How are you doing, Mama?" Jan asked.

Marisa eased herself down on a pile of moss. "Still alive. Qilla, take your people home. You'll know when we come back."

The quine nodded and led the others down the slope. They stopped a little way down and grazed. Jan and the other women found places to sit, Brian beside them. Loren wandered around and peered at the bridge.

When the sun hovered above the trees, Marisa said, "We need to at least cross the bridge today. We can camp just under the trees."

They rose, picked up their bags, and Marisa led the way across the bridge. Loren carried Marisa's bag. Maybe she was just getting old, but there was a distinct mistiness over the meadow. She stomped along with her walking stick, Jan at her side. Glori and Brian behind, followed by Kaylyn and her brother.

Glori kept blinking her eyes. "Does the landscape look fuzzy to anyone else?" she asked.

"Yes," said Jan. "I thought it was just me."

"No, it's real," Marisa said. "Do you see it, Kaylyn?"

"Straight ahead, yes, but if I look to the side. it's clear."

They reached the trees and found a place to camp. Something Marisa perceived as a protective bubble surrounded them. She relaxed into sleep.

Marisa dreamed of another world below hers, like a picture on a piece of thin paper laid over another similar one, and the black and gray over the top. The image remained in her mind when she awoke.

The group followed the trail into the forest. It grew dim and narrow, so they had to walk in single file. Loren followed Marisa, and Brian walked behind the other women.

They stopped at a wide place to rest. "This is not like it was before," Jan said.

"This is the only way we can go." Marisa looked around.

"I didn't know the forest was so thick," Loren said. "Will we get to where we're going today?"

"Probably not. We'll have to sleep in the woods."

"There's mountains beyond, but we're not going uphill," Brian noted.

They marched on, Marisa stumping along behind, and presently found a glade to camp in, but it was not the same, either. Marisa was too tired to figure out the differences.

"Those blue flowers weren't there before," Jan said.

•　　　•　　　•

Late next morning, they came to a wide, misty meadow. Patches of red and yellow dotted it, blurred by the mist. At their feet, tiny blue flowers speckled the grass. Cool dampness pervaded the air.

A wide path at the right led along the side to a structure with no right angles. Reddish-brown tentacles sprouting from it looped into the meadow and the forest on either side. Black squares and circles moved around in the air, morphing into triangles and ovals when Marisa looked away.

"Okay, now what?" Brian demanded.

"I don't know." Marisa blinked and leaned against a tree.

The sun shone down on them as they shuffled around the small space.

"Something will happen," Glori said.

The deep tolling boom of a huge bell surrounded them, causing them all to jump. Brian caught Glori before she fell. Marisa held onto the tree.

A tongue of darkness crept from the meadow, another from the forest, and the structure darkened and appeared to move closer.

"No," Marisa cried, pulling Jan and Kaylyn to her, Loren's arms around them all. Brian and Glori, in each other's arms, stood close by.

The tongues grew and met behind them, the sky darkened, and the group slowly descended to the grassy ground in a huddle. The darkness surrounded them as they shivered.

'What are you doing?' Marisa asked Asiram in her mind.

'You will be safe,' came the answer as she slipped into sleep.

54

ASIRAM LEANED BACK in her chair in her workplace and said, "We are ready."

The Keepers linked with Asiram. :We have connected with inhabitants of Peace One and Peace Three. Conditions are optimal.:

'What will occur?' Asiram asked.

:Make sure no loose items. Magnetic field may change. Make self comfortable. Changes go through you, will not harm you. When you are ready, send link. You will subside into sleep. When you awake, you will be on combined world, same location.:

'How does this occur?'

:No words in your language to describe it.:

'This will work?'

:Yes.:

Asiram removed a box of scribers and several scribe sheets from the table and put them in a cabinet behind her. She leaned her chair back to a semi-reclining position. 'I am ready.' She closed her eyes, and the Keepers drew her into sleep.

• • •

The first thing Asiram noticed when she came to, was the quiet. All the odd little sounds of objects running into or brushing by others were gone. She took a scriber from the cabinet, held it out, and let it drop. It fell to the floor and stayed there.

"Ah," she said aloud, and rose. The air was clear and free of flying objects. Now she was able to see the green hills around the valley and the mountain peaks beyond to the east and north. She turned to the southeast and sought with her mind. In the far distance she sensed groups of sentient beings.

Her niece, Nanj, ran out to her. "What happened? What's going on?"

"The others who took our gravity are gone. We are one with two other parallel worlds. You no longer need wear the iron belt."

"Aunt, there are others here." Nanj peered into the distance. "I can see so far."

"They are from the other worlds. We may meet them someday."

55

PING OPENED HER EYES to a new world. At first, she saw only the trees and the trail between them. She sat up, opened her mouth wide, and tasted deeply. It took her a moment to recognize what was different here. Tastes of both her world and Marisa's mingled with a strange one, but all had the same physical structure.

How could this be?

She rose and touched Gogi's shoulder. "Wake up."

He stirred, rolled over, and snored.

Ping stepped over to the opening and saw a bright light at the end of a straight stretch.

Gogi mumbled behind her. Ping turned; he was struggling to sit up.

"Morning, I guess," he muttered.

"Us must go. I see light." Ping danced with impatience.

Gogi dragged himself to his feet, staggered behind a bush to deposit his waste, and collected his bag.

"You have nuggets?" She had already eaten hers.

He nodded, fished one out, and consumed it.

Ping led the way down the trail, which widened until they could walk side by side. These trees kept their feathery branches to themselves.

At the end, they found an open meadow speckled with red flowers and a bridge in the distance. Ping blinked, and Gogi squeezed his eyes shut. Ping led him out, and they dropped into nests of bright flowers.

Ping tasted again. Still the same combination of worlds, more fulfilling than each separately. She sensed groups of citizens, both north and south.

"This our world?" Gogi asked after a while, squinting.

"Yes." Ping opened her arms wide. "And other."

"What?"

"Come, I show you." Ping started for the bridge.

Mumbling to himself, Gogi followed.

After they crossed the bridge, the same gray arc as the other bridge, and turned south, Ping stopped and looked around. Downslope, she saw the buildings of the clanhome and, back at the forest, people stood just outside the trees.

"Look." Ping pointed.

Gogi turned his head and blinked. "Who they? Where they come from?"

Ping *reached.* "Marisa, Jan, Kaylyn and three others. How they get there?"

Gogi shrugged a shoulder.

"Maybe there was other trail. Us wait for them."

Ping watched as they shuffled along the path. Marisa staggered across the bridge and sat with a thump. Ping went to her.

"Are you well?"

Marisa shook her head. "My knee. I shouldn't have done all this walking, but Asiram gave me no choice." She took a deep breath. "I'm not surprised to see you, Ping. Quines are coming, we'll ride from here." She introduced the men. "Brian, Glori's mate, and Loren, Kaylyn's brother."

"This Gogi. He fly travel pods."

"Hello, Gogi. Welcome to this world." Marisa looked at Ping. "What happened to your head?

Gogi nodded and sat down. Ping felt he had questions he was unable to ask.

"Not important," Ping said, looking away.

"Ping, how did you know to come?" Marisa asked.

"Something inside me said to come to you. I think us all one world now."

Marisa *reached* all around her. "Yes, we are. I hope it works out for the better."

Ping nodded. A pounding drew her attention. A group of quines came galloping up the slope.

Gogi jumped up and backed away.

"Is well," Ping said. "They quines, let humans and me ride them."

"Here they are." Marisa let Brian help her to her feet.

Qilla snuffled all around her head and shoulders.

"I'm all right," Marisa said to the quine, who tossed her head.

After Marisa and Kaylyn mounted their quines, with help, Gogi approached the animals.

Loren brought his quine to Gogi. "You ride. I don't mind walking."

"You sure?" Gogi asked, eyeing the creature.

"Yes. Here, put your foot in my hand and jump up and put your other leg over."

Gogi looked at Ping.

"It safe," she said. Kaylyn called her to come ride on her quine. Ping sat behind her, and Jan mounted her quine.

Gogi put his foot in Loren's cupped hands, swung his leg over, and fell on his face on the quine's back. He pushed himself up and looked around.

"Hold onto the neck hair," Loren said, patting the steed.

Brian mounted and the group took off.

During the ride, Ping watched Gogi's face change from apprehensive to gleeful.

Ping settled in her seat and recalled the pleasure of riding. A warm day with little breeze, the quines took off at a slow trot along the line of tall trees next to the roaring river. When they reached the quines' trees, and the quines knelt so the riders could dismount, Loren, with his sharper eyes than most, said, "I see round structures and people down there." He nodded toward the beach.

Warmth and joy flooded into Ping. This *was* one world now.

Marisa took a deep breath and grinned at Ping. "We made it. You are welcome to stay here tonight."

Ping glanced at the fuzzy blobs on the beach, then at the houses around her. "Gratitude. We will."

"I have a spare bed," Loren said to Gogi. "You come with me. Be good, Gramisa." The two homs strolled away.

Ping followed Marisa to her house. Inside, Marisa settled in her chair nest and Ping on the long nest.

"I noticed you squinting. Do you have trouble seeing distant things?" Marisa asked.

"Yes. Us not need distant sight inside."

"Open that cabinet door there. See that tube?"

Ping picked up a tube wider at one end than the other.

"That's Allen's spyglass he brought from Earth. You may have it if you wish. Go out and try it. Look in the smaller end."

Ping stepped out and peered through the device. *The pods are clearer.* She looked at trees and houses. *Much clearer.* She returned to the house. "Much better," she said as she settled back on the couch.

"Did you see the misty meadow and the weird building?" Marisa asked.

"Yes. How you know ..."

"Asiram told me."

"Asiram?"

"She lives on black and white Peace and brought us all together." Marisa told her about the first event, when she was young with a newborn, and her latest conversations.

"Ah. You come from your world and I from mine, and us meet here together."

"Yes. How are things with your people?" Marisa tugged a silver curl.

"Not good." Ping pulled at her chest fur. "Eruption in sea brought habitats on land, many hurt. Power broken, most live in sleep pods that broke off and came on land."

"Oh, my." Ping felt Marisa's concern.

"Head chief and others die, new Head Chief Mola want everything like before. I think it best us set up new colony on land."

Marisa shook her head. "I sense you two do not get along."

"No. I cannot go back, Chief Mola banished me. But my family, my mater, sisters and aunts are there. And all other citizens. I owe duty to them. So I must go back."

•　　　•　　　•

In the morning, as Ping prepared to leave, Marisa said, "I would like to loan you a couple of quines, but they refuse to go down there. Come visit soon."

Loren and Gogi arrived. The four made their farewells, then Ping and Gogi headed down the slope. They found mud strips and damp grass not far below the community.

"So the tsunami happened here, too," Gogi said.

"They well, their place above where water came."

At the area where their pods had first been, Ping stopped, pulled out the spyglass, and stared down at the broken community. She saw the curving row of pale colored structures, but nothing else had changed. Sleep pods still lay scattered about, their group's pods still in the same place.

After a short rest, they continued down.

At her sleep pod, which had not been touched, Ping stopped. "I stay here. Go down and see what happens."

"No. Us stay here until others come up." Gogi went to his sleep pod.

"Gogi, I need know ..." Ping began.

He turned. "I not go until I know is safe." He stepped into his sleep pod.

Ping glared at his back, then stepped into her own sleep pod.

Sister Bede was the first to come up to the sleep pods. "Ping! You back. How did you get here?"

"Never left. How repairs going?" Ping and her sister touched hands.

"Not. Citizens have no knowledge and cannot access bioputer. They try things that not work. No power, cannot do much else."

Ping nodded. Just what she'd expected.

"What is situation regarding me and Gogi?" she asked.

"Citizens who know you, are angry. Can hide emotions only so much. Chief Mola trying to get people move back inside Science, but air bad and no power. Maker took material from broken connectors for power hose and extended it enough to get some power, in Maker. Citizens moving in there."

Bede waved her arms. "Chief Mola trying to get Chief Rody to move nugget maker back inside, but he not do it. Citizens from Central must stay outside until they decide how to fix. Want to turn module over, but too heavy. Trying to detach nests from ceiling. Medical set up outside, but no equipment that runs on power."

Sister Juni with her baby and Cori came up. Juni hugged Ping, squashing little Peni, who howled.

"Oops. Sorry, Peni. How you here, Ping?"

Ping explained.

"Good thinking, Gogi."

His mouth widened. "First time I disobey chief. Just not want do that to Ping. She just stayed in her pod, and I flew up out of sight and parked for night."

The aunts and Nela arrived, followed by Cale and Otie.

"Us left Mang in pod down there," Cale said.

"Why he not adapted? He here long enough," Ping said. "What I do now?"

"Stay up here," Aunt Dela said. "Not let Head Chief Mola see you."

"I need be down there."

"Us keep you informed," Bede said. "Us found another citizen with exobrain and she has memory module. Chief Dano do surgery on her like yours."

"Good." Ping fished her module out of her bag and held it out. "Plug in now?"

"Yes." Aunt Dela pulled off the covering on Ping's head and eased the module in. "Can you access it?"

Ping felt an added presence in her brain and touched her head. She thought the key word, and new data opened up, almost overwhelming her. "I must digest this. Too much." She crept into her sleep pod and curled up in her nest.

"Be well," Aunt Dela said as she and Bede trotted back down to the colony. Gogi moved to his sleep pod and sat on the hatch step.

Ping spent the rest of the day exploring the files in her exobrain, first the ones she'd seen before, then others she did not recognize. These held information about history of the habitat and the chiefs.

56

THE NEXT MORNING, Ping packed her bag. Everyone except Gogi accompanied her as they marched down to Science module, meeting groups of citizens who welcomed and joined them.

Someone stuck his head out of the Science hatch, looked down, and said something to someone behind him. Soon, Head Chief Mola appeared.

"You! How you here? Where Gogi? Find Gogi," he barked.

"Greetings," Ping said. "I not disappear well."

Head Chief Mola glared, scrambled down the ladder and almost fell off the last rung, keeping his eyes down, glancing up occasionally.

"How you return," he repeated.

"I here. How repairs going?"

"You!" he screamed, the dam of frustration breaking.

Ping and everyone else stepped back.

Chief Akoi took Head Chief Mola's arm and pulled him away from the crowd.

Shocked to her toes, Ping could not hear what he murmured to the angry chief. The two chiefs walked away together around the side of Science.

Ping stared after them. *Head Chief Mola must be under terrific stress to blow up like that. Chief Akoi handle him. I must take charge now.*

She turned around. Everyone gazed at her. "Too much for one chief to handle."

"Yes," said Aunt Dela.

"Return to your tasks," Ping said. "I visit each group. Us must succeed in building colony out here."

A few murmurs floated in the air as the crowd disbursed. Ping and her family looked at one another.

"Perhaps, if Chief Akoi gets him calmed down enough, I can show him my information." Ping brushed her chest fur.

"Not likely," Nela said. "Once he get idea in his mind, he never let go. He infuriated my chief when he demanded us do something not physically possible. Only when us started doing procedure and it not work, did he see it. Then he told chief to find way to do it."

"Ah," Ping said. *Too bad one man block the way. If he be eliminated … She* only dared think it in her private mode. She wondered if anyone else was thinking it.

"Let we go talk to citizens," Juni said. She led the way to the children's compound, where she took Peni out of her snuggie and handed her to a caretaker.

"How things go?" Ping asked the fem in charge.

"Well, considering what us have, children seem much healthier out here. Food is problem, but us make mash out of plants you show we. Us fems ate it first, and when no problems, fed bits at first to babies, they thrive. Most nursing fems not produce enough milk."

"Ah. Do what you can. Us shall survive."

Ping and her sisters went on to the education compound, where she saw supplies mostly sorted. "Children learning reading from sorting papers," Aunt Lee said. "Gratitude, Ping."

At Medical, the main problem was the crowding. The fem with the child, both well, was now in her sleep nest. More citizens were hurt, not knowing how to use tools or do repairs properly.

Chief Rody welcomed her at Nutrition. Someone from engineering showed them how to increase speed of hand cranked mixer. Most citizens worked well inside structures, as inside the habitat. Only a few still had problems viewing distant objects.

After completing their rounds, Ping and the others returned to their sleep pods. When Ping told Gogi about Mola's blowup, Gogi whooped with laughter.

After a rest, Ping and her sisters and aunts returned to the colony. Head Chief Mola did not make his usual afternoon announcements. Ping went to see how the new bioputer was doing.

Chief Miki showed her several buds. "It take time, but grows back. Maybe two, three eight-days you can use it."

"Good." Ping continued on her rounds when someone grabbed her arm and whirled her around. She came face-to-face with Head Chief Mola.

"Now, Ping, since you keep coming back and you make this mess, you fix."

"I made water come up?" Her insides began to curl on themselves.

"Habitat fine until you began going on about problems." He glanced up at her face quickly and looked down again.

"I not make problems. Problems exist." Ping wouldn't let him see how she was shaking inside.

"You have disobeyed your duty. You will be punished."

"I regret." Ping bowed her head. Although the rules against protesting were no longer meaningful to her, she felt it would be a waste of her time.

"Come." Head Chief Mola led her to Maker. At a pace that caused her to have to take occasional running steps, he took her through a rarely used workroom, to a small storeroom at the rear.

Why here? Ping thought uneasily.

He shoved her in and took her bag.

"No, I need my bag, my nuggets." The words escaped involuntarily.

"I bring you more." He pawed through it, removed a nail file and small scissors, threw the bag at her, and shut and locked the door.

Ping felt for a light button but could not find one. She stood in total darkness. Not even the glow of the dot of a screen. No sound except her heart pounding in her ears. Fear stalked her. *Great One, help me. Did Mola leave me here to starve? What he planning to do with me?* She took a deep breath and gathered her courage. *I not give up. I must proceed.*

She took another deep breath. Mostly stale, barely breathable air. Turning in a circle in place, she tasted the walls. Stale, musty.

No one had been in here for a long time. But there. A faint trickle of air. Ping exhaled, stepped to the place, and felt around. A wall panel was loose.

"Ah," she murmured. She moved her hands over the panel until she found the edge, and a place where she could stick a finger under it. Ping pulled and something popped. With three fingers under, she pulled more, accompanied by more poppings.

Ping remembered her lightstick, tucked away in a hidden pocket, for use if the power went out. She pulled it out and aimed it through the hole. Another wall with a hole in it. If she got through one, she could get through a second. Fear faded and hope welled. If she could make the hole big enough, she could escape.

She pushed the wall back in place. Head Chief Mola would be returning with nuggets. After Ping sent the narrow beam of the lightstick around the closet, she grabbed some old cloths off a shelf, made herself a nest in a corner, and tucked away the lightstick.

Ping curled up in her nest and planned. If she could get into the next room, most likely another storeroom and unlocked, and get out, she could find a hatch to the hullway. She thought there were entrances into the outer hatches from the hullway. If she could find one, she could get out. All the way out.

But then, she still needed to help build the new colony, for her family and the rest of the citizens. She did not know how to do that yet; something else she must learn.

Sometime later, she awoke to the creak of the door sliding open and blinked in the bright light.

Mola tossed in a brown supply bag. "You stay here until habitat repaired and closed." He slammed the door and left.

"Meaning forever," Ping muttered. The bag held nuggets and a jug of water. "If he not accomplish anything by now, may be long time, if ever, it get done."

She returned to the wall and peeled back the panel. The inside of the panel in the other room was rough, easy to use fingers to pull and push. A section gave, and she pushed it away. Ping shone her light around. To her left, a bare wall with a clear bioplaz sheet over it covered a hatch to the hullway. Besides the hatches to the outside, there were hatches to the hullway on every level, to be used in case of emergency.

Ping sensed someone coming. She scrambled back and pushed the panel down.

Head Chief Mola and a hom wearing the medium red of a surgeon opened the door.

Ping stood. "I am well," she said.

The medic took a quick look. "I see nothing wrong," he said.

"Remove her extra brain," Head Chief Mola said. "Here."

"Not here. If you wish, I prep operating room in Medical Central."

"Why not here?" Head Chief Mola demanded.

"No operating table, no instruments, no supplies, no anesthesia, not sterile."

Ping's astonishment at the demand echoed the medic's.

The medic continued. "I must have my chief's permission to perform surgery anywhere except operating rooms. Who is this citizen?"

"I Ping." She touched her necklet.

"I outrank your chief," Head Chief Mola said. "You have your bag. Do it."

"Where is light? Cannot see in here."

Head Chief Mola shone a strong beam at Ping who closed her eyes.

The medic poked around her head. "I need x-ray to see where connection is." He turned and looked at the head chief. "I cannot do surgery here. I need special equipment in Medical Central."

Ping sent gratitude to him.

"Tomorrow, I have time and place to do it."

"Very well." Mola turned off the light and they left. "I be back tomorrow."

Ping let out a sigh of relief and dropped to her nest. "Great One, help me," she murmured. Her exo brain held the information the citizens needed to repair the habitat and set up a colony outside. *Citizens must live somewhere. Better outside, but even* inside *need to be made safe and healthy. Why does Mola not see this? Why does Mola want to destroy it? Why is he afraid of me?*

57

P ING'S THOUGHTS ROILED. *Take my brain? Even if I survive surgery, what kind of life I have?* Ping sat there numb, trying to get her mind to focus. *Get out, get away. No life here. Family. Must go. Wall.* Finally, thoughts coalesced, and she dug out the tool Marisa had given her. A rounded stick with a sharp stone set in the end.

Ping pushed fear away, stepped to the wall, and pulled back the panel. The whole thing popped off, leaving an opening plenty wide enough to go through. She pushed on the other panel. It moved a little way then stopped. Something was blocking it.

No.

She continued to push, with no success. Leaning against the wall, Ping wiped her face with a cloth from her belt pouch. There must be a way. *I must do.* With the lightstick in one hand, she took the tool with her left hand and pounded the sharp end against the panel near the open edge. The material tore, her hand went through, and she had to drop the lightstick to grab the edge of the opening. Catching her breath, she pulled her left hand back, picked up the lightstick, and pulled at the edge of the hole. Her fur had protected the back of her hand, and she saw only a small scratch amid a patch of torn fur.

The panel ripped all the way up and all the way down, leaving her a space she could push through.

Gratitude, Great One.

Ping picked up her bag and stuffed the cloths in it, turned, and pushed her way through into the next room, dim and musty. Swinging the lightstick around, she saw more shelves with odd bits of materials on them, the hatch, and the door. She stepped over to the hatch and tried to open it. It was sealed with something she could not make a dent in, even with her tool.

No.

Ping turned to the door. It was stuck tight also.

She recalled noticing three storerooms and attacked the far wall. One long strip hung down. She pulled it and the panel came away. It took longer to get through the next wall, it didn't tear as easily. For once, she was glad for the lack of maintenance.

Ping dropped to the floor and managed a drink of water before she slumped into sleep.

When she awoke, she had no idea what time or day it was. She took a nugget and drink, left her waste in a corner, and tried the door.

It was also locked, but there was a paper-thin space between the door and the frame. She pawed through a pile of tools on a shelf and found a thin strip of stiff metal. Pushing this into the crack, she managed to move the lock back and open the door enough so she could get her fingers into the space.

Ping stood and *reached*. No one around outside. She pushed the door open enough to ease out, then slid the door closed. She found herself in a large work room. Three dim lights in the middle and one on the far side showed tables and benches thick with dust. She sneezed. A door at her left side drew her.

Where to go?

She tiptoed through the doorway. A long corridor extended to her right, and to her left, a hatch to the hullway. She trotted to it. It was sealed shut with several hundred years of crud.

No.

A corridor stretched in front of her, parallel to the hull, small rooms off both sides. Still no one nearby. She trotted down the corridor until she came to another open space with no hatch. Walking more slowly and breathing deeply, she finally reached a space with a hatch. She tried it, but it wouldn't budge.

No. Please, Great One.

Gasping for air, she pushed on. After two spaces between rooms, Ping found a hatch that did open. Being emergency hatches, they were kept unlocked.

Ping pushed it open and crawled through into another dim, dusty corridor. Again, no one. The air tasted little better. Sometimes, citizens used the hullway for running exercise, but most of them were outside the habitat now. She headed upslope, not sure where she was or when she would get to the next outside hatch. She figured anyone coming after her would go down because it was easier. Chiefs always looked down.

The tiny emergency lights in the hullway gave only enough light for her to see the floor in front of her. Patches of darkness where some lights had gone out forced Ping to use her lightstick. The only sounds were her faint footsteps and gasping breaths. The place pushed in on her, forcing her to keep moving.

She began to wonder whether she was above the highest hatch. A light blinked out, then another. Hopelessness crept over her.

After hours of nothing, Ping had to stop. She found a place between two inner hatches, sat and rested, gasping, her ears listening for any sound.

Half asleep, she heard a distant unidentifiable sound below her. She jumped up and trotted up the unending slope. Around the next long curve, she came to a hatch that opened in the ceiling. *This must be top of habitat.* There was no way she could get up there. *Whoever used that must have tool to pull it down.*

The sound again, no closer.

Ping trudged down the other side of the spiral. The sounds came closer. When she thought she could go no farther, the noise stopped, and she heard the clunk of an inner hatch. She leaned against a dusty wall and inhaled stale air.

Faint and gasping, Ping plodded on and soon came to an outer hatch. She found the small personnel door and slid it open. A gust of fresh air assailed her. She crouched there and inhaled great gulps of sea air, from an opening to her right.

She stood in a large dim room where a couple of travel pods sat waiting. On her left, the door to the interior corridor stood wide open. She couldn't see the far wall, but suspected it held an exit to the next section of the hullway. Faint rustling sounds came from beyond the pods.

I go in and find regular exit, or go out here? Her oxygen depleted brain couldn't focus.

Head Chief Mola stepped out from behind the pod. "There you are."

No!

Ping ran for the opening and out onto a platform and rickety walkway on the outside of the hull. The sea spread out down below, land to the left. Far below. He followed her and stopped at the end of the platform.

She stared at him, breathing deeply of the fresh sea air. "How you here?" *This was end – or beginning.* "Come and get me."

"Footprints." He took a deep breath, then a step out and hesitated, squinting. "I have you now, Ping. You at end of line. You have nowhere to go."

Never thought of footprints – everything dusty. "There the sea." She looked down, a long way down.

"You cause me and habitat much too much trouble. You be banished to other part this world, well away from your friends. I choose citizen to take you, not Gogi." He took a step out onto the walkway, holding onto the rail, and squeezed his eyes shut.

Ping stood still and said nothing. A breeze ruffled her fur. She glanced down at the sea below. *Return to habitat not option. I survive fall. Life outside is feasible.*

He took another step out and stopped, fists clenched, eyes slits.

Ping stood on her tiptoes, then thumped down on her heels. The walkway bounced a little.

Head Chief Mola shut his eyes and grabbed the railing with both hands.

Her brain cleared. She remembered his inability to look up at the world. *He must be terrified out here.* She wiggled the railing, saw it was loose and shook it. Nobody had done any maintenance out here for years.

He squealed. The breeze picked up.

She took two steps closer to him and pulled hard on the railing he clutched. It broke off and he grabbed at her. She held on to him as she leaned over the gulf.

He pushed, and Ping pulled him with her as they fell into the sea. She shoved him away toward the side of the habitat and, recalling a water scene she'd seen on her screen, formed herself into an arrow, hands stretched out in front of her.

She slashed into the water heading away from the habitat, farther and farther down. Suddenly something large grabbed her and carried her upward. Although she'd only seen images of it, she knew it was the sea serpent. The creature gave her a shove as it let go. Everything went dark for a moment, and she flailed, trying to reach the surface.

Someone clutched and lifted her out of the water. As she gasped for air, Ping saw it was Kaylyn.

Gratitude, Great One.

She felt the strong strokes of the fem who carried her to the beach and laid her on the grass above the sand.

"What is it, Mama?" a child asked. "It fell out of the big ball."

"I Ping," she gasped, a confusion of water, sky, sand, people in her mind. Kaylyn sat beside her on the grass and patted her arm. The habitat, Maker, loomed well down the beach. *Did I fly?*

"Are you all right? What happened?" Kaylyn asked.

"Mola want me gone," Ping mumbled. "Railing broke. Shoulder painful."

Others came. One fem touched her limbs and other parts.

"Shoulder only bruised," she said. "Nothing broken."

Ping's mind began to clear. She was out of the habitat for good. *Let Mola live in his mess. If he lived. If not, Chief Akoi do good job.* She was glad to be out of there.

She climbed to her feet and shook herself, scattering water drops over the nearby Peace people, then sat again. "I well."

A young child toddled to her and touched her fur. Ping pulled away, recalled being forbidden to deal with children. She sensed Kaylyn's concern about her fading.

"It's all right," Kaylyn said. "You may spend all the time you wish with our children. You are always welcome in our home."

The child crawled into her lap. Ping put her arms around her and held her tight. Joy coursed through Ping's being. The ache of childlessness was gone. She could see herself in the childcare room surrounded by little children.

Ping could also see herself returning and announcing that Mola was dead. She would visit Kaylyn and Marisa and the children often. She would build a new colony for the citizens and live life fully aware of other citizens and the world, as she was meant to do.

ABOUT THE AUTHOR

Lorna Hopkins Keith, born in Hollywood, California, with a B.A. in Mathematics, has been writing since her teens. Fascinated by both numbers and words, she is also a musician, photographer, and puzzler. Lorna has self-published a science fiction trilogy, attended many science fiction conventions and writing workshops, and has read science fiction most of her life. She grew up in California, lived in Colorado, and moved to Florida with her physical therapist husband, where they live by a lake with a chatty calico cat.

ALSO BY THE AUTHOR

CITYFALL

by Lorna Hopkins Keith

After Samanda Lar destroys her ex-husband, the Volen hand her the mission of saving the people of City and establishing their new home.

BUBBLES OF TIME

by Lorna Hopkins Keith

When Janni's mindtalent leads her to space, she discovers other human colonies ... and a threat to them all.

Available from Water Dragon Publishing in
hardcover, trade paperback, and digital editions
waterdragonpublishing.com

YOU MIGHT ALSO ENJOY

THE CERES ILLUSION

by Sue Eaton

Something is definitely rotten in the experimental settlement on Ceres.

REBIRTH ON XARBO

by Diane De Pisa

Yearning to reunite in the afterlife, a couple's search runs afoul of the materialistic Technists on Earth and the intransigent laws of Commensuration on their adoptive planet Xarbo, where rewards and retributions fly fast.

SMASH THE WORLD'S SHELL

by Laurence Raphael Brothers

t's the end of the Age of Kali and our world is dying, its bounds shrunken to encompass a single city.

Available from Water Dragon Publishing in
hardcover, trade paperback, and digital editions
waterdragonpublishing.com

www.ingramcontent.com/pod-product-compliance
Lightning Source LLC
Chambersburg PA
CBHW061342310726
48974CB00001B/153